TWIN SPIRITS

Creola Thomas

Name: Thomas, Creola, author

Title: Twin Spirits/Creola Thomas

Description: First edition. | Flamefire Publishing, Chicago, Illinois, 2026 | Summary: "When a cruel prank leads Margarita to Leona — the mirror image of a dead woman — the bond they build over the years will shatter the moment Margarita discovers the truth about herself." — Provided by publisher.

Layout and cover by Inksnatcher.

BISAC: FICTION / Psychological | FICTION / African American & Black / Women | FICTION / Sagas

Identifiers: ISBN 9780981455341 (paperback) | 9780981455358 ePub

For information about special discounts for bulk purchases, please contact the author at creolaxoxo@gmail.com.

Printed in the United States of America

This book is lovingly dedicated to my late mother, Annie Thomas. You taught me that words have a rhythm of their own, and that stories live all around us – like sound – waiting to be heard and told. You showed me never to give up, to always search for another way, and when life becomes difficult, to pray. You are truly missed!

CONTENTS

THE POETIC PARABLE

We all live to speak to a soul that would hold, our truths as
mines hold gold; unearthed and buried deep, become
memories that we sometimes watch like cinema, memories
too painful to remember, so we hide.

We want you to know that we are small particles of dust,
moved around by a powerful force, tucked in our happiness
that is walled by our tears, emotions, sealed like storages
all we hear are our fears.

A sound with no strings, just base and treble, that reminds
us that we are fragmented pieces, dismembered
hearts in search of a home, or simply a place to belong.

We traveled like pilgrims, migrated from you, but your
words linger, and your whispers clothe us like wool for the
winter,

but remember, seasons will change, and wool won't be
needed, then we will dress ourselves in September.

Settling for nothing more than time, as we breathe for
normal

but not normal, just calm and maybe not even that, just the
unknown.

Time not only heals wounds, it kills hope, it waits like a
grudge for its day of reckoning,

dust from the booths of the Choctaw Indians,

will summons the wind to take revenge and curse the
memories that won't let guilt in, until it kills, again, and
again.

But there is hope, I'm not like the ghosts of my past.
I'm new and unimaginable kaleidoscope of vision.
Walking the path of an individual.
Following the invisible steps of the strong.
Unplanted and unhinged weary legs wander into love, and
meet hate.
A creative emotional scapegoat covered in duplicity,
or was it serendipity
leaving us to contemplate,
have we met hate in the interval of time, and we never
separated?
Loved but unwanted is an accepted bad habit you can live
with or rehabilitate, you can divorce and remarry misery.
When the flesh has nothing to call its own, when betrayal is
an inner stench, an aroma that perfumes the air.
And everywhere you go, it smells.
Or could you have imagined it all, and maybe you feel
nothing at all?
When your own thoughts can't be trusted, your action can
be ruthless, and feeling can be bypassed,
you become padding for marching or running feet
or discarded things, that are gone without a second thought,
the lingering effects, of being guided by your feeling, in a
world that hides hope, disguises lies, and gives high praise
to pride institutionalized in the bark of trees, where your
dreams live or die.
Until you realize that all
have purpose, and your pain had only a season,
eternal gifts defy imagination,
hope births revelations,

and overturn doubt.

We move like syncopated beats that draw your soul into the
deep

so the story repeats, and you get all angles.

Remember there is light.

Remember to seek after the light.

Remember you are the light.

And

that's that.

PHRASE 1

MEET MARGARITA

Margarita

My sisters reacted as if they had been handed a life sentence when they learned they would have to keep me—thirteen-year-old Margarita Carter—the Friday of the last summer house party in the building. I often felt like a baby roach crawling slowly behind a big mama roach as she wandered through cracks and crevices searching for a place to hide. The little roach didn't choose its own path; it waited to see where Mama went, trailing behind her, unsure and afraid, hoping not to be crushed by human hands.

My sisters didn't want me anywhere near them that day. I knew it, even if nobody said it out loud. It was the end of summer, and the older teenagers were desperate for one last story to carry into the first day of school—a slap-down, be-there-or-die kind of party.

It was the last day for hot pants so tight they hurt every possible woman part, and braids pulled so hard you needed Crisco oil just to loosen the knots and think straight. No sister wanted the burden of babysitting me when she was trying to catch the eye of boys who cared more about baseball games, basketball tournaments, or her handheld games than any girl.

This was the house party of the year. The song "Shake Your Body" would play over and over, walls vibrating, kids shouting the words, and nobody caring how late it got or who got in trouble.

————

I had watched them, my sisters: Cindy, the older of the bunch, who already was secretly dating and who for sure wanted to be there to keep an eye out on her boyfriend; Nia, we call her Batty, because she was on the same page with my sisters to attend this party, even had her outfit laid out, but on the day of the party, she changed her mind; and then there is Janet, Wanda, and Andrea, the hammer heads; they would be there, and they would dance, and they probably would risk smoking, hoping not to smell like smoke by the time Mama came home. Those three were thick as thieves, a cute group of robbers and liars.

On this particular day, they had been huddled together, snickering to each other and planning so carefully how they would solve the "little sister problem." I was always the problem when my parents decided my sisters would have the unenviable duty of watching me when I was too young to attend a house party.

As unbearable as the remembrance of this very day is, I wouldn't change it for the world because it was the careless actions of misguided teenagers that brought one of the brightest lights into my life and changed my life forever.

————

I can't forget growing up at 1158 North Cleveland in Chicago, Illinois — vacant lots, broken glass, thin grass fighting for space through pockmarked fields. The only place in the neighborhood where people were treated with respect was the funeral home. My wayward sisters and their friends went there often, turning it into a game. They would whisper and guess who lay in the center chapel — a man or a woman — and place bets on what color the person was dressed in.

I thought it was wrong and always waited outside while they walked in to look at strangers laid out in caskets. Sometimes they even touched the bodies, then ran back out laughing and describing how cold the skin felt. I never wanted to hear about it, but they told me anyway.

Death felt close in my neighborhood, but I never understood it. I only knew it frightened me.

It's strange how things that once felt enormous shrink with time. That week they teased me, called me names, and acted as if they wished I would disappear. Still, I stayed. My sisters had a secret plan, but it wasn't a very good one. They thought that if they treated me badly, I would ask to stay with someone else for the weekend. But you know what else is strange? Once you get used to being treated badly, you sort of like it. So their plan didn't work, but they made one last attempt.

Everyone knew I hated going near the funeral home, much less stepping inside. Many times I had no choice but to wait outside with my eyes squeezed shut and my fingers crossed while they went in and, to me, disturbed the peace of the place. My sisters came up with a plan to make me enter. They meant to frighten me badly enough that I would beg my parents not to leave me with them. Then my parents might let me go with the adults to their gathering, as they had once before.

Had they shared their mindless plan with me beforehand, I could have helped them revise it, which would have given them their goal of not having to watch me. But they didn't give me prior warning; in fact, they waited until the very last minute to tell me the plan. When they revealed it to me and I outright refused, they threatened to run off and leave me if I didn't go in and touch the body in the casket they chose.

"Why me? Why this? What for?" I can remember resisting as my sister pushed me inside the funeral home. The name given outside the main chapel was Lillian Smith, and I was headed in her direction.

"This will help you get over your fear of the dead. We all got to go one day," my sister whispered.

I actually would have thanked her if I hadn't felt an urgent need to use the bathroom. My sister was pushing me quietly down the aisle. When we were halfway there, I pushed her hands away from me because I felt drawn to the woman in the casket. I slowly began to pick up the pace. After a while, I found myself facing her.

"Lillian, oh Lillian," my soul cried out. "What happened?" Then I remembered she couldn't talk, so I stared at her silently. She was beautiful. She had long, curly, sandy-brown hair with streaks of gray. Her tan skin had been perfectly made up—well, powdered. In fact, the powder had sort of a caked look, but it was beautiful anyway. Bronze lipstick had been evenly placed on her slightly chapped lips.

"Touch her and let's get out of here," my sister was saying, and I was trying not to listen. She lay so silently. I noticed a strange burn mark on one hand and realized there must have been many accidents and unexplained pains in her life. I wished I knew, but it was too late now.

"Let's go!" my sister Wanda shouted.

I once again thought to myself how peaceful Lillian was, and then I touched her hand and walked away.

As I was walking from the casket, my sisters were saying in bewilderment, "She really did it."

Yes, I really did it. I had also wet my pants, which made the experience all the more memorable.

"You touched her?" Nia asked me. "You really touched her?"

Every second or so, they took turns asking me how it felt. I didn't answer that question until we had almost made it to our project housing.

At first I thought I really shouldn't share this, but for some reason I felt Lillian wouldn't mind. So reflecting back on it, I said, "She felt nice."

"Nice?" they repeated after me, somewhat surprised.

"She didn't feel cold?" Janet inquired.

I tried to think back on it, but I couldn't remember everything. I only knew I was wet, the heat pressed against my skin, and all I wanted was a bath and my bed. I ran up the stairs into the house, hoping never to relive that day, even though I knew I would never forget it.

I wanted to tell my parents about my sisters' actions, but that would have meant they had won, and I wouldn't allow it. My memory was already reshaping the moment. At night I told myself stories about the person I had touched. I still feared the dead, but I was no longer truly afraid.

Lillian was dead. Later, on the day of her funeral, I thought about her. She'd had on a pink silk dress, which had lace around the collar. That dress was much too beautiful to be just the protector of bones. Had her family chosen that dress because it was something she wore that was special to her? Maybe she'd met an important person like a king or queen of another country, or maybe she wore such an exquisite dress for a social-elite party where she was being honored. To me, that was much too fancy a dress to be on a corpse for one day.

I began to think about life and our scars in life. How many scars hadn't healed on her? How many scars would I die with?

Lillian's death had a strange effect on me. My sisters realized this and felt sorry for me because they didn't understand. I heard them arguing among themselves about who was to blame.

A week or so later I found myself craving ice cream and cookies. I took out my paper tablet and began writing down small things I noticed—things that seemed strange only to me. I was convinced bees preferred the color orange, even though everyone said they liked yellow. I wondered if the bees in my neighborhood were the same as bees everywhere else.

I thought about the sky too. Did it hold the same secrets in my neighborhood as it did in other places? Did it cry the same? Did it watch the world the same way? I wondered if there was another child somewhere like me, someone who understood that shadows do not always trail behind you. Sometimes they walk beside you, and you can feel them fade softly into the sunlight. Maybe shadows don't follow us at all. Maybe they wait for us to reach the light so they can become part of it.

Just thoughts (of a young girl trying to figure it out). I spent a lot of time inside my thoughts. They kept me busy and entertained, and I didn't need or have the companionship of my sisters. I often wondered if I was truly original or if there was a whole army of people like me somewhere in the world—people I might one day meet and have everything to talk about. That idea made me happy.

I would put on my favorite gray shorts and my pink-and-white polka-dot shirt, and even my sisters would smile. Since the Lillian incident, they had been a little kinder to me. They seemed to understand that whenever I wore those few favorite outfits, I was simply back to being myself.

They said the "spookiness" since the day at the funeral home had finally worn off me. And I guess this time they were right. Besides, I couldn't sit and think about Lillian all day; I had to move on and get along. There were ant stories I needed to narrate; I hadn't done that in a while, but it kept me busy, just watching the ants search and find food and find places to hide out. I would give the ants names and purpose, and I had several ant stories, but there was always room to write more, and that day after chores, that was exactly what I planned to do.

A few hours later, as we walked to the store, I had no thought of the dead, but rather how free it felt to know that we were alive. Once we got inside the supermarket, my sisters and I split the grocery list and went in search of our items. As I was selecting cold cereal—Sugar Pops or Peanut Butter Crunch, sugar or peanut butter—I played an internal heads or tails over this life-altering choice I had to make when I felt a light touch on my shoulder. I turned around.

A woman with long, curly sandy-brown hair, streaks of gray fused perfectly in the mix, stood in front of me. She was older, thin, and wearing a light-pink dress with a lace collar. I couldn't believe my eyes. It was her. I couldn't move or speak, and I was about to faint until she spoke.

"Excuse me., I— Oh, I'm sorry."

I blinked to show her I was human, but I still couldn't speak. I looked away, but sound was still coming out of this woman's mouth, this woman who was supposed to be dead. Surely I was dreaming.

Then she spoke again. I tried to simply walk past her, but she lightly held on to my shoulder and said, "I just wanted to know, does this box say 'no salt'?"

I looked quickly at the box and nodded yes, then nervously bent down to pick up the boxes of cereal I had dropped. I didn't want this lady to think I feared her. I did, of course, because I feared the dead. I was a tough preteen, but I was terrified. Then I started to think that somehow I was trapped in a horror movie. The movie *Candy Man* had come out a few years back, and people were still trying to instill fear in youth in our community by yelling or implying the Candy Man was coming, and I thought that if the Candy Man could somehow be real, what horror movie was this trying to pull me into? I needed to pick up the boxes. But while I was on the floor, I figured I would look around to see if maybe I had dropped something else. If I didn't see her, she couldn't pull me into the soon-to-be blockbuster fright movie. Her soft, sweet voice was still breaking through my reality, though, as real as the boxes that had fallen on the floor. I kept hoping this dead person would stop talking to me and walk away. She was telling me about how the doctor took her off salt because of her blood pressure.

After I put the boxes in place, she smiled at me and said, "You're such a sweet little girl."

"Thank you," I said.

She reached out to shake my hand. Her hands were soft like a baby's and somewhat cold. I backed away from her slowly, and she turned and walked away.

When I was sure she was out of my sight, I ran to find my sisters. My sister Cindy was selecting the sugar.

"Cindy, Cindy!" I said excitedly. "I saw her! I saw the lady in the casket!"

"What?" she asked, somewhat confused.

"I saw her. Come here, I'll show you. She just went up aisle five."

My sister dropped the sugar in the cart, and we ran down aisle five. I looked both ways, then ran to the end of the aisle.

"I just saw her," I repeated several times as I looked down all the aisles and checkouts. *She must be outside*, I reasoned. *She couldn't have just disappeared.*

I grabbed my sister's hand and we ran outside, looking all around. No one, only two plainclothes cab drivers who often hang outside the supermarket, looking to assist with bags and hoping to give someone a ride. These two men looked comfortable, as if they had been there a while, both drinking a soda pop and talking to each other.

I ran up to the one I thought would be more observant—he had an alert look in his eyes—and asked him how long he had been waiting outside. He said twenty minutes or so. I asked him if he had seen an older lady, late fifties, with long, curly, sandy-brown hair with gray streaks. "Wearing a pink dress," I added quickly.

The cab drivers looked at each other before saying no.

"But she was here!"

My sister sighed and walked back into the store.

On our walk home, I tried to explain my encounter with the strange lady, but no one would believe me.

"Stop. Wait a minute. Maybe it's time to tell Mama what you guys did to me," I said.

Then they started to listen and even look around as if they wanted to see this lady as well.

———

Months passed, and I saw the lady several more times. She would greet me nicely, and when I ran to get my sisters, she would no longer be there. I didn't know why she only revealed herself to me, but I hoped I would soon find out.

That day, fortunately, came soon enough. My sisters and I were waiting outside the currency exchange. I spotted her trenchcoat and silently signaled for my sisters to look at her. They turned slowly around, and they couldn't believe their eyes. The lady gave me a familiar smile. I waved, and she got in her car and drove off. I was filled with excitement because my sisters had finally seen that I was right. This lady knew me, liked me, and for no apparent reason, felt at ease communicating with me.

"Wow, that does look like her," my sister Wanda said disbelievingly.

"But it's not her," Janet quickly interjected.

"Then who is she, and how does she know me?" I asked, looking at Janet.

"I don't know," she said.

Unfortunately, this was not a satisfying answer.

We researched the topic of spirits as much as our fear would allow. We looked up the word "ghost" in a dictionary. We saw this woman around the neighborhood a few more times. She only ever spoke to me, and at times she seemed to disappear as suddenly as she appeared. After a while, I decided I had to know who she was and put an end to the mystery. If a ghost keeps following you, you follow it back. The others agreed. The next time we saw Lillian Smith, we would trail behind her and speak to her, just to make sure she was real. After all, she was only a woman — about fifty years old — and we told ourselves she couldn't hurt us.

Off and on, over the next two months, I continued to see her. Once, I was looking to buy a pink outfit for our church's summer picnic when she appeared and said she really liked pink and that it would look nice on me. I turned around to thank her, and she was gone. Then I remembered Lillian had been wearing a pink dress at her funeral.

I decided to go with the green outfit; let's just say it was too much of a coincidence for a thirteen-year-old girl to handle.

We met again on a brisk fall afternoon. My sister Andrea and I were trying to pick up orders for our Girl Scout cookie drive, and we saw Lillian leaving the cleaners and walking north. I told Andrea I was going to follow the lady, and before she could protest, I was out the door. I found myself making many strange turns until we stood in front of an upper-class square complex. The sign outside read, "Evergreen Plaza." Lillian went inside the building.

Andrea, scaredy-butt, was pleading with me to turn around, but I had come too far to turn back. I knew two things would happen when I faced my fear: I would feel nervous, and I would wet my pants. But learning the truth was worth it to me.

We walked up to the board and looked at the names. I had made an agreement with my sister that if we didn't see Lillian Smith's name listed, I would turn around and count it as a case of mistaken identity. We looked down the "S" list until we came to "Smith," and just as sure as I'm the youngest of nine, there was an L. Smith, Apt 904.

We rang that bell, hoping to speak to someone on the speaker first, but instead, we were instantly buzzed in. We walked shakily past the guard — who eyed us suspiciously — got on the elevator, and pushed the button for the ninth floor. Andrea was telling me it wasn't too late to turn around, but I wasn't listening. You see, a person ready to face fear becomes more determined.

We got off the elevator and knocked on the door. A nice, sweet voice from inside asked, "Who is it?"

In my excited state of mind, I stated my real name, which caused my sister to nudge me in the side. Before I could take it back, the lady opened the door.

"Oh, dear, it's you." She smiled gently. "Now what can I do for you today?"

We were lost for words. After a few awkward moments, I said, "My sister and I are selling cookies for the Girl Scouts and we wondered if you would like to order some."

She looked pleasantly at me. "It's nice that you should think I was fit enough to still desire sweets," she said laughing. "Well, dear, come in, and I'll place an order with you."

I looked at Andrea, and before she could object, I walked in. Lilian's house was beautiful: small but lovely. The color scheme was light orange and gray.

She had pictures of herself all around. *How vain*, I thought. *But then, if you look as nice as Mrs. Smith, I guess it's okay to hang pictures all around.* She had plants in almost every corner, a small couch with handmade pillows on it, and a small coffee table in the center. On top of the table was the Holy Bible. The house had somewhat of a historical feel to it, but it was very homey. In the corner was a baby grand piano, and on top of the piano were more pictures of her. She had life-size sculptures and beautiful handmade dolls everywhere; the place sparkled with creative energy. It pulled me into her reality. Never had I met someone so intriguing. I needed to know about this lady.

"Well, now, let me see." She placed her eyeglasses on her nose as she looked over the assorted cookies for sale.

I was hoping she would sign her first and last name on the slip, but she didn't. She signed "L Smith." That meant we would have to stay there a little longer, because I wasn't leaving the house without knowing more. I said the only thing I could think of. "So you play the piano?"

"Yes, madam!" she said excitedly, and before I could ask, she walked over to the piano. "I've been playing all of my days." She gently played a scale. "I used to hate it when I was younger, but I love it now. It's good company. Would you like to hear something?"

I nodded, and she played the sweetest love ballad I had ever heard. Then she played a gospel song, and Andrea and I tried to sing along, but it was obvious who the real singer in the room was. I told her my other sisters could sing too.

Well, it was getting late, and as much as I liked Mrs. Smith, we really had to go. The time was at hand, and I didn't know any other way to ask, but I had to know. So I just came clean with the lady. "Mrs. Smith, may I—" I swallowed my spit, and for one brief moment I almost lost my nerve. Then I looked over at Cindy, and her anticipation of my failure recharged me. "Mrs. Smith, may I ask you a question?"

"Sure," she said confidently.

"Well... are you a ghost?"

She smiled at me and then gently touched my face. "Ghosts don't have flesh and bones. Why would you think I was a ghost?"

"Well..." I hesitated for a while and then I explained how I was made to go in and view Lillian Smith's body.

Tears came to her eyes.

I wanted to cry too, because a conscience had suddenly visited me, and I felt sorry for disrespecting the dead.

"You visited the funeral home?" she asked.

I nodded yes.

"Well, do you believe in God, dear child?"

I again nodded yes.

"I do too. Don't feel sad that you visited. I was so disappointed when I didn't see one kid there, but now I hear that you were there after all. What is your name, child?"

I hesitated, then I spoke softly, "Margarita." I wanted to hide. Why did I tell her my real name? To lighten the mood, I said, "I know I can't ever be president with that name."

And to my surprise, she laughed.

The nerves melted from my body. That laugh did it for me; I had a connection with this woman. We were alike in some cosmic way that binds spirits together.

After a long, easy silence, she finally said, "God knows." Her voice sounded somewhat questioning. "You do believe in God, don't you, Margarita?

I said confidently, "Me too."

She smiled, then she said rather eerily, "He answered my prayers." Then she continued. "I prayed for just one child, any child, to visit that funeral home. And that child was you. He's still answering prayers." She smiled. "Lillian, my dear, was my twin sister. My name is Leona."

Twins. Andrea and I both gave deep sighs of release. *Not a ghost after all*, I thought.

I thanked her for her time and told her we had to go.

She smiled as she said, "Yes, yes, I understand. But if you would like to stop by for a while and just talk, I would like that. I'll tell you all about Lillian. She was a fascinating person, an extraordinary cook, and studied kung fu in China. She was a very interesting person."

"Well, I'll try," I said nervously.

"Please try hard, dear." She hugged me and then opened the door for us to leave.

In the days that followed, I visited Leona often. It wasn't only because the church members thought highly of me for it and sometimes slipped a little extra money into my hands, or because I later received the mayor's Good Citizen Award twice, appeared on a local cable show, and even earned scholarship money. It wasn't because I worked summers in the generation-gap program that paired youth with older adults in the community. Those things happened, and they mattered, but they weren't the reason I kept going back. I went because of her.

Leona shared a kind of life wisdom with me that I didn't know I needed. She fed me ice cream and full dinners, gave me small gifts, and even bought a comfortable chair for me to sit in when I visited, along with handmade pillows stitched with my name. With her, I felt special. I felt wanted. We spoke, and I counted myself fortunate to be the chosen listener.

PHRASE 2

MINES HOLD GOLD

Margarita

It didn't take much time for my parents to meet and like Leona. Before long my mother was not only selling Avon to her but to others too—Leona was introducing her to many others in the complex who enjoyed that personal shopping experience. I could tell that my family, and even others, admired my friendship with her.

It turned out she was well known for serving on countless committees, raising money for charities, and helping people throughout the community. She was an important person, yet she was my special friend.

One particular day, we took a walk for nearly twenty minutes. She believed walking refreshed not only the body but also the mind. Afterward at her apartment, when I settled into my chair and she into her favorite window seat, she began to talk. I listened as her words painted colorful brushstrokes in my imagination. I hoped they would never fade. I only wanted to remember.

"Life at its beginning is just a dot," Leona said. "That dot grows, and somewhere along the line of growth, souls become polluted. This pollution embodies itself in people who possess the ability to focus on themselves and even center the world around themselves. Some may call this their true and only talent." She leaned toward me. "You didn't know it was a talent, eh? You must be quite artistic and inventive to see out of eyes so glued to yourself that you can ignore the cares of the world. Life becomes a chase to make money, hire people to work for your money, and secure enough bonds and such that your money earns you more money while it's sitting in the bank." She put her hands on her knees. "Sadly, money can buy many material things, but it has yet to purchase a conscience for its many twisted victims, who may have the world but lack the ability to feel. For without a conscience, one can't have a soul. It is unimaginable how people wake up and greet the sun soullessly, but this miracle of the sun rising happens every day, and people are so blind that they never stop to wonder or ask why. You know what I mean, dear?"

I looked at her, still stuck on the sentence about the chase to make money, but I said the only thing I knew would be acceptable: "I understand."

She nodded. "I think that they, these people, must know something is missing, which is why they seek out doctors and counselors. There is always this need or rush for excitement, which is why they are always under reconstruction, searching for total beauty that can never be achieved. My mother was like this.

"That being said, please understand that it's a privileged position, because these select few will always be admired, no matter how sick, selfish, and degrading they are. Meaning, when bad things befall them, people don't worry at all for their well-being; they only shake their heads and think, *What a shame, all that money*. And with this floating thought, they begin to wonder what they could do if they had all that money." Her eyes pierce mine. "It's funny that when these people are in the pit—the bottom of shame—others, even if just for a brief moment, wish they were them. This could very well be the biggest societal problem that has not been addressed or recognized." She smiled.

"You may be thinking that this old lady just rambles on and on and on. Never think that I'm old. I may be a bit of a rambler, but never think I'm old. I'm fifty-four, and in the grand scheme of things, that is not old at all."

I felt relieved she seemed focused on her age, but I was still afraid she would catch my thoughts in midair and expose that I wasn't quite following her.

Changing the subject, she said, "Have you ever smelled blood before?"

I wanted to say I try not to, especially during my monthly visit, but what I simply said was no.

"Good, good." She nodded her head. "If you ever smelled blood, you wouldn't ever forget it. I remember the day I smelled blood, but I'm sure you wouldn't want to hear about it."

"But I would," I quickly interjected.

"If you are sure, then I will tell you, but remember, you wanted to know."

She stood up and walked over to the window. The smell of flowery perfume filled the air, but I didn't care. I wanted to know about the smell of blood, and what she told me would forever live in my memory.

"I think I will take you way back," she said. "I often long to forget this day, for in many ways our lives were altered and my destiny changed, just like that. There were times when I felt my worst nightmare would have been a better reality." She settled into the chair and began.

Leona

This story begins with my father. He lost both of his parents at a very early age and was raised by his grandmother, a strong woman who held her community together. She was a leader in the Order of the Eastern Star, an organization devoted to service and helping others. I grew up hearing stories about how hard Grandmama worked, always caring for someone in need. My father took whatever work he could find and often labored as a sharecropper. He valued hard work, but he loved his wife — my mother — even more.

My mother was only thirteen, like you, when she migrated South with my grandmother, who'd decided to teach in Belzoni after my grandfather died, and Mama was not a poor southerner. At times this made her very popular. Grandfather had been a train operator, and he had married a teacher from Chicago whose father was free. My mother didn't have much to say to us that I remember, but I do remember her saying often, 'We ain't descendants of slaves, like folks 'round here. Grandpa was a free man.'

My parents met in the late 1940s, when the world itself seemed to be changing. Neighborhoods were growing, brick homes were replacing older wooden houses, and people gathered for simple pleasures like outdoor movies that families watched from the tops of their cars. Courtship was changing too. Marriage was no longer only a partnership for survival or work; people were beginning to marry for companionship and attraction. My parents were part of that shift.

I was told my father was the kind of young man who dreamed of building a big house in the woods with his own hands, and he talked about it often. While many boys his age dreamed of sports and fame, he dreamed of porches, lamps glowing at dusk, and a swing moving gently in the evening air. Somewhere in his mind he had already chosen a place in the woods where he stored his hopes—the picture of the man he wanted to become and the things he held sacred.

My mother was a beautiful and proud woman, and she carried herself as if she knew it. She believed she was meant for more than struggle, and she expected life to provide comfort. In her mind, a man's role was simple: He was to work and provide so a woman would not have to worry about money.

My father was a quiet boy, and everyone loved him because he worked hard. He rose before daylight, picked cotton, and still went to school afterward. As far as I was told, he had only one close friend, a girl named Clare, the minister's daughter. Her father pastored several churches—six, I believe—which seemed unusual, since there were only four Sundays in a month except for the occasional fifth.

My father's grandmother attended one of those churches, and that is how he came to know Clare. They formed a close friendship. They fished, swam, laughed, and shared secrets, and she cared deeply for him.

Up until then, my mother had never seen a friendship so close that wasn't physical or adult-like—I hope you know what I mean. Well, my mother would follow them and watch and study my father for a long time. She figured out that the connection between them was church, so when school was out and she was away from her friends, she began to attend church. She started asking my father questions. Clare warned him from the start about her, but he didn't listen. He felt sort of flattered that a girl like that would even talk to him. Then my mother started inviting him over and going out with him without Miss Clare.

From the beginning, my mother made lots of demands on my father. She made him cut his hair and buy himself decent clothes. When school started back, few people recognized him, and my mother was proud to call him her man. I hear he never really talked to Mama like he did Miss Clare, but he loved her.

My father arranged to lease a field and pay the owner a share of his crops. He saved some money, bought a shack, and fixed it up himself, putting in new floors and all. Three years later, he asked my mother to marry him.

My mother was quite impressed, and she accepted, for she saw, as most people did, that my daddy, though not well educated, was well-liked — not to mention, he'd become the youngest council member on the board of Belzoni Township. She had plans for him, and being a working man, he was well able to keep her in the lifestyle she was used to. After they got married, Mama made Daddy work a lot while she entertained people.

Miss Clare never really liked Mama, but Mama never really cared. In fact, she enjoyed stopping by Clare's parents' house just to chat. After Mama got married to Daddy, Clare left for a higher education because she didn't have much else to live for in Belzoni. She wanted something my mother couldn't take away, and going to college came close.

I was told that on the night of the going-away party for Clare, my mother announced the arrival of her new baby. She knew Clare wanted a baby more than school, so Clare's moment in the spotlight was stolen by my mother again. When I think back on it, it's not that Mama hated Clare; she just wasn't going to be outdone.

My daddy was like a baby with candy when he heard of this pregnancy. He was happy for Clare but much happier for himself, and Clare knew this. She was going to ask him to help her take some of her things to the train so they could talk like old times, for in her heart she still loved my daddy, but after seeing his joy over the pregnancy, she decided not to. Nine months later, Mama had twin girls, and she vowed never to have another baby. Everybody knew Daddy wanted a few boys, but Mama said no and she meant it.

Our house sat quietly back in the woods. To reach it you had to drive down a long, tree-lined path, surrounded by nature on both sides. My father loved fishing, and the property held a private pond, along with a small building behind the house that I was told he used for peace of mind.

Though the house felt isolated, it could still be seen from the main road. People often said it looked like something from a postcard, so beautifully placed among the trees. And if you ever became stranded on that road, our house would have been the only house you could find for miles.

Daddy didn't like Mama going out without him. People whispered about her, and those rumors followed her wherever she went. He worked constantly to buy her nice clothes, yet we rarely went out together. As much as people admired my father, I don't think they cared for my mother. I still remember the looks they gave her, even when we were only small. My father often told her to speak very little, especially around other men. She didn't always listen, but it was something he felt needed to be said.

Four years later, Clare returned. Her appearance alone showed the difference time had made. Her hair, once natural, was now pressed bone straight to her shoulders. Her skin looked smooth and carefully made up, a light foundation evening her complexion. Soft pink eyeshadow highlighted her dark brown eyes, and her full lips shone with a rosy gloss. She was tall and slender, with curls placed just right.

When the church held a welcome-home picnic, every available suitor seemed to appear. My mother could always turn heads, but that day the attention belonged to Miss Clare, who had returned as the town's new schoolteacher. I remember thinking to myself, *I would love to have Clare as a teacher.* She was so different from the women down there. And she talked like Mama talked when she recited poetry to us. Clare was also a brilliant piano player, in fact, that is how we learned to play.

I imagine my mother was surprised by how nice Clare looked. My mother was still beautiful, but after giving birth to us girls, her body had softened in the natural way motherhood brings. Her beauty was no longer the kind that stopped a room, but a gentler grace.

Mama left before they cut the cake. She never let Clare see that anything was wrong. She smiled, laughed, and spoke to people who slowly drifted away, yet she kept smiling as if nothing had happened. That day belonged to Clare.

Even then, I sensed something had changed. My father seemed distant, almost embarrassed, and soon after, we were leaving. I didn't understand why then, but I just remember thinking these people really do not like my mother.

In the months to come, I wanted to see my father more, but he was just not around. On a few occasions, after church, he would give us money and watch us run to the candy store, but that was it. Sometimes I felt my father resented us girls a little because we were the reason Mama wouldn't have any more children.

My mother, I guess, loved us in her own way. There were times she sat down and told us how she was desired by so many men, and how she was born free and all. She had a flair for the dramatic, especially when she recited poetry. Then there were times she didn't cook because she wanted to lose weight, so none of us ate until Daddy came home, and most of the time that was too late to eat.

I don't know exactly when Randy Crawford started visiting our house, but we were around six or seven. I remember because it was after Grandmamma had died, Daddy's grandmother, and Daddy said it was a great loss to the community. We met Randy when he had car problems. I guess he saw our little house in the woods and stopped by for help. Mama took to him right away, and so did we girls. He was slender and tall with the complexion of a shiny new penny. His face glowed like he had put Vaseline on it. His hair was cut low, so low that at night he looked bald. And he had a small mustache, just a straight line across.

What was special about Randy was that he had long arms and bulging knuckles. His arms were so long that he could pick us girls up in one arm and hug my mother with the other arm. My mind always wanted to hide from the small, unspoken hope that I really wanted him to be my father instead of the silent giant that came home and looked at us as if we were born the wrong sex.

My mother and this charming gentleman would go into her room and laugh so loud. They listened to music together and acted as if they had known each other for years. He would look at us with slanted eyes that looked pitch black at night, yet they were always inviting, and they held a smile much longer than his plump lips and perfectly white teeth. He was that type of cool that made each of us girls feel special in different ways.

We knew he had worked hard all his life because his hands were rough. But something had changed for this Randy guy in that he wanted to work hard no longer; he was free and on the run. He came over often, but only when Daddy wasn't home. Mama would tell him that he was gonna have to calm down and get a family of his own, but he would give her a hearty laugh, one we enjoyed hearing. It was a loud sort of chuckle. He'd say the life he was living was the life he had always dreamed of.

He was different from Daddy. He did great magic tricks, laughed with such enthusiasm, and could sing. He would go deep in the woods and serenade my mother, and it sounded like he had a megaphone in his throat, we could hear him so clearly.

But once, Daddy came home in the middle of his song. He yelled at what was making noise in the woods and threatened to shoot the person if they didn't stop all that bellyaching. Mama wouldn't let him, and you could see in her eyes that Daddy had just ruined a moment for her. Right after dinner, she went and stood on the porch as if waiting for Randy to finish his song.

Daddy often said that if he ever caught Mama with another man, that was it. Even as children of seven or eight, we understood what he meant by 'that's it.'

Randy had been visiting for about two years before Daddy got wind of the affair. Daddy stayed away more after that, but when he did come home, he wanted everything to feel the same. I felt we were a family only in appearance, and that somewhere my daddy had another family he truly loved.

It was late, and you could hear the crickets singing outside the window. Nothing moved that night except heavy breathing coming from Mama's room. Then came thumps on the wooden floor, steady and deliberate. I hoped Mama heard it and somehow got away. For a moment I hoped it was Randy, but the steps were much heavier than his and moved too fast. I heard a click, like a latch opening. Then loud bangs—*bang, bang, bang, bang*—followed by another click, like something being pulled back, and then three more bangs.

Lillian jumped up, grabbed my hands, and pulled me to the kitchen. We huddled beside the table. Heavy footsteps moved quickly through the house. The smell of burned metal filled the air. It looked as though fog had settled inside our home, lingering around Mama's bedroom.

We heard shuffling—clothes or covers—then a heavy thump, like a body hitting the floor. We saw the shadow of Randy's limp body being dragged out the back door. Daddy may have carried him to the small cabin behind the house; he was gone for about an hour. When he came back in, his eyes were red and wide. He didn't look at us and we didn't look at him. He walked past, pacing back and forth as if searching for words to explain what had just happened.

We saw Mama lying on the bed, her lifeless hands covering her face. Blood soaked the sheets where bullets had struck her neck and side. My father cried for hours. The sun forced its way through the cracks in the closed shades. Morning had come. Then he went back into her room and stayed for what felt like hours, though it may have been only minutes. Time had stopped for me and Lillian. We watched him as if he might bring her back to life, because that was what we wanted.

Mama had loved us girls in the only way she knew how. On the rare occasions she called us beautiful, we believed her, because we carried her face, her smile, and a curlier version of her light brown hair.

Finally, Daddy lowered her hands and pulled a sheet over her body, leaving only her face uncovered. My sister and I held each other as he came out, head bowed and still covered in blood. He asked if we wanted to say goodbye to Mama, and we both ran to her.

The smell of death filled our noses and brought tears to our eyes. We each said goodbye and ran back out. We'd loved her so much. The pain was unbearable, and we returned to our hiding place. We wanted to talk to Daddy, but we weren't used to doing that, so we stayed quiet. Then we sat on the kitchen floor, clinging to each other and trying not to show any emotion at all. That silence would live in our consciences forever … a silence that gave birth to years of fear and self-hatred.

Then Daddy said, almost calmly, 'Good, now that's over.' He covered Mama completely, packed our clothes, and walked outside. We thought he had gone to the truck to get something. Instead, we heard the engine start and the truck drove away. He didn't even look back at us. He just left.

We were children, incapable of caring for ourselves, but we ate crackers, drank water, and cried on the floor. Sometimes we ran to the door or stared out the window, waiting—for what, we didn't know.

It might have been two days later when Clare came to the house. She saw what she saw and called the police. The look in her eyes when she saw us … it was as if we were ghosts. Then she noticed our suitcase was packed. She grabbed our hands and pulled us out of the house. The smell—it must have been the smell—made her cough and clutch her chest. She kept staring at us, especially at Lillian. Lillian gave a small smirk, and Clare immediately turned and vomited just as the police officers pulled into the driveway.

Later that week, they let the townspeople have a funeral for Mama. I don't know what happened to Randy; we never went to a funeral for him. I don't remember much about Mama's funeral. She had a casket. It was closed. The only thing I remember clearly is saying goodbye to Mama a few days before—a goodbye I would never forget. Sometimes, it's the painful things we say goodbye to that help us understand this: You can't truly appreciate the pleasures of this future until you've first learned how to let go of the pains of the past. Now, my child, that one is for the book.

———

Margarita

We sat and talked for a little bit longer, mainly about the plans for the day, but her story lingered like a leftover meal, which I nibbled on for weeks to come.

PHRASE 3

MEMORIES TOO PAINFUL

Margarita

My mother was yelling my name from the kitchen, "Rita!" at the top of her lungs, trying to get me out of the house so they could drop me off at Leona's and pick me up a few hours later.

I lagged, slowly putting on my light jacket, breathing heavily as if it were a weight I could barely lift. I combed my hair back and moved as though it hurt to move. With each step I stomped, hitting the floor with my shoes as if they had personally offended me.

There were six pairs of eyes that watched my purely awkward acting, but only one pair of eyes spoke.

"Just stop going. Why do you keep visiting the lady anyway?" It was Janet.

In a family where I was often an unwelcome guest, time with Leona changed that narrative, and that made all the difference. Those mini-visits became something I protected. If my sisters knew how much I truly enjoyed them, not to mention the school credit I earned, they might have wanted to join in. Cindy had already mentioned she needed service-learning hours, and I didn't want anyone infringing on my time.

If only my sisters understood how much I learned from Leona. Some days it was color—how to coordinate and contrast, and lessons tucked into conversations about hair and nails. Other days it was cooking: frying and baking chicken, stirring pots of gumbo. When I felt like talking, I did, but mostly I preferred to listen. Her life was far more interesting than the one I created for my ants.

My father was blowing his horn, and I had to conceal my urge to get out of the house, which became confused with my rushing to appease my parents. I think the family still believed these visits were torture. When I was seated comfortably in the car, my mind was free to feel pleased that I got to visit again.

I could barely contain my joy for this visit: It felt like watching the next episode of an exciting soap opera. Leona would tell me about Clare today. She always left me hanging when she ended her stories. She had told me Clare killed her artistically, and my next probing question was how? How did that happen? Was she so mad that she made them practice all the time and punished them unnecessarily? I guessed I would know today.

When I made it to her small apartment, she had a big bowl of ice cream on a small tray in front of my chair. Leona liked to stock my favorite ice cream, black walnut. The chair—my chair—covered in soft orange upholstery, made me imagine I was a queen riding a caterpillar, ruling over my ant subjects.

At times Leona's house felt more gray, but today it felt more orange. The tall orange vase in the corner really popped with the orange placemat under my bowl and the orange coasters Leona had set out on the coffee table.

She smiled at me, which always made me relax. "How many siblings do you have?" she asked.

"There are six girls altogether, and three boys, so nine."

"Wow, that must have been nice. All by the same parents?"

"One was adopted." I pushed the bowl away from me and sat back to show her I wanted to listen, not talk.

"Tell me about them, the sisters I have not met," Leona said. "Let me see, I met Andrea, Janet, and Nia? Who else?"

"You haven't met Wanda or Cindy. I know you remember Andrea. She's only three years older than me, but she does bad things, which is another story."

"What's so bad about what she does?"

"She'll do anything for money."

"Is she rich?"

"No."

"Well, they say rich people will do anything for money, and they call it 'ambitious.' "

"Ambitious. She's only a few years older than me. She lies a lot and steals my stuff."

"You all don't like Andrea?"

"To say the least. She's rather stupid. Janet says she might be pregnant. She's only sixteen, the dummy." I shifted slightly forward. "Can't I hear *your* stories, Miss Leona? I mean, there's not much I can say about Andrea."

"Sure there is. I'm just curious as to why you dislike her so much."

"She's just stupid, that's all! The guy she likes? He's a nobody. He gets high and gang bangs, and that's what she likes about him! She wants to be grown up until she gets in trouble, and she calls on Mama, and Mama just lets her back in again. Mama's probably going to have to raise her baby."

"She's your sister." Leona's tone held no malice.

"I know."

"Are you just a little bit glad that she isn't your real sister?"

"Just a little," I admitted.

She laughed. "Child, you just told me you knew she was your sister. She can't be your sister a little bit; she either is or she isn't."

She had me there. Warmth flushed up my face. I said the only justifiable thing I could say. "I love her like all the rest. I just don't like it when she does stupid things. And ... and she keeps saying me and her are just alike. I am nothing like her."

"Why do you suppose she says that?" Leona's face was full of curiosity.

"I don't know. Because we both are allergic to watermelon. It started as a joke when I was little. Now when she says it, I don't like it. I am nothing like her."

"Well, you both are allergic to watermelon. That's a shame within itself."

I laughed. I guess she had a point. My family loved the stuff, but it made me and Andrea itch, and we would stay in the room until the eating and the sticky hands and the red-juice-running-down-the-face feast was over.

Then Leona scooped me another spoon of ice cream. The fact that I had satisfied her so easily was strange to me, but I wanted the conversation to end, so I didn't say anything else.

"Do you remember the first time you had ice cream?" she asked.

"No, not really."

"You know why you don't remember?"

I wanted to say because it's not important, but I had learned that Miss Leona didn't like to be challenged or smarted off to, so I simply said, "I must have been too young."

"Yeah, and because you have it so often," she said. "I didn't have ice cream until I was fourteen. A day I shall always remember."

"Why's that, Miss Leona?"

"Well, Clare didn't let us have much of a life. I never had a pink, flowered dress, lights for Christmas, or turkey for Thanksgiving unless we got it from the church, which I hated. We cried many tears, hidden behind pretend smiles. If it wasn't for the music, I probably would have ended it a long time ago."

"So Clare was that mean?"

"I wouldn't say that. Let's just say she was a closed spirit with many secrets to hide. When we finally were allowed to read her spirit, we learned to understand and eventually worked toward forgiveness. My sister and I were around ten years old when we moved in with Clare, right after Mama's death and Daddy's disappearance."

———

Leona

Clare lived in a large Victorian-style house on Fox Valley Road, which was a main street at the time. I heard she had the house built from the ground up, and my daddy helped with the work. She was one of the well-off Black folk in the South — living in a big house and driving a car — so people saw her as important. She had money and lots of it, but she lacked flair. My mama had style and flair.

The inside of Clare's house was nothing special. There was a couch covered in handmade pillows, a large china cabinet with a matching dining table, and a grand piano in the corner of the living room. She played that piano sometimes three times a day. That's how we learned to play — by listening to her pound out songs. She was a good pianist. Music was her lover. We were just spectators. She would close her eyes and play Beethoven with fierce intensity — right notes, wrong intentions. We listened, pretending to be somewhere else, while her presence crushed the sparks of creativity inside us. Each note burned within, but opening our eyes drowned the melodies like cold water on flames. When she was away, we imitated her music, piece by piece, trying to resurrect our own creativity and just breathe.

Clare didn't want us there, though she never said so outright. She had made Papa a promise, and above all else, she was a woman of her word. The church people often praised her for her good heart in keeping us, but she never accepted their compliments graciously because deep down, she knew there was nothing good about it. She fed us, clothed us, and kept us in school, yet she had a way of tormenting us that left lasting mental bruises.

When our mother's personality came out of us, she would get so upset that she would lock us in our room until dinner. Then she wouldn't cook, and we would eat cheese or liver cheese and crackers. She would take pleasure in breaking up the crackers into pieces so small that it would be difficult to eat the meat with them. But it's strange how when people try to do mean things to you on purpose, it doesn't always work. We learned to love to eat meat with broken crackers.

What was also peculiar was that there were so many things we never really knew about our mother; we didn't know what not to act like. So when Clare reacted with hostility toward us, she was helping us get to know the woman we never knew. And although she meant it to hurt, it was strangely satisfying. Sometimes, we would do things just to learn more about our mother.

I remember when Lillian sort of liked Tom—you know how young kids just play around. Tom, of course, said he liked another little girl named Mattie until Lillian talked to him.

Clare got so angry that she shouted, "Just like your mother! Always wanting something you should not have. You hear me, you?" Then she would whisper things like, "Slut," and, "Just can't wait to grow up and be a whore like your no-good mama."

Those words cut like a knife, but we didn't understand until later what they really meant. Those kinds of words just.... She stopped talking, looked at me, and smiled, letting me know that she was okay now, and the story continued.

Don't get me wrong: Clare was mean, but as long as we were quiet and didn't look at her too long—because we looked just like our mother—she allowed us to live in her house. However, there were times when my sister and I would be in the room laughing and she would burst in, shout "Cut off the light!" and say somewhat breathlessly, "Bedtime." We knew that meant no more laughing.

We only had each other in the world, and we knew it, so we never fought. Oddly, Clare didn't resent our closeness. She didn't encourage it, but she didn't resent it either.

When she was in one of her good moods, she would tell us about Daddy. She would always start off saying, "Your mother was capable of almost anything, but your father was a good man, angry because of the cards life dealt him, but a good man. He worked hard all the time. When he was a boy, he was determined that he would always carry his own weight."

I sometimes wished we looked more like Daddy, because Clare loved him.

In that large house, there was one room Clare didn't want us to ever go in, but one day she left us home alone while she ran errands. Now this was strange, because she never wanted us in the house unless she was there. At times she even watched us go to the bathroom. And the woman would sometimes burst open the door of our bedroom late at night when we were asleep and scold us for talking.

That day, she left us alone in her precious house. We figured this was a perfect opportunity for us to see the room she'd barred us from for life. We had learned early on that life was short, so we decided to go inside. This room was full of pictures of our father when he was younger. There was a box full of letters, some old and some from within the last few months. Then we found a newer picture of Daddy in the middle of a wheatfield. He was alive and well, and they had obviously been keeping in touch. I didn't like the feeling this gave me, but we knew she would be coming back soon, so we ran back to our room.

After that visit, she barricaded the room door. You see, what we didn't know was that she had a piece of thread on the doorknob, and when she came back, the thread was on the floor. She knew that we knew, and she hated us for this, but she never said a word.

Clare was strange indeed. She never dated! But I remember one young man she brought home for dinner. He complimented us girls for having beautiful eyes, and we never saw him or anyone else again. Clare just continued to work hard, fix up her house, and go to church. Church was our escape. We didn't believe much of what we heard from the pulpit at that time, but it was our ticket out of that silent torture. After Clare found out that we knew about her secret room, she rarely said two words to us. And she put us in the school across the bridge so that she wouldn't have to teach us.

We were only ten, and we had another thing to endure. The town's rumors had turned us into monsters in people's minds. We learned you can't fight rumors. Rumors are invisible spirits that can't be defeated because they are carried on the breath of so many people. They move around with pride and indignation, creating images from the imaginations of people who never really knew you. They spread fantasies about what you are, and many times you are the very opposite. So most of the time we let them talk, because it was senseless to defend ourselves against unthinkable lies.

One rumor said we were twin spirits — you saw two, but really we were one. That one was almost funny. We were supposedly ghosts. Simple people with small minds needed a story, I suppose. I hated that they gained it at our expense, but some good came from it: Those who had nothing had us to talk about.

I used to wonder why life was so hard for us. Why didn't God do something? But after you live with something long enough, you stop wondering.

On numerous occasions, we tried to make Clare like us — really, we did. We didn't complain about the fact that she never talked to us or gave us Christmas gifts or allowed us to get involved with Easter plays at church. And with all the money she had, and she had lots of it, she never bought us one new dress. Our clothes came from the secondhand store, or from friends, and if the dress was pink or yellow, we couldn't wear it. We just lived in dark colors, inside a house that was equally as dark. She didn't allow us to have friends in the house or go out much; it was school, church, and home. What she forced us to live, she had to live too.

She never told us outright that she was in communication with our dad and that she was planning to be with him. But she told us that if we ever saw our father again, we should be happy, hug him, and remember that he didn't have it easy. We smiled, for we didn't know how to respond. But I know how I felt inside. I wanted to shout, "Are you crazy? I saw my daddy kill my mother, and he's the one who hasn't had it easy?" But Clare was talking to us, which rarely happened, and she seemed happy, so we listened. That brief moment of sanity ended a few weeks later, when Papa didn't show up.

I would catch her looking at Lillian with such hatred. If you were ever hated as a child, you know how real hate feels and how it can cut deeper than a knife. In the seven years we lived with Miss Clare, I did only one rebellious thing. Lillian and I wanted brighter-colored clothes; the kids at school were beginning to talk, and we were young and searching. I decided I wouldn't go out of the house until I got a promise of at least one bright-colored dress.

Clare simply said, "You are leaving this house at nine o'clock, even if you have to wear a bathrobe." She kept her word, too.

I wore a bathrobe to church that day, and that was the same day I realized I hated her. When we got home, I dressed and told her just that: "I hate you." My sister looked surprised. She felt the same way, but she just wouldn't say it. I ran to my room, and she ran after me. We held each other like we usually did when we were hurting.

Three years later, we graduated with honors from grade school, and we were accepted into the best high school in Humphrey County. Clare came to the graduation, but she left in the middle of the ceremony, so we had to walk home. When we got home from our graduation, our clothes were packed. Clare was standing there as if she was fighting this decision, or it could be that she just felt we had it coming. It was a strange look, not a smile and not a frown, just rather relieved. We heard her take a deep breath, like she had something to say but would wait to say it.

Lillian looked at her and asked, "What's this, Miss Clare?"

Clare responded rather boldly, "You girls are fourteen now, old enough to live by yourselves. My mother started out at twelve."

The silence in the room made time stand still. I wanted to yell, scream, and hit this woman, but pride—or maybe respect—wouldn't let me.

Then she continued, in a tone that told us this decision had been made years ago. "I did all that I could do. Now I just want peace." The mask of hurt was slowly peeling from her face right before our eyes. We could see how she had aged with us in that house. Her hair was now completely gray. There were small crow's-feet at the corners of her eyes and deep lines across her forehead. And if I hadn't been so afraid of what would happen to us or where we would live, I might have felt pity instead of hatred for her.

She handed Lillian and me a brown envelope with money inside. She had packed a box of food and a suitcase of clothes. "You girls are old enough to make life's decisions. You could work, go to school, or get married. It's your choice. I just want to be left *alone*, that's it. Nothing more—just left *alone*."

It was something about the way Miss Clare stressed "alone" that caused me to run away without looking back at her. As I was leaving, I heard what was to be the true nature of the woman named Lillian: My sister said sweetly, "Thank you." She picked up the small suitcase and box and struggled off the porch. When she caught up to me, I helped her carry our few things as we walked toward the woods. We knew that this woman had not only put us out of her house, but had also uninvited us to be a part of her life. She wanted nothing to do with us at all.

The smell of the red dust itched my nose. We sat on the side of the road in silence, waiting for a miracle that never happened. When it got too dark to see that the dust was red, we got up and began to walk. We both knew where we were going, but we didn't say a word. Lillian had never forgotten the last day at home, and she still had nightmares. Clare had anointed her with holy oil and made us both read the twenty-third psalm each night, and after a month or so, the nightmares stopped. But there were still times when she remembered and had to sleep with the lights on. Neither of us had ever imagined we would ever go back to that place.

Once we got to the house in the woods, we both stopped and stared at how little it had changed. The same sloping roof covered the little porch with a swing on one end. There were a few new cracks in the stairs, and the shades were pulled halfway down, but otherwise the house was the same. I walked up the steps and turned the knob. The door opened easily. I looked back at Lillian, then quickly closed it and sat on the porch, leaning against my suitcase for support. Lillian joined me, and we stared at the stars. When they faded, we watched the slow turn of the moon. Somehow, we fell asleep right there on the porch.

The next day, the wind started sprinting around the house, forcing the branches on trees to bow in submission, rattling the windows, and shaking the unstable porch. Then it began to rain. It rained so hard that the water dripped through the weathered shingles and down on us. We prayed to God for a miracle: not for the seas to part or a mountain to move, but just for the ability to look up, for we both knew if we could just look up, we could get up and remove ourselves from this situation. We looked up at the rain, then at the door. Somehow, strength came, and we got up and walked into the house, fearless.

Soaked and wet, we went in and started the business of running that house. There was a bag of canned goods in the box Clare had given us, so we found some old pots and began to make supper. We washed our sheets and things by hand, and once the rain stopped, we cut enough wood so that we could sleep in a warm house. Reality had set in, and we realized what we had to do was make the best of a bad situation.

We shut Mama's door and put a lock on it. It was no longer a part of the house. Then we started to scrub away ten-year-old bloodstains. We didn't wonder where they came from; we just cleaned. We cut more wood for the fireplace, threw out old food, and restocked the cupboards. I tried to persuade Lillian that we could go to high school in another county, but she wouldn't hear of it. We were smart and would finish right there. As time went on, we learned how to prepare full-course meals and save money from sparse work.

Not everyone in the South believed that Clare was an angel waiting to ascend to heaven. There was one such woman by the name of Mrs. Bell. She had married young, we were told, but no one had ever seen her husband. When we came in her presence, she smiled. It was rumored that she was our mother's friend, but that was never confirmed. We did not see her much growing up. It was the way she looked at us—with such sad eyes—that let us know she understood our struggle.

Her appearance was plain, and she wore a simple, flowery dress straight against her shapeless body. Most days she wore a scarf to protect her hair from the heat, and she wore gloves all the time—even in the summertime. She spoke softly, and when greeted by others, she smiled. She rarely wanted, or was given, credit, but whenever there was a funeral, she was there, front and center, passing out obituaries or helping to serve food. She knew what it was like to struggle and to hurt, and somehow she had discovered that easing the suffering of others dulled her own pain.

When Clare asked us to leave, a week or so later, Mrs. Bell showed up with a pot of greens and another pot of beans. The only thing she said was that rationing it into small portions should last a week. We nodded, and she walked back the way she came. We wanted to say thank you, but before we could get the words out, she was already on her way, walking quickly down the paved road.

She would bring over boxes of clothes and winter wear, even though it was summer. She only spoke to us when she had something important to say, and her voice was almost a whisper — low, slow, but direct. One day she told us to meet her around 7:30 a.m. at the Evans home, and we did. There we found ourselves employed to clean houses a few days a week. She even taught us to garden. So that first summer in our new home was spent beautifying our own house while cleaning the houses of others.

Ms. Bell introduced us to a lady who showed us how to take care of our hair. Our hair was soft with very light waves, a much different texture than most folks' in the South, so we learned how to wash it daily to keep it from getting too oily and looking stiff, like paperboard. By the time we started school in the fall, we had learned how to do nice pinups and how to do braids, which never stayed up long with our hair, but for a day or so, it was a style similar to what the girls in our age group were wearing.

That summer of '54 was a time to remember and reflect. The sound of running water from the nearby creek dripped slowly, a steady reminder that we had survived another day. The most important lesson we learned was this: Whenever you find yourself trapped in a situation and don't know how to get out of it, just look up—then get up and step out of the rain.

PHRASE 4

WE HIDE

Leona

Dandelion flowers, heat, sweet bitter tears, and adventure are how I would sum up the year 1955. It seems so long ago now, 1955, but it was a year to remember. Lillian and I had adjusted to the house and were excited about branching out and trying new things.

Our high school principal was a realist who didn't believe in ghosts or spirits; she understood our predicament and wanted to help. She hired Lillian to tutor the younger children during the school year. Lillian was a little afraid of the job because she had never worked with children before, and since we were the town outcasts, she assumed the children would dislike her too. I reassured her as best I could that everything would be all right, and thankfully it was, because I was afraid for her, as if it were me going before those young people.

After her first day of school, the verdict was in: It was really going to work out. Lillian had met "real people," as she said. They were special children, all struggling with learning, and she felt honored to be able to help them.

She worked so hard—making up spelling songs, writing lessons, and grading papers—that I was forced to take an interest. I had found a job with one of the local churches, cleaning and doing odd tasks, but it was Lillian's work that eased us into adulthood and covered many of the hurts we weren't yet able to face. Each day Lillian came home with a colorful story. Those children loved being around her so much that I found myself wishing I was their friend too, and eventually, I was.

Lillian and I had so much fun. We took long walks when we were bored, or we would take a little money from our rainy day fund to go see a matinee cowboy movie. We listened to old, very old, episodes of *Amos and Andy* over the radio, and yes, we bought ice cream. We never understood the word "fun" until we ate ice cream. It was one of our goals that year to taste every flavor—all eight of them. We accomplished that goal, ultimately deciding that chocolate was the best. We did what most adults didn't do: We bought a TV. It was black and white and sat on four legs in our living room. Most people still only had radios, but we had ourselves a television and were privileged to watch the world around us. Of course, we had to pay someone to modernize the house just a little, but we did that. We had electrical outlets throughout the house, an electric stove, and heat in most rooms. At times we couldn't help but think it was not bad for a couple of teenagers.

In fleeting, unpredictable moments, the hurt would hit us like tornadoes—so strong that all we could do was cry. And we would hide—from sound, from thought, from anything that reminded us of what was real. Then somehow, the sun would shine through a crack or corner of a window, and a burst of energy would invade our space. We would rush out and have a bowl of ice cream, and the thought of fun would return. Then we would talk about the future and what each of us wanted to do. We both agreed that one day we would leave this town, but we just didn't know when.

It was important to Lillian that the house be sold to a family with many children. She wanted their laughter to fill it again.

At work, she would sit out back where the children played and simply listen to them laugh. Then she would come home and describe it to me. She believed that if everyone could remain a child forever, we would never have more than petty problems in this world to solve.

Lillian had read in the Bible that Jesus instructed us to be childlike, and this made her fall in love with Him—because He loved children, she said. With that notion, we found ourselves back in church. I didn't mind; I liked the music, and once again it kept us away from our thoughts.

When you have lived through trauma, or just hard times, rest doesn't settle easily. We were always on guard that something was going to happen, and like a change in air pressure, an unseen sense caused us to watch and wait. We had learned that everything in nature moves underground before it hits the surface. An earthquake was coming.

High school was upon us. In a small Southern town, you attended school with students from the surrounding communities. There was a mixture of children, and the ghost stories about us were not readily believed—at least not at first—but eventually they would be.

We held on to happiness loosely, because each day felt as though darkness were slowly approaching. We sensed something big was about to happen, for fear lay buried deep in the pits of our stomachs.

PHRASE 5

SMALL PARTICLES

Leona

The troubled souls who struggled only to remain poor did not deserve any more sympathy than anyone else. Yet it seemed, in the end, that our divided world would reach the same sad fate. We had settled into a life that was too settled for us, and still we could not run.

We had money, and much of it was soon taken for the mere privilege of living. Most children our age had some sort of aim—marriage, sports, music, or college—but we had only each other and the sound of the piano. We had bought it and played it often, and its music filled the house, yet at times it felt hollow, as though it were only strings vibrating, beautiful but unable to quiet what lived inside our thoughts.

We had been living alone for a year now. Even so, fall brought new hope for Lillian and me. Lillian had been asked to stay on as a tutor after school, and I was to take care of all our household chores. Now that we were back in school with less time to work, we knew things would get tight, so we put every extra dime we had in a pot for rainy days. We even stored canned food away. For a couple of fifteen-year-old girls, we were doing pretty well. Over the summer, we had bought nice, colorful clothes, ribbons for our hair, and household appliances. We had quickly adjusted to our new role as adults, and I had even managed to hold on to the two hundred dollars Clare gave us when she asked us to leave. I didn't want to touch that money. In fact, secretly, I vowed not to and hid it in the third drawer. I figured one day I would give it to a very special person, and it would help them out a great deal, but I would never use it. Lillian understood my secret vows, though I never told her, and she never questioned me about the money. We just never talked about it, and because we were able to save money, we never needed it.

We had completed a year of high school and covertly hoped it would change how the townspeople saw us. But in the South, your past never disappears. You are followed by the shadows of hundreds of people who never stop to say hello, let alone get to know you. Ours was a life they had never lived and one very different from their own, so they added to and subtracted from our experiences, turning our story into unholy fables. We no longer wore dark colors, yet we were still regarded as strange. It made Lillian and me a little self-conscious, but we learned to live with it.

There was only one person in the whole ninth grade who spoke to us. Her name was Tara. She was considered very unattractive, so it seemed natural that we would become friends, and that is exactly what happened.

Tara, like the others, had questions about us. She wandered about with nowhere to go, studying us as if she might see herself in a mirror and counting how many times we finished each other's thoughts. It was almost humorous to us. At first she was afraid to touch our hands, and when we offered her food, she sometimes let it sit on the table for hours, until her stomach forced her to eat or be sick.

We wanted another person in the house, another voice besides our own, so at first we allowed it. Finally, I spoke plainly to her. "I was born the same way you were—to two parents. My father did a very bad thing to my mother, so life hasn't been easy for us. But if you don't want to be here, or if you can't see that we are human just like you—" I paused. I could feel Lillian's heart beating faster as she grabbed my hands, almost as if she was praying.

For a moment, I couldn't continue. I knew Lillian wanted her around; just being with me wasn't enough. She wanted what I wanted—voices, smiles, hand slaps, jokes, and laughter.

As life would have it, Tara didn't stop being our friend. I think she understood the message. Besides, I never begged for enemies, and I wasn't going to beg for friends. Tara looked at me and smiled, letting me know her notions, like those of the other backwoods southerners, were silly, and our friendship blossomed.

One crisp fall afternoon, as we all sat on the porch, Lillian was the first to share with Tara the story of Mama's death, our daddy's disappearance, and our time living with Clare. Tara, in her own way, shared a similar bond with us. She had also lost her mother at a very early age—not to death but to selfishness. Her mother had been singing in a band since Tara was only three years old, so she remembered very little about her. Her father was still alive, but she rarely saw him. The only thing she ever said about him was that he was a drunk.

We made a pact that we wouldn't talk much about the past unless it was truly important. We knew each of us was hurting in ways we couldn't yet explain, so most of the time we left it alone.

I have fond memories of us cooking meals together and having late-night pajama parties. We moved back and forth between the adult and the child worlds, and that was all right. Tara would come over to study, and then we would play records and record ourselves singing. That was how we discovered that Tara had a beautiful voice. Lillian would play a jazz tune on the piano while Tara sang along. We replayed the recording to see if we sounded anything like the record, and soon our attention settled on Tara's voice. She had a beautiful voice — second soprano, I believed. She could hardly accept that it was her own voice on the recorder.

This helped Lillian and me too. For the first time, we had a dream we could share: the dream of stardom. Making it in the music world wasn't what I truly wanted to do, but it was something to think about. Growing up, I had a vivid imagination — probably because I wanted a life other than my own, and also because the imagination is a very powerful tool in covering up pain.

For the first year and a half of high school, we continued to do quite well. Lillian was bringing in a little extra money, and I was keeping up our house and, from time to time, cleaning the homes of others, which also brought in cash. Tara helped by cleaning our house, and most nights she actually stayed with us. But that winter, as I chopped wood in the cold, the storm we had felt brewing finally struck. The H2N2 flu found me. I had chopped wood all the previous winter without so much as a sniffle, so my illness came as quite a surprise.

Lillian worked hard doing homework for both of us and keeping the bills paid. I knew it must have been really hard on her, but she never complained. That little church started holding prayer meetings every night, since the flu had become an epidemic. Every evening she would go there and listen to the people pray, and then she would come home and help me. Much later, she told me it took her weeks to pray for me because she wasn't sure God loved her like the rest of the people, so she stayed quiet. There was something about the prayers of others that took her mind off me.

I was losing weight and seemed not to be doing any better. Lillian had taken every nickel to buy medication and old grandma remedies, but nothing was taking away the fever.

One day, Lillian was cutting wood, and she almost fell. Henry, a tall, dark stranger, came out of nowhere, caught her, and carried her in. As he placed her on the couch, he belted out,

"What you trying to do, kill yourself too?"

As Lillian rested on the couch, that question stayed with her. If I was going to die, who would she have in this world?

Henry finished cutting the wood so the house would be warmer than with just our space heaters. In fact, he cut enough wood for a week. Every day Henry would come by and visit, bringing over soup for me and sweets for Lillian. He even stayed with me while Lillian reluctantly attended school.

Henry gradually grew on Lillian. He wasn't what either of us would have called attractive — certainly not as striking as the other stranger who had once found the house in the woods, though that stranger had to be carried out of it.

At first, Henry's shadow reminded us of him; I think they were about the same height. But Henry was dependable. He must have heard about the two girls living alone in the nice house in the woods. It was also rumored that Ms. Bell sent him our way. He wasn't bad-looking, just not handsome. And although he had aged gracefully, aged he certainly was. I remember his hairline was slightly receding, and one of his front teeth was shorter than the other, which made it seem as though he was missing one. I always thought he looked like a clown without makeup — there were smile lines in his cheeks even when he wasn't smiling.

Lillian never felt comfortable when Tara and I joked about his appearance, so we saved our comments for when she wasn't around. For days, Henry had wanted to get Lillian by herself; he wasn't a native of our town, so his eyes saw Lillian in a different way. She was of average height, with curly, long, sandy-brown hair and a nice figure, and she was very smart. She told me much later that he finally got her alone in the kitchen; Lillian was putting away some food as he watched her. The way he eyed her both moved and disturbed her, which made her move faster.

"Don't—don't be afraid, Miss Lillian," he said. Henry had a slight speech impediment that prevented him from completing sentences easily.

"I'm not afraid. I got to feed Leona, then study my lessons," she answered.

He grabbed her by the hand and led her to a seat. "What do you fear the most, Miss Lillian?"

She thought about it for a while, and she answered honestly, "I guess I fear being alone."

"Well," he said sort of nervously, "if you married me, you wouldn't ever be alone, even if we lost Leona."

She stared at him, half angry for implying that she might lose me, but happy that someone wanted to take care of her if such an event did happen.

"What do you th-think 'bout that?" he asked.

"I don't quite know."

"Man can't always stay around if he ain't wanted. You just think about that."

I seemed to be getting worse, and Lillian had begun to fear my room. Tara didn't. She still came in, wiped the sweat from my face, and sang to me. Lillian fed me when I felt like eating, then quickly left the room.

That weekend, Lillian asked Tara to stay with me, and in secret she married Henry. He had promised the marriage would remain hidden until she finished school, and she had promised him her heart—two promises that could not be kept.

A week later, the strangest thing happened: I got better. I don't know if it was because Lillian finally found the nerve to pray for me, or because Tara washed all my linens so the sweat and sickness could no longer cling to me, or maybe the virus had simply passed. However, it is said I recovered. Soon I wanted to bathe and sit up, and two weeks later I was back in school.

Lillian then told me about her marriage and that Henry was now staying with us. I understood. I never liked it, but I understood. As with all things, when the truth needs to be revealed, it will be.

I wasn't afraid of Henry. I neither liked nor disliked him; he was like fine dust—moved by powerful forces, drifting until it settled on things still and lifeless.

PHRASE 6

MARGARITA GOES TO HIGH SCHOOL

Margarita

It had been two years I had spent with Leona, and I was on my way to high school—not just any high school, but a selective-enrollment one—and I had already decided that someday I would be a writer. I had passed the Iowa Basic Skills Test, and I felt good. Not because I was smarter than those who had failed, but because I knew I was good at guessing.

Plus, I was graduating. There is something about a girl who has accomplished a hard task—you feel lighter in school, and the air around you almost seems perfumed. So when people asked what I had scored on the test, which was rather high for a girl who spent most of her free time in her own fantasy world, I didn't give details. I simply said I passed.

That was what I told Leona when I came joyfully through her door. "I passed, and I'll be going to high school in the fall!"

"That's good, dear. I made popcorn," she said.

As I grabbed a handful of her fresh white popcorn, I decided I would sit with her for about an hour. Then I would go home, watch television, and dream about going to high school: the journalism club, work after school, and of course, the boys.

"Your mind is so far from here that the Grand Canyon could fit between the distance," Leona said.

"I want to hear more of your stories," I lied.

"I have never told you a story in my life. Everything I told you was the truth."

"Well, I want to hear more truth."

"Tell me, dear, what happens to the people who did not pass?" she asked.

"Some will stay in the eighth grade, and others will go to high school after the summer."

"Must be a horrible thing to be left behind. Those young students must feel terrible."

"I don't know," I said.

"Think about it. It's not hard to imagine; just imagine if it was you."

I put my head down, for the thought was too painful to fully imagine. I would rather have held on to the fact that I didn't have to think about it. "I passed; let's just celebrate that fact."

"I'm happy you passed, really I am," Leona said, "but we must be living organisms."

I thought to myself, *Okay, this again.* I wondered if it was a good time to tell her I never really understood her parables. None of it made any sense to me. Parables were a literary tool when Jesus walked the earth, but they weren't very popular anymore.

She looked as if she was deep in thought, so I decided it wasn't a good time. That day I promised myself I would be bold enough to tell her all the things I longed to say, but for now I just wanted an extra bag of popcorn, a couple of dollars, and something to celebrate the fact that I had made it.

My eyes drifted to a box sitting on the end table, and I wondered if it was for me.

"It's for you," Leona said. "Why don't you open it?"

My wondering ceased. With much enthusiasm, I opened the box. There lay a beautiful light-blue dress; it was perfect, just beautiful. At sixty years young, this lady still had style. "Thank you, Miss Leona! It's beautiful! I could wear it for my luncheon and graduation."

"You shall, but there's something I want you to do first. I want you to look at the other side of the coin."

"The other side of the coin? Okay," I said. If the truth be told, I would have said anything to ensure that I got to wear that beautiful dress.

"I want you to invite all the people you know who failed the test over, and we will have a little party. I'll buy ice cream and cake, and we'll just have a little celebration."

No way, was all I could think. Actually, falling or fainting seemed like a more comforting idea. "I can't do that, Miss Leona," I said.

"I bet you can."

"I'll tell you, and I hope you don't think poorly of me, but most of the people who failed are not my friends," I said. "I have to be honest, Miss Leona — they are mean people. Really. I think they expected to fail. If I invite them to a party, they'll think it's some kind of joke. Please don't ask me to do this."

"I just did."

"And what if I can't?"

"You can! I just said you can. Now you just have to do it!"

She smiled and had very little else to say to me. Usually, when she didn't want to talk to me about her life, we would talk about politics or things happening in the news, but today there was nothing, so I finished eating the popcorn and left.

I was glad to be out of there, but sad to leave the dress behind. She didn't remind me to get it, just asked that I come back on Friday. She said that she would have the party set up in the group room on the first floor.

As soon as I got home, I went straight to my mother to tell her about this thing Leona wanted to do, in the hope of finding a comrade, but she actually agreed with Leona. For the first time, I had the mind to just leave the lady alone. Nevertheless, I thought about the dress, the light-blue lace dress. Knowing that my parents couldn't afford something so beautiful, I tore myself away from the thought of leaving her just yet.

I thought about telling Leona the truth about myself — that although I wasn't a troublemaker, I fought often and could end a fight with a single blow. We were a large family in the heart of the ghetto, which meant people tested us, and we had to defend ourselves. I never enjoyed it, but if someone forced me to fight, I tried to end it quickly so they would never want to come after my sisters or me again.

The rule in our family was simple: If one of your siblings was fighting, you helped, which was why I fought so much. Now this crazy lady wanted me to invite some of the very people I had once had to beat up to a party. What — did she think I was an angel?

Maybe I should tell her I used more foul language than a drunken sailor, and I was good at it. It was one of the few things us preacher's kids could do that helped lift the halo people thought we wore. We preacher's kids had struggles like everyone else. We had challenges and enemies like everyone else, and poverty was no place to be weak. You had to fight or at least be willing to, and I was.

Still, I had a writing career, a future husband, and children — at least in my imagination — to look forward to. My mind searched for some creative way to wiggle out of the situation, but I found none. I thought about lying, about just inviting my friends who passed and having them lie to the lady and eat her ice cream and cake. That was it: I would ask a few friends to come over and we would trick the lady, I would get my dress, and I wouldn't ever see her again.

On the day I was supposed to put the plan into action, I gained a conscience. I found myself face-to-face at the pencil sharpener with one of the girls who had not passed the test. That day was her last day of class until summer school began.

I wondered what it must be like to be her—to have taken graduation pictures, applied for high school, and been measured for a graduation robe, only to be told she might have to do it all over again the next year.

So I told her, rather nonchalantly, about this crazy lady who was having a party in the condo square, which for years we had thought was a senior building, and how she had asked me to invite everyone who failed—how silly! She asked for the time and location and then walked away. I realized she didn't find the idea silly at all.

That encouraged me to invite the other students who had failed, and I did so with a little more enthusiasm. I told them that, if nothing else, the cake would be worth the walk to the square.

I walked home that day feeling good about myself. I had never felt that way before. I had invited fifteen or more kids to the party, and none of them rejected the idea.

Friday came, and it was just Miss Leona and me. I felt like a fool. I must have looked like a fool to those kids, actually inviting them to a party. What did I think—that they were really going to attend a "Congratulations, you failed" party?

In my mind, the scene began to change. I imagined the kids I had invited whispering behind my back and laughing at me, and that as soon as I walked out of the square, I would have pea balloons thrown at me. The thought brought tears to my eyes.

Why did I even listen to this confused twin? I thought. *Isn't she really just half of a person?* What they must have thought of me! I prepared myself to fight to get my reputation back. This was an act of weakness; I wouldn't ever be this weak again.

"What time did you say, dear?"

Not that I wanted to say a word to the lady, but I still needed the dress. "You said 5 to 7 p.m."

"Oh my, it's 5:15. I guess we can cut the cake."

I nodded; I didn't much feel like eating, but I would play along with the game. Besides, I needed something to keep my mind off the fact that I must have looked like one big fool to all those people I invited. How would I amend this? Maybe I'd have to beat up all the people who told me they would come.

Just as I was thinking all this, Mark Granner walked in. He smiled at me and sat down. We were friends, I suppose. I was honestly sad he hadn't passed the test, though we had often asked him to sneak candy out of Jet's store for us.

Ten minutes later, Sherice, the girl I had met at the pencil sharpener, came through the door. She was nice, I suppose, but not someone I would have ever considered a friend. She sat down awkwardly at the table with Mark and me.

Before I knew it, seven more kids walked into the room. One girl I recognized, Brenda the blabbermouth, came right in and immediately began talking. But in the middle of her chatter, she told everyone there would be a study group that summer after school, one that would help them pass the test the next time around. It was free and run through LaSalle

Street Church, a place many kids in the community already went for tutoring.

We talked and we laughed. Even though they still had to go to summer school, we somehow found a few fun moments in it. They all talked together, and for a moment I actually wished I was going to summer school too.

Before the afternoon ended, Sherice said to me, "You know what, girl? I thought you were lying,"

"Thought I was lying?" I said in disbelief, knowing that almost all the time, I lied.

"Me too," Mark said, "but I said forget it, so I came anyway."

I didn't address the issue of my possibly lying in front of Miss Leona. I knew they had reasons to feel that; I was known for stretching the truth, and it is at this very moment that I decided that I didn't want to be known as a liar.

We sat at that table and talked about future hopes for high school. I didn't know I could be encouraging, but I was. All I said was that summer goes really fast, which was a truth they could agree with.

Life had opened a new door for me. You can get to know people who seem to have nothing in common with you, and when difficulties happen, you can change a situation simply by sharing a meal together. I wouldn't have traded that day for the world.

Miss Leona said a few encouraging words to them and gave each of them a preparatory book of some kind. Then she let us continue our conversation as it moved on to all the things that had happened that year—the good and the bad— and she didn't interfere.

An hour or so later, the group left, and I remained with Leona. I felt no ill feelings toward her at all. I felt she had taught me something in the larger scheme of life that I would one day need. I think she knew it too, and in a quietly satisfied way, she was proud that she and I had shared the moment.

"You want the dress, don't you?" she asked me.

"I—I guess."

"Now you know we have to listen and we have to hear," right?

"We hear?" I asked.

"Hear the pain of others. It's in understanding their brokenness that our brokenness is healed."

This, oddly, I understood. I couldn't explain how I understood, and not even what I understood, so I just nodded yes. Then she continued.

"I always thought gray, pink, or black would be your favorite colors." She stopped and looked at me proudly and said, "That was a good thing you did, dear."

"You did it, Miss Leona, all this," I said. "I just told people—"

"I know. That's okay. You could have invited all your friends and cousins and had them lie to me, but you didn't. I'm proud of you. You are so much better than I imagined."

She got up, placed the box on the table, and left. I remember how she sort of floated out of the room, smiling and satisfied.

My curiosity drew my eyes to the box she had left for me. I opened it and found not one but two dresses: both blue, my favorite color. I was excited for the dresses, but nothing could surpass how I'd felt when Mark, Sherice, and the other kids walked through those doors.

I wasn't going to come back for a while, but this lady was wise, and a thinker and interpreter of thoughts. I saw what she meant when she said the opposite side of the coin was nothing to fear. We are all fragmented, looking and hoping that the opposite side of the coin brings us to wholeness.

PHRASE 7

SOUNDS WITH NO STRINGS

Margarita

Today we would not fight, and we would be cleaner than purified water. Boys would have fresh haircuts, with their favorite logos etched into their heads, and girls would wear fresh braids or newly permed hair. Everyone would strive to look their best on this day. Legs would not carry fear, but bold steps of accomplishment.

Balloons would float high in the air, and cards would be decorated with caps and gowns. The organ would be playing "Pomp and Circumstance," and on this day our feet would not dance—our spirits would. We wouldn't need a dance partner because each person would move to their own rhythm, shaped by the struggles that brought them here.

The balloons, covered in congratulatory signatures, the cards with a few dollars tucked inside, the smell of soft perfumes or Old Spice, the smiles on our parents' faces that said, *My baby did it.* The yells and applause from the audience as we walked across the stage to receive the rolled-up piece of paper with our name on it, simply saying: *You graduated.*

Yes, today was graduation day.

We would hear sounds without strings and beats without bass. Laughter would create a rhythm of its own, and the applause would become lyrics without words. These were the moments we longed for.

I invited Leona to my eighth-grade graduation, but to my surprise, she declined. She was not a person for formal events, and after hearing her stories, I understood why.

I arrived at her house on a Saturday at my usual time. The door was open, so I walked right in and took a seat in my chair. She sat at the piano and played a very slow melody. When I started to ask who had written it, she hushed me.

She played and I sat. I can't say I wanted to leave. I just knew I shouldn't. She had helped me through some very hard times, and for the first time, I realized she needed me not just to hear, but to listen too.

She rose from the piano with tear-filled eyes but said nothing at first. Instead, she fixed herself a cup of coffee, and I basked in the smell of it, freshly brewed and warm. She sat on the edge of the piano stool and spoke.

"Graduation is a monumental step in everyone's life, and it is necessary. I just don't have happy memories of graduations." She paused. "When we graduated from grade school, we were put out of Clare's house, and by the time we reached twelfth grade, we had other things to face—some good and some not so good—but we made it. We made it with all the odds against us."

Then she explained why she had declined.

"I declined your invitation, dear, because I want this day to be for you what it wasn't for us—joyful. Do you want to know what high school was like for us girls?"

"I guess."

"Come on, you can do it. Say it like you mean it."

"What was high school like?"

"I thought you'd never ask."

Then, instead of talking, she sat at the piano and began to play. It was a strange tune, one I had never heard before, though Leona could play almost any genre of music. After she finished, I asked her the name of it, and she answered as if she was giving a music lesson.

"Scott Joplin," she said. "Such a tragedy that we sometimes put music through."

Then she turned from the piano and began to speak.

———

Leona

I never could quite figure out what the word "strange" meant, especially when it was used in reference to my sister and me. We both worked hard and studied even harder, yet in the minds of those with limited space and a small vocabulary, we were considered strange. We were even voted the strangest people in the senior class. Our good friend Tara tried to put it mildly, saying that we kept to ourselves and people feared what they didn't know. Nevertheless, we knew the truth. This town had never given us a chance, and they weren't going to start now that we were attractive adults. We looked like our mother, so we were called ghosts.

Our dream, before Henry came into our lives, was to leave Belzoni and pursue a music career. Now we had a new dimension to consider: Henry. Lillian always honored her secret marriage to him and wouldn't allow us to disrespect him. I could sometimes feel her sadness. It was clear she would never give him her heart, but what she did give him was respect, and she refused to let anyone else take that from him.

I was jealous at times — not because I wanted to marry an older man, but because I longed for someone to love me. I was beginning to feel the sting of rejection, especially when Tara got a date for the senior dance. She waited until a week before the dance to tell me, I suppose because she didn't want to hurt my feelings.

We had accepted her and helped bring out her talent. Now, when people heard her sing, they could finally see her differently. She was going to the dance with Dan, a thin boy with a stick-figure build and a filthy mouth. He was always making crude jokes I couldn't stand to hear.

I asked Tara why she would want to go out with someone like him, and she simply replied, "I want to go to the dance."

Don't we all, I thought, but she deserved to go more than anyone else.

Lillian was able to cope with not having a male friend and not being asked out because she had Henry. As time moved on, he was panning out not to be all that, but he was her husband, and a broad shoulder to lie on at night and tell her secrets to. At times, he didn't know how to complete sentences. He just sort of hoped she got the point, and in most cases she did. He was not a talker, but he was a good listener.

I experienced a glimmer of hope in the twelfth grade when Dan's cousin Mike passed me a note in history class asking if he could have lunch with us that day. All through class I daydreamed about what he might want with me. Like Tara, I didn't really find him attractive, but I wanted to be asked to the dance.

The three of us sat quietly at the lunch table waiting for him. We shyly glanced back as he laughed and talked with the other kids about the dance. When the bell rang, my heart sank so low it felt it could touch my toes, but I kept my head high as I left the lunchroom. I was disappointed, but I wouldn't let it show.

Just as we were about to walk into class, Mike came up and tapped Lillian on the shoulder. I stepped in front of her, determined that he would speak to me, not her.

"Hey, where y'all going?" he said, smiling as he lightly grabbed my arms.

"To class," I answered, assuming he was speaking only to me.

"I said I wanted to talk with y'all. Come on now, give me a break."

"Okay, what do you want? Let's get on with it!" I hoped for a quick question so I could say yes and get on with the business of being the prettiest girl at the dance.

Mike had swagger and a charming smile, though his skin was rough, marked with dark spots and a few large bumps on his cheek. Still, the girls liked him. He was good at sports and talked constantly — always about sports and how he was going to be the next Jackie Robinson or Hank Aaron. If you weren't careful, you might even believe him. For now, though, he was mostly known for pleasing the ladies. He looked at both of us, though I hoped he was looking only at me.

"I wanted you to go to the dance with me. After the dance, we could all do a little something. I hear things about you, and I could take every one of you."

"Which one of us are you talking to, Mike?' I asked innocently.

"I want all of you. Every single one of you. Besides, who can tell you two apart?"

I stared at him, one inch from slapping his face, when Lillian gently grabbed my arm and said calmly, "Pick us up at seven-thirty."

He looked shocked. "All right … that sounds good." Then he walked away.

"What did you do that for? I'm not going out with him—I can't!" I shouted.

"Neither am I. He doesn't want to date us," Lillian said mischievously. "He wants to date ghosts." She gave me a look that assured me she had a plan.

Lillian warned me not to tell Tara, fearing she might repeat it to Dan, Mike's cousin and best friend. I promised not to say a word, and the plan was set.

As we walked home, Lillian revealed her idea, and once again I felt proud to be her sister. We hurried home to fix Tara up. In a strange way, the plan brought excitement to my life.

Maybe we really were a couple of unusual girls.

THE PLAN

Leona

If only I had known then what I know now. Since that time, I have learned a great deal about tricks and illusions, but back then Lillian and I knew very little. We only wanted to scare Mike and maybe cause a little bodily harm.

I understand now that when you lower yourself to the standards of others, you become what they believed you were all along. The lie becomes the truth, and you find yourself living inside the very nightmare you once hoped to escape. We probably would have made better decisions had we understood that.

I could have simply said no and left him to invent whatever story he wished about being turned down by a couple of "ghosts," as the townspeople called us.

———

The first thing we had to do was get Henry out of the house, which wasn't that hard, considering for the last six months he'd hardly been home at night anyway. Lillian had been telling me that Henry was becoming a stranger in her bed. He would wake her up at night just to make sure she was alive. I noticed that when I walked into a room, he would quickly exit, but I just figured I didn't have time to nourish Henry's fears. I was three weeks from graduating and still didn't know what it felt like to be liked by a boy, so when Lillian complained or complimented Henry, I paid very little attention.

To make sure he wouldn't come home, we told him we were having a girls' night and needed to be left alone. He agreed, or rather grunted something, and walked out of the house, taking nothing but his bad attitude, which had been his constant companion for months now. We were just glad he was gone and would stay gone long enough for us to plan our revenge on Mike.

This was the plan. We took two white sheets and stuffed them with old clothes and newspapers, then tied strings around them to form heads. Using a black eyebrow pencil, we painted eyes, a nose, and a mouth on each one. Lillian put a little lipstick on her ghost figure, and then we strung them up from the ceiling so they floated flawlessly back and forth. We rigged a bucket of milk to fall on Mike when he knocked on the door, and recorded all kinds of weird sounds and laughter that we planned to play after the milk dropped. Lillian suggested that we jump from behind and start hitting him with sticks or something, but I decided against it. He would be a mess and wouldn't be able to attend the dance: that was punishment enough.

At 7:15 Mike arrived. He was dressed in a nice black tuxedo—the 1950s' kind with wide lapels and a white shirt. His black shoes were spit-shined, and his coal-black hair was slicked straight back as if wax held every strand in place. He walked with a swagger, side to side, making soft crunching noises as the grass and leaves bent beneath his feet along the muddy path to our house.

When I saw him, I had second thoughts. I told Lillian we should just pretend we weren't home. But it was his hands— freshly shined with Vaseline—holding two long-stem red daisies that brought tears to Lillian's eyes. We were many things in that small town, and some even believed we could fly, but we were not immoral. The sickening thought that he intended to defile both my sister and me made our bodies shake with anger. The plan stayed in place. Now all we needed was for it to work.

As he stepped toward the place where it would happen, I thought of what he would later say to his small band of misfits—that he had conquered both of us. I imagined them throwing their heads back in laughter, slapping their knees and clapping their hands in disbelief, each secretly wishing they could be so lucky. Our house would be reduced to nothing more than a place for wayward men. What hurt most was what we would never say aloud: We feared it would prove everything Clare had ever believed about us was true. We would have finally played our whore card and she would have been right. That's why we did it, and although the consequences would never be lived down in that small town, I'm glad we did it.

The night came, and so did our fear, but I pulled the string. Milk drenched him, the music began to play, and the stuffed sheets floated back and forth. He was so shocked that he was afraid to move at first. We had to throw rice at him just to unstick him from his fear. Besides, the tape was only ten minutes long, and we needed him out of the house. When the rice hit his face, he ran so fast that he left his dress shoes behind. That was the last we ever heard of Mike.

But the town had much to say. They said Mike was traumatized and rushed to the hospital. I knew that wasn't true, but once words begin to spread, they have no boundaries. Soon, people young and old pointed and whispered as we walked by. Laughing it off as a joke didn't work. They argued that it took very strange people to imagine a joke so cruel. I thought it had already been decided that we were strange. My only real regret was how the school reacted. The principal listened to our explanation and was rational enough to understand it had been a prank. However, she had to inform us that some parents no longer wanted Lillian working with their children, so we would have to find new jobs. Lillian was crushed. She lived to care for those children, but we understood.

What struck us most was that no one seemed troubled by the fact that a boy had asked out two sisters at the same time. It did not make a single soul uncomfortable with what that "innocent" boy had been implying.

This single event was all the evidence Henry needed to walk out of their marriage. I remember when he left for good. He had heard about what happened to Mike, and fresh rumors developed. He came home one night and asked to speak with Lillian. He sat on the edge of the bed and quietly removed his jacket. Lillian walked into the room prepared with explanations, but the sight of him sitting there—jacket off, shoulders heavy—pulled her mind away from every word she had planned to say.

Henry had reached his end. He wanted out of their secret marriage. Although she was convinced that what she felt for him was not love—it couldn't be love when you imagined a life with a totally different person—what she felt was obligation, something that can hold you in a bad relationship as strongly as the pretense of love.

Before he could speak, she went to the closet and pulled out the pretty green dress she had bought. She thought maybe with him seeing the dress, he might like to see her in it. "Like this, Henry?"

"It's, it's—"

"Beautiful," Lillian said, completing his thoughts. "I bought it for myself. It was sort of an anniversary present." She held the dress up to herself and twirled around. "Do you realize that it will be three years this winter, Henry? I was only fifteen, a babe when you walked into my life out of nowhere. Right through the fog, you walked right up and started doing things for me — cutting the wood, making warm soup. Did I ever tell you thanks?"

"You did, I'm sure. I mean, I, I—"

"Thank you." She ended his struggle for words. "Least you say I was rude. You want to talk to me about the rumors, don't you?"

He stayed silent and just looked at her. He was searching her face for something, but she didn't know what, and this frustrated her to the point of anger, which changed her tone with him.

"What do you want to know?" she asked.

He turned his back away from her, as if to gain strength.

"Well, I can't tell you if something is true or not unless you tell me what you know, okay?"

He nodded yes.

"Now tell me what the juke house is rumbling about and I'll tell you the truth," she said sternly.

He looked away from her to avoid her penetrating glance, but his body was still turned toward her. She was about to witness a miracle: It was the first time Henry had ever finished his own thought. "Well—" He started slowly but sped up until he was running sentences together, and she had to sit down close to him to make sure she was hearing him correctly. "Well, they say this house is full of the haunts, ghosts, that people's ghosts is round it all the time, and if you come out at night, you'll see them. They say you two sisters communicate with these spirits, and can even become one of them because of how you grew up. They also say we see one, but actually you are two." He sneaked a quick glance back at her, catching a half-felt smile. "Well, well, I'm convinced people say anything, and people believe anything."

He bowed his head, and Lillian got angry. She had lived with this man, slept with this man, bathed him, cooked for him, and grown to appreciate him despite all his faults, and he questioned whether or not she was real. She internalized her need to cry aloud. Instead of crying, she sweated like a field worker. "Well, big boy, do you want to know if I'm real? Do you?" she asked.

He looked away from her.

"Well, now, you just touch my hand. Not as if you haven't touched me all over, because you have, but that didn't convince you, so maybe if you just touch my hand, this subject will be forever settled."

Henry slowly moved over and held her hand, which was wet with sweat and very warm. In his mind this heat was unexplainable. He pulled away as if he had just touched a hot stove. Lillian laughed, then got up and walked out of the room.

We heard things shuffling around, then heard the suitcase open and shut. Lillian watched that 250-lb. man run away as if he had stolen something. She longed to tell him that she was sorry, because he was a nice man and all, even if he was rather dense. But he left and didn't look back.

I came to the back door seconds later, and all I could see was a figure fading into the darkness. I knew he had left but didn't quite know what to say to her.

After about ten minutes, she looked at me and said, "I will move back into your room, and we can make me and Henry's room a guest room."

"Who's going to visit?" I asked sarcastically.

"Well, according to the town folks, lots of people."

She smiled at me and I smiled back. We were connecting again. I didn't want to let on to the fact that I saw the traces of failure written on her face. Lillian was a strong woman, much stronger than I. She managed to see good in people who hurt her; I had to learn how to do this. She had hoped that she could have convinced Henry to listen to her and not to the townspeople. As he ran out of that house, so did her dreams and hopes of reconciliation.

Nevertheless, from this experience came a lesson in life that would be stored in our memory for keeps: If a person would rather run away than stand, let them run away and hope that they will run fast, for eventually they will fade into the darkness and be lost, just as Henry did.

Belzoni had chopped us into many parts. We were disassembled bodies, walking through fallen places, waiting for a magnet to pull the pieces back together. It was sounds with no strings, just a heavy beat for a heartbeat. There are moments in life when you want to run out of your own skin — pretend it isn't as bad as it really is, until it becomes worse. But the strange truth about life is that you are always much stronger than you realize, and resilience is forged during the hardest times.

Now, my child, that one is for the book.

PHRASE 8

REHABILITATE

Margarita

I must have been born into the wrong family—that has to be it. I, Margarita, was born into the wrong family. If I could jump out of my skin, be transported away, or be beamed out of this life, I would.

I'm a junior in high school, and I'm going to college. I just have to get through one more year. I also have to keep my grades up because I'm hoping to go to Northwestern in Evanston. Even though it's only about forty minutes from my house, when I visited, it felt like a completely different world—not just a different city, but a different life too. It's a world and a life I long to live, which is probably why I'm still here.

I sit and think about things the "twin way," as Leona always accused me of being afraid to do—to just sit and think. Well, I do on a day like this. A day when I have to face the fact that my mother's heart is too big for her life.

I often wonder where people like my mother come from. She lets people just move into our small four-bedroom house. We moved from 1158 N. Cleveland to the West Side of Chicago, and now that we finally have an actual house, this week it's filled with visitors from some small town in Iowa who have come to "save the souls" of us urbanites. Give me a break. I'm pretty sure these two vagabonds are homeless—I know because they smell like it—and I refuse to shower in this house again until they leave.

Why would my parents allow them here in the first place? They must be desperate for adult friends, which I don't understand because they have an entire church full of adults they talk to.

Here is what I've concluded:

Being poor is like a curse, except there's no spell-breaker. All you have is a small, thin crack of light—so small that very few people are focused enough to find it. The rest stay trapped in darkness, lost and blind to it and unaware of their blindness. I must be one of the lucky ones because I found the light.

It was education, and for this reason my grades, my book knowledge, is what I needed to hold on to.

Sometime in the early eighties, everyone in the neighborhood began to anticipate tax season. People would work at McDonald's or any other low-wage job so they could get an income statement. The rush would be on to find kids to claim to earn more money, and long-lost family members appeared to see if they could get taxes for themselves or get some of your tax money. At times like this, I felt like I must have been born into the wrong family, or maybe I was the only one who saw the light. Whatever the case might be, I had run away from my parents' apartment to my only place of comfort, Miss Leona's house. She was also the only person I'd told about the small voice inside of me that was convinced I wouldn't make it and should end it all, give up, and travel to the world of the unknown. For once you have seen the light, if you don't make it out, you can't live, you just can't, and you would rather die.

When I was in high school, I needed a place to study, and I needed to invite my friends over to hang out. That was how life seemed in the normal world. Yet my mother and father, both struggling to make ends meet, had a house full of homeless adults. I hated that house. Each day I felt dismembered, like someone was taking me apart little by little, and forcing me to watch, and what I had to watch was a horror story.

My sister Andrea is now a committed addict, and my mother has the honor of raising both of her children. Let's clap it up for Andrea—she accomplished her goal.

Leona hates when I talk badly about Andrea, but I don't care. I don't understand how someone can live in constant chaos and still wake up every morning acting like life is normal.

I think that's the real reason Mama keeps these "sin breakers" in the house—people who travel the world trying to break sin off other people's lives. My uncle meets these people and invites them to speak at my father's church in Chicago. And we would have the honor of giving up our space and our peace of mind for about a week.

Honestly, I half expect Andrea to steal from them if she ever gets the chance. She probably would.

Her kids—those boys—don't have an Off switch. They're actually really cute. Bright brown eyes, curly hair, and Shirley Temple dimples. They replaced me. I'm no longer the youngest. Now there are two little boys in the house who can be claimed on my mother's taxes, even though she doesn't care much about money. She'll probably give it away or buy more outdated, mismatched furniture to add to this already cluttered house.

This is my life right now, and I'm just trying to catch a ride out of here.

I forgot to mention in my *tale of woe*: My beloved brother had just come back from the Army a few weeks earlier. He started fussing at us girls for eating food he had brought into the house for himself. My father told him, "If you buy for one, you buy for all." We were a large family, and no one could realistically monitor the refrigerator to satisfy him.

So what did this Army enthusiast do? He threatened to put rat poison in his food. I remember thinking, *Really*? You'll be gone again in two weeks. The government gives you a check. I should probably question what he does with his money, but I won't because he'll be leaving soon anyway.

Wanda and Janet decided to go to City Colleges together — how lovely. They're both in love … or maybe just lust. Wanda has a wedding on the way. I guess she's gotten herself in a "womanly" situation.

My parents like Wanda's mother-in-law to be. She's one of those South Side Black rich—I'm told she owns several buildings, and her son is about to move my sister into one of them. Apparently he'll also be the manager. Besides managing the building, he plays guitar and sings Prince's *Purple Rain*. He even wears purple tights. I suppose that might be impressive if you weren't six foot one, squeaky-voiced, and mysterious. Instead, he looks ridiculous.

My mother, however, adores my sister's husband-to-be. He brings her sugar cane—actual sugar cane—and nobody knows where he even finds it in Chicago, but she loves it. To her, that alone proves he's a good man. She clearly sees something in him that I don't. I've watched him take the stage in purple stockings and a purple wig, crying while singing *Purple Rain*, dark as baked mud, doing a very poor job at being

Prince. I swear I couldn't make this up if I tried. Sometimes I feel like I'm the only person in my whole family who can see clearly.

As for Nia and Cindy, I won't even start. I have nothing kind to say.

On a more positive note, my mother won a pink car from selling Avon, largely because Leona's friends bought from her so often. But my dad refuses to drive it. It's pink.

A few ants have crawled back to their safe place behind the door. They comforted and confused me today. They scatter at the sound of my clicking keys, though that used to bring them out. I hope my mother hasn't found the spot and sprayed it again. I've told her a thousand times: they're ants, not roaches.

I go upstairs and glance into my parents' room. I want to be sure my dad is downstairs before I go down. I pass my brother in the hall. He's holding a big bottle with a red X on it. He smiles as I walk by and continue toward the stairs.

When I reach the kitchen, my dad is sitting at the table, eating that familiar bologna—the lunatic bologna. He's going to die soon, but I won't tell him.

"Dad, are you ready?"

He nods yes to me.

Good, I think. I'm going to my other house—the condo square—to do homework, after which I hope someone will tell me a story that takes me far, far away from my life.

As I exit the kitchen, I see Janet opening a box of powdered white donuts.

"That might be poisoned," I tell her.

"He always says that," Janet says, enjoying her powdered-covered donut. "You want one?"

I look at her powder-covered white lips and take one anyway. My thoughts are clear: Things are not supposed to be normal here. We have to leave one day, and I might as well go with powdered-covered lips.

I was born into the wrong family. That's my thesis, and now, after careful contemplation, it feels like a proven fact.

My dad is actually walking out the house now, with my mother and the sin busters. They smile all the time. I smile back because I can't remember their name. I think the lady is called Gloria. We drive in the car, as they speak about how Andrea is now going to be a better person, after receiving oil and prayer. I was right, they were on a mission to save my sister's soul.

I leave that house hoping life won't swallow me whole so I won't have to face any of it — my family, their issues, and their problems somehow became my problems. Sometimes, I can't study because I feel like I'm the part-time mother of two kids, while their biological mother is out living it up somewhere without a care in the world. This churchgoing family is deeply messed up in a holier-than-thou kind of way.

I wonder if Leona knows. Does she know? Is that why she chose me? Does she know she gave me walls — something to hold back the pain and the turmoil I carried inside?

Death feels fascinating. Quiet. Appealing in a way I hate admitting. And although I know I shouldn't flirt with the idea, I do. I must have murmured those words out loud, because for a moment I forgot I was in Leona's house, wallowing in my self-pity, telling her everything I had just experienced.

She looks at me as if I just handed her a secret. Then she finally says, "You really don't want to do that now, do you?"

"Hell yeah" I repeat. Then our eyes meet.

I was brought back to reality — I had cursed in front of Leona. She had listened to me for the past thirty minutes without saying a word. All I could think about was what I could take back, what I could make lighter. I had bared my naked soul, and now I was searching for mental clothing, even though this was the very place I had tried to escape.

"Have I ever told you about Tara?" Leona asked.

"Your friend from high school?"

"My best friend. She was a good person, but she had become one with the very dirt she migrated from. It took some time to help her find her own identity, but eventually she did. Her soul had to be rehabilitated, something we all will experience at some point in time. Let me tell you about her beginnings."

———

Leona

After the incident with Mike, it was a while before Tara visited us again. Not because she believed everything she heard, but because she was in a sensitive position. As a senior, she was well-liked for her singing, and she had even been asked to perform at graduation. It was also well known that we played the piano, so I suppose that made it acceptable for her to start coming around again. At first, we didn't receive her warmly. Still, she was our friend, and it felt good to have someone else to talk to again. Besides, we knew the truth. We also knew that no one else really liked Tara. She often told us we were the first people to accept her for who she was, and we knew she meant it.

You see, Tara was the middle child. She had a strong older brother who was oddly attractive. He was good at baseball, and that gained him a place in the world. It was rumored that her younger sister Rose wasn't their father's child, and from the looks of it, that rumor was true. Tara told us that her sister had been fathered by a guy from New York. Her mother came home pregnant, and her father let the girl live in the house. He grew to love her the best he could, knowing his genes could never have produced something so cute. Then there was Tara—her father's child and her mother's mistake. Tara told us her mother said it was the first and biggest mistake she'd made in her life.

Tara's mother wasn't exactly pretty, but she was beautiful. She had the kind of face cosmetics were made to accentuate. She was articulate, too—she sounded educated, though she'd only completed the sixth grade.

In the three years we'd known Tara, we saw her mother maybe twice, and even now I shiver when I think of her. Her long nails clutched a cigarette as if it were an extension of her hand, the smoke curling around her like invisible worms. Her hair was bone straight, her makeup carefully applied. She was so thin, she looked like she could slip through cracks in the walls. When she walked, she didn't really walk at all—she glided, as though the air carried her.

The day our eyes attached an image to words spoken about her, she was lying on the couch, gazing at the television as if she would see herself appear on the screen at any moment. I looked over at Tara's father, who had walked into the house wearing one dress shoe and one tennis shoe. One had to wonder what the local hobo and drunk of the community had in common with such a lady, but when you looked at Tara, there was no mistaking that she was a product of the both of them.

It would soon connect what she saw in Tara's father. He worked, he was a provider. He had also inherited a beautiful home, left to him by the kind people who raised him. Nothing else is known of his biological parents. When he wasn't drunk he had an even bigger problem: He never believed his children could tell the truth. This is why Tara rarely told her father anything, because he never believed her. If she said, "The store is out of bread," he would swear up and down that the store had bread and that she was just too lazy to walk.

If anyone ever had a reason to run from life, it was Tara. Even when she minded her own business and tried to just exist, somebody would remind her she looked exactly like her father. As she grew older, people began calling her his female version. God never leaves you without an ace to play. Besides the fact that Tara could truly sing, she had a nice shape—a thin waist, runner's legs, and a full figure she couldn't hide even when she tried.

Tara used to tell us stories. Strange men would come to the house late at night. Her mother would let them in and try to get Tara to take them back to a bedroom, but she never did. When she told her father what was happening, he called her a liar.

Late one night, she came to our house crying. Her drunken father had drifted off to sleep, and Tara had found a man in her bed. He covered her face and had his way with her. When he left, she ran to our house. She was hurt because she had just gotten raped, but what was even more hurtful was that he had covered her face. We let Tara and her sister Rose stay with us for about a month after that happened. Her mother had somehow gotten the money to go back to New York. Tara was afraid to go home, and her father didn't believe this nice, respectful man had done such a thing to her; besides, this nice, respectful man had a beautiful wife, one that no man would cheat on. Tara said to us she had nobody, until we reminded her she always had us. Her mother's sister came and got Rose. She had decided that she would raise her. Tara would live with us. No one would hurt her at our house.

Tara didn't see her mother again until Rose was around twelve, and Tara was a senior in high school. Her mother came running back home, with a plastic bag full of clothes and an obvious drug habit, and she didn't come alone. She brought this Todd fellow, who was apparently on the run with her and quite possibly her lover. Her daddy, like a sad puppy, let them both back into the home under the pretense that this Todd fellow was a manager. For some reason, Tara moved back home. She liked being around her mother even though she claimed to hate the woman, but the opposite was the truth. Tara wanted to be just like her mother. She wanted someone to want her and had decided that this someone should be her mother, and as bad as this woman was in our sight, Tara wouldn't let us talk too badly about her.

Tara kept telling me that her mother would leave the music business and support her as she was the real talent in the family. It was clear her mother was not going to do this. We witnessed Tara's mother come into the living room and flop on the couch next to her manager. Everyone knew this man was not just a manager. He was obviously her lover too, which could have been the real reason Tara had treated us so strangely. Nevertheless, we were there, and they asked us to sit, so we did.

The mother and the manager both eyed us as if we were ghosts, then she said, "You must be the ghost bitches everyone is talking about down here."

How do you answer such offensiveness? What do you say? We said nothing. We didn't agree or disagree. We just looked at her. We didn't want to embarrass Tara more, so we decided it was time to leave, but the mother oddly wanted us to stay.

"You came all this way, might as well stay," she said. "What do you want with Tara ugly ass anyway?"

Tara smiled and teared up at the same time. She remained silent, but her mother, feeling some sense of emotion, followed up with another offensive remark. "Don't be acting sensitive. You know I call you ugly all the time, but you're my ugly child. My first big mistake, and my dumb ass made two more after that."

Lillian and I knew it was time to go now. We'd had more than we could take of Tara's mother. She was mean and unlikable, so I guess her being gone so often was a good thing. Their father may have been insane, but he was not as verbally abusive.

Tara told us that her father had noble intentions. All he ever wanted to be was a hero. He would have gotten a hero's honor for trying to save some people from a fire, but people suspected him of starting the fire himself in order to save lives. When he went into the burning house, the smoke was stronger than he had expected, and he was not as strong as he had imagined. He was able to save only one man. The man's wife and two kids died. Out of obligation, the man refused to let the authorities pursue the case against Tara's father. I guess he preferred not to know, for he was dealing with the loss of his wife and kids and didn't have the strength to deal with the possible murderer who had saved his life.

Did Mr. Daniel start that fire? Or was he cheated out of his hero status? He claimed he was a hero and he'd been cheated because he was colored and the family he saved was White. Later on, Tara would seek the truth, but that's another story. We know for a fact that he lived his life looking for the next big fire to either save a life or die trying. As fate would have it, that was how he met his end.

Tara's brother had hopes of becoming a sports star. He distanced himself from the shame of his family. He would later settle for a conductor job with Amtrak. He married, had a few kids, and settled in Michigan. Her younger sister Rose was protected, taken in by the mother's sister, her biological aunt. This sister had nothing to do with Tara's mother, but Rose, she and her husband took good care of, and she would never return to live in the house with her mother and father again. It was clear she was loved in this world. Lastly, there was Tara, who was neither loved nor liked, and certainly there was no beauty to buy her favor. She was blessed with a body that she had grown to hate and a face she couldn't love, forced to live and not know why.

Tara could also sing. She never sang for anyone without a reason. But in close earshot of her mother's friend Todd, Tara started to sing. We asked Tara what made her sing for her mother's lover, who was disguised as her manager. We wanted to know what made her open her mouth and show her talent, and here is why she did it: She wanted him to stop looking at her, so she gave him something to listen to. When she sang, Todd, her mother's lover, heard that incredible, untrained voice that sent chills down one's spine. He rushed her out of the house, looking for the nearest bar, but she convinced him to come to our house. Tara brought Todd to our house to show him how she sounded when accompanied by music. His attraction and need to control her were obvious. He wanted not just her talent, but also control over her life. He was seducing her mentally, and as a girl who was a stranger to love, she was willingly accepting.

Todd invited Tara to return to New York with him instead of her mother, and she accepted. The day, she told us, felt surreal. She had dressed in some of her mother's clothes and wore heavy makeup, including almost orange lipstick. She looked older, but also strange. Only a few months remained before graduation, yet she no longer cared about high school. She was leaving with Todd. He would take her, and her mother would have to find her own way to New York. We thought it strange, but it was happening, and words felt useless, so we said very little.

She wanted to leave, and in a strange way, we felt she meant to hurt her mother by doing so. She kept saying, "My mother is going to be so mad," yet she also said she could now be with her father. "I'm the star now." Maybe she wanted to hurt her mother and help her father. I'm not sure, but she was leaving.

It was hard to believe that Tara left only two months before graduation. She ran away—a decision I can tell you she regretted for many years. Still, we stayed loyal to her. We begged the principal to let us collect her assignments and send them to her in New York, explaining that Tara had to leave because she was being hurt at home, which was not entirely a lie. The principal finally agreed. We did her work along with our own, and although Tara never knew it, she graduated.

I cried on the day I graduated from high school. I'm not sure why, but I cried—maybe because I didn't know what would come next for us. Lillian and I needed a reason to get out of the house, so we picked up Rose and took her out to dinner. We knew Tara would have wanted that. Tara didn't have much in this world, but she had Rose, and Rose looked up to her.

Rose was glad to see us. She liked it when we took her places and never treated us as if we were strange. After we dropped her off, Lillian and I went for a walk. Rumors had already reached our house. Lillian heard them all, and even though she didn't want to know, we both knew.

Ms. Bell, our special proctor, spoke to Lillian very softly and deliberately after Henry went public with his new relationship. She said, "Now you can live your own life." She said the words so strangely, but Lillian was only thinking that she needed to get to Henry. Henry had not been back to our house in six months. Some days Lillian was enraged, just waiting to pick a fight with anyone who dared to speak to her. In many ways, Henry was as innocent as the virginity he took the day he said he would stay with her forever. She had to face this battle by herself, but she wouldn't be alone.

As time permitted on a lazy weekend day, when not even the wind visited the house, the heat held everything in place but your thoughts. We followed the whispers and stood facing the house that Henry apparently shared with some woman. It was blue and incredibly small. It looked almost as if humans could not walk straight inside the place, but it was cookie-cutter neat. It had white shades that were half pulled down, exposing a window lamp and the small table that held it.

The yard was well-maintained — something we missed him doing at our small house. There was no porch, just a few steps that led you to the latch, which was used to knock on the door. Directly to the side of the house was a child's swing.

At the sight of the swing, Lillian stopped and took a few breaths, remembering how he had been building a swing set at our house. On the few occasions when they'd had deep conversations, he'd revealed to her how he longed to have one child's set of feet that belonged to him. She would listen to him talk about the kind of father he would be: He would teach the child—he hoped for a boy—to save ten percent of everything he got, and he would teach him how to work with his hands, but this boy he would send to college. Lillian liked listening to that sort of talk from Henry, as it reminded her of all the things she wished her father would have given her.

I silently begged her to leave because she didn't need to see what we both already knew.

Lillian walked slowly up a few steps and knocked on the door. A little boy opened it, then quickly shut it and ran for his mother, who came seconds later. Lillian stood face-to-face with her husband's lover, a person she should have hated but suddenly felt sorry for. She was a short, slightly overweight woman with short hair pressed so straight down to her head, it looked plastered or painted on.

They stared at each other for a few seconds. Lillian saw no remorse in the woman's eyes. As much as I quietly begged Lillian to walk away, she didn't hear me, and the woman, roundheaded and solidly built, was not going to intimidate her into leaving. Lillian stood on those steps as if to say, *I dare you.* She finally said to the lady, which ended the stand-off, "Go get my husband, Henry."

Then the woman called for Henry. A moment later she heard his heavy, clumsy footsteps coming to the door.

Before he got there, Lillian had figured out where she had seen the lady. She'd seen her at church, in grocery stores, and pretty much all around, for she was a community person who had loved badly once, and when she met Henry, I guess she thought she was about to do better. Okay, maybe marriage wasn't as official as it is now, but there was a committed relationship that should have been honored or at the very least dissolved before another one was entered.

Henry came to the door holding a baby who appeared to be a newborn. This explains why he was rarely at home. This woman was with child before he left her house for good. The lady took the baby out of his arms and watched them intensely. She was better than Lillian in this one way; she had something that she was willing to fight for.

Lillian looked at him with eyes that wished him dead. She was more disappointed that he left her to find out this way. She was disappointed that he listened to the fables of fools and did not talk to her first. As she stood still and looked at him, she became even angrier because he had created a whole family with a stranger, and as he looked back at her, she knew he couldn't comprehend that he could have one day had that same family with her.

The child began to reach and babble. His mother calmed him down. She didn't want to miss a word.

"You come for?" Henry asked, shuffling his huge body from side to side. At that moment, she realized it must have been hard for him—a stranger in a small town trying to create a life that others would respect him for. He had helped her sister stay alive. He had brought food to that house and didn't want to blemish her name, which is why he agreed to keep their marriage a secret. At times he made her laugh, cooked her food, and brought a male voice into her world. Both of them had been victims, so why should she be mad at him for finding what he had come to that small town to find in the first place? She was no longer angry.

"It's a beautiful night," Lillian said. I don't know why she said that, but she said it anyway.

He nodded in agreement.

She looked straight into his bashful eyes and sensed his fear. *Poor man,* she thought. This time she noticed something new — gray hair beneath his nose and along his chin, fine lines creasing across his forehead, and small wrinkles circling his eyes. He had aged. *What he must have gone through, hearing what they said about us,* she thought. They convinced him we were not real, just a couple of freaks. Henry's life was rooted in nothing but hard work, which had limited his imagination, so he believed them. It wasn't altogether his fault.

Lillian realized a truth she had known long before this meeting: No one was to blame. "Why don't you have those divorce papers drawn up, and I'll sign them before we leave?" Then she added, "Thanks, you hear."

She walked away with the image of Henry, the whore mistress, the pretty, wide-eyed three-year-old boy, and the new baby, all staring as if someone was about to take a photograph of them — and in fact, someone did. Lillian didn't look back to get a lasting image of what she left behind, but I did.

When we made it home, she announced that we were leaving Belzoni, for in that town we couldn't love, and if you can't love, all that's left is hate, and we had lived with hate long enough.

I shouted for joy — it was what I had longed for since my childhood — to actually be leaving Belzoni.

Henry brought the papers and left them on the table for Lilliana to sign. She did and returned them. We got a local handyman to help us find a nice car, and we paid him to give us lessons over the course of six weeks. He did. He was afraid of being with us at night, but in the wee hours of the morning, he showed us how to drive. When we felt we were good enough drivers to take to the highway, we padlocked all the doors and shut all the windows of the house, packed us a suitcase full of clothes, and off we went, leaving behind pictures, nice furniture, pots, pans, stares, rumors, fear, and two hundred and fifty dollars hidden under the china cabinet. I never was able to touch that money Clare gave us, and Lillian never pushed the issue. We were just glad to be going and starting over. It's okay to feel dismembered. Just remember to let life bring you back together because that is one thing death can not do, and that is make you whole.

New beginnings are like being reborn, but in our running away, we learned that sometimes you run back into the same dirt you migrated from. Your mind can be like feet and travel in many places that give you no peace. It can lounge a little too long in nonsense, making you unhappily married to your failures. Watch your thoughts, they are the strongest predictor of the future.

Now, my child, that one is for the book!

PHRASE 9

MIGRATED

Leona

Every three hours, we stopped and rested. We were good drivers but slow drivers. This is how I developed what others have called my "car-top comfort." I would lie on top of the car just to hear my own thoughts and whisper personal prayers to God. We were leaving Belzoni. I asked God to lead us to a place where our past would be untraceable, and about nine hours later we found it.

We were two seventeen-year-old girls, fresh out of grit-eating, fish-frying Belzoni, suddenly standing in Memphis. We hadn't gone that far — the people still spoke with Southern accents — but Belzoni people typically didn't leave Mississippi, so we felt safe. We knew we were finally away when folks treated us any way but mean. They actually looked at us and sometimes smiled. We were complimented on our beauty and on something called grace, which we never knew we had. We didn't plan on staying in Memphis long, but the people were so welcoming that we just couldn't resist.

One of the first people we met in Memphis was a lady named Jean. She was a short, dark-complexioned woman with short curly hair, a razor-sharp tongue, and a huge personality. She had a long scar about her left eye which almost reached her ear. It looked like someone could have cut her with a razor blade. It wasn't so deep, but it was very noticeable, the type of scar that drew attention away from her subtle, attractive features. Jean cleaned rooms at a roadside hotel, and she was the kind of person who tells you her whole life's history in a day. She had a very scarred past, which must have been what attracted us to her in the first place. Jean opened up a pack of cigarettes, took one out, lit it up, and began to smoke.

"All my life, shit's been happening," she said. "It just keeps going on and on and on. Sometimes you have fun in between, but most times you don't. My father said that, the f—ing drunk, and you know what? He's right." And that was the basis for her philosophy of life. So simple, so childish, but the best fiction couldn't have read better than Jean's life story.

Other than getting abused and falling in and out of love, she lived to watch television, and she worked a little until she found the next man who would for sure make her a victim. Another childlike characteristic that attracted Lillian to Jean was her faultless honesty about her life and circumstances in general. You wonder about people like Jean until you get to know them. Then the wondering stops.

Jean introduced us to Olivia. Olivia and Jean had a complicated relationship—in short, they didn't like each other. Olivia didn't want Jean around at all, so we made sure they rarely saw one another. Jean was more Lillian's friend, and Olivia was mine.

Olivia represented something different for us because she was a businesswoman. She used her nice seven-bedroom house on a corner lot as a boarding house. Of course, I rented a room there when we made it to Memphis. I always liked her, though it took Lillian a while to see what I saw. Yes, she was plain and only dressed up for church on Sundays, but she ran a respectable business—no funny business in her house, just people who needed a temporary place to stay.

Olivia wasn't unattractive. She was simply plain in a way that fit the town. Still, you couldn't help but notice her hair — so thick it gathered into a large knot at the back of her head. She only let it down on Sundays. At first Lillian thought she was lazy and wasn't impressed, but that would change with time.

It took a while before we truly got to know Olivia. She wasn't like Jean, who was an open book anyone could read, rewrite, or tear pages from. Over the course of a year, we learned her story. She had married young, to Big Paul, and her son was called Little Paul. Big Paul was accidentally struck in the head by a baseball and died suddenly. Big Paul, whom she loved dearly, left her a good house to raise her son in, and she later rented rooms to help pay the bills.

I loved hearing her talk about Big Paul — she had stories for days. She had loved someone who loved her back, and what wasn't there to admire about that?

Just the thought of Memphis and 12 Oak Circle — Olivia's home, which still stands today — brings it all back. What I wouldn't give to have one of Olivia's pumpkin pecan pies. On hot nights the guests would sit on the porch while someone fiddled or recited poetry. We were living some of the best years of our lives in that house. It was there we began making friends, and there the bond between the three of us formed.

Jean stayed close to us. She felt that since she had introduced us to the community, she was obligated to be our friend. I could see why Lillian liked Jean from the start. She was easy to talk to and very funny. She could stretch a joke for thirty minutes and have you laughing until you cried. She was friendly, and people enjoyed talking with her. What made me uncomfortable, however, was her need to know everything about us. At times I avoided talking to her. Lillian and I had promised each other there were two things we would never tell anyone, no matter how close we became. First, no one could find out where we really came from. We agreed that Jackson was safe enough since we knew the town from shopping there on many occasions. Second, we wouldn't tell people about our mother and father. We would die with these two secrets if our lives were to end in Memphis.

We had to get used to being asked out all the time. We were having fun and gaining a reputation, but we were careful not to keep the company of too many strange men, just the ones Olivia felt it was good for us to know. Olivia wasn't too much older than us, but she acted like our mother. She was also housing us. People who didn't live in the house paid for breakfast and dinner at her house. We were told they wanted to be near us. Olivia was pleased because she had all of her rooms filled. We were actually bringing more attention to her roadside boarding house, which she certainly appreciated. It wasn't hard for us to find work either.

The first week we were in town, we found work: Lillian worked at a preschool and I worked part time at a law firm. With our high school diplomas, we were planning on going back to school but knew we had to save money first.

During those rare moments when we actually missed Belzoni, we attended Olivia's church, which was the community hub, a few times. But a town over across the river had a little church of around fifty people. This church was more for us because they were more welcoming to traveling evangelists. Every so often a new family would visit this church.

I liked talking to the new families. This was a way I learned about new places. There was one family Lillian especially liked. This husband-and-wife duo had a lot of children, and they were all so respectful, especially the kids. A lot of the church kids played and sang well, but she just admired how talented this one particular family was. They may have lived in the big city, but they had Southern hospitality.

We didn't regret giving Memphis the next fifteen years of our lives at all. We had entered our September season — the heat beneath our feet, the sweat on our backs, clothes hanging off our shoulders and draping across our necks. September, you had been missed in the seasons of the past, but in Memphis, it was September at last.

PHRASE 10

HEARTS

Margarita

Time had passed like hospice patients, some fast and some slow, all with the known destination of moving on without permission. I was a young adult now — well, I was sixteen — and there was something about being alive that I wanted in my life: a touch, a soft kiss on the cheek, a tight hug … simply put, love. It was everywhere, but it had yet to rest on me.

Time had passed in my life. My sister Wanda had gotten married first and divorced first, and now Janet was getting married. She already had a child, and she wanted to know whether she should do it or not — that is, get married. I wondered if I had told her the right thing, because I didn't know if she knew what love really was.

I looked up at Leona, who was watching me, waiting for words I could not find to articulate. Then I finally said,

"Well, I just wonder if she's doing the right thing, and if I'm doing the right thing by letting her do this thing she's doing. Seems like nobody cares. They all just want to eat cake. They want love and red hearts and bright butterflies."

"Do you like him, this boy you've been thinking about?"

"I'm not talking about me," I said. "I'm talking about my sister, who is getting married. I have a boyfriend, but I know I'm not in love. When I think I'm close to love, I'll be sure to read a book or talk to the pastor or something."

I had not been totally honest. I didn't think I had been in love, but I was in a strong *like*, and everyone was doing it — sex. I thought about it all the time, and he had asked me to do it. I wondered if I should, or if I should do the marriage thing first, like Janet. I told her.

"And this is not about you." She laughed as she got up to fix herself a cup of tea.

When she did things like that, trying to read my mind, it bothered me. "It's not about me," I wanted to shout at this lady. I was just dating a boy to have a boyfriend. I wasn't in love, although I had wondered how our children would look if we got married, and I had jotted down my name with his last name a couple of times. When we were together, I wondered if it was destiny or just a coincidence that landed us together. I was sixteen going on seventeen, soon to be a senior in high school, and I needed someone I could confide in, but this was not about me at all.

"Did you like the event in your honor?" She had changed the subject to me, but she knew I was not done with it.

"You didn't show up," I said.

"That's okay. You deserved it. I don't like to feel like you are visiting me out of pity. I'm far from old, you know. When I can't wash my butt, that's old. I'm still in my prime — ask my husband next door."

"He says he's not your husband."

"You asked him for real?"

"Yes."

"And that's what he said?"

She eyed me, searching for a change in my facial features as a reason to doubt my words.

"Yes," I said. I lied. I was afraid of him, but I knew he worked in the funeral parlor. I just didn't think they were married, or ever would be, so I said what I said with lie-proof hesitation in my voice.

"Well, I guess he told you the truth. We don't have much of a marriage now—he's sick, early-onset dementia. He not only worked at a funeral home, but he owned a few of them, and that work can take a toll on you, especially when the secret is out.

"What secret?" I asked naively.

"The secret of knowing that what you did to others all those years, someone will do to you. I guess that's why he asked to be cremated. When the condo next door became available, I bought it too and hired full-time, around-the-clock help so he could live out the rest of his days in peace. I'm surprised he talked to you—in fact, I know he did not—but the story you tell is yours. Even if we tell ourselves lies, it's still our story to tell."

She laughed, not to correct or embarrass me, but simply to remind me that she liked stories as well. Then she added,

"I always said my husband would have been just fine if only he could have died a few times before his physical death. That's possible, you know."

I didn't say anything because the thought of dying before your physical death was unfathomable. I simply let her continue.

With a shy smile, she said, "When you can't love someone the way they want to be loved, or when you can't be loved the way you want, it becomes torture for both people. Then you realize the person you never loved was yourself, and you blame them because you didn't know how to love them—it was you who you hated. Do you understand?"

"Sure, this time, in a weird way I understood," and I thought to myself, *There's a really good story coming*.

She walked to the window, and this time she did not take a seat. She told me this story standing up.

"Tell me, dear, what books one might read to learn about love. It's such a tasteless topic to feast on."

"Just books." I perked up a little, for we had come back to the topic at hand. As I became more engaged, I realized she was right. It was about me. Then I clarified my question,

"I guess my question should have been—when do you know for sure that you have actually experienced it, and you are ready for love?"

"I will tell you that if you ever have to ask, you are not there." She said, and this time I fully understood.

"You should stand for this one," she said.

I reluctantly obeyed, hoping the standing would not be long.

"The world can teach you how to get laid and how to get laid right. It can teach you the art of kissing and strange sensations, but it can never teach you about love. If you ever fall in love, you will surely fall out of it. Love is a word that must belong exclusively to God. It is much deeper than we can ever imagine or comprehend. It must happen by choice. It can't be forced, manipulated, or reasoned.

"The only truth about love we can claim to know is that it is a choice. We choose to love the people we love. Remember this when you think you must feel something, hear something, or be given something to truly be in love. It's a choice. You must be careful whom you choose to love, whom you attach that word to, or it can destroy you, the only part of you that matters: It can destroy the heart. Your heart and his heart."

PHRASE 11

CLOTHE US

Leona

Standing on a rocky road, watching the moon fade into midnight, you reach for it, wanting to hold on and not let it go—never realizing that if you released that seductive moonlight, the sun would rise even brighter. That is the greatest lesson love can teach.

I've been through many relationships. Some I remember, and many I don't. Often we broke up soon after confessing our undying love for each other. Some people simply like saying the word *love*. In your heart you know when you don't mean it. At least I always did. When you truly love someone, you don't have to keep saying it. You fall into a rhythm and do life together, and sometimes it feels so ordinary, you barely notice you're living at all. Days move slowly, like garden snails, until one day you look around and realize one of you is covered in the dirt of it all.

I never thought I was the marrying type, but two years after we got to the great state of Tennessee, I got married. It was exciting to me. It was a covering. I felt he clothed me with an identity.

Lillian really didn't like the idea that I had settled so quickly, for when a twin gets married and the other stays single, an unwelcome interference happens. We weren't as connected: I couldn't always read her thoughts, nor could she read mine. I had tried to explain this to her when she was married to Henry, and she just couldn't imagine or understand what I was trying to say, but after I married Jack, she understood.

Jack had been married before and had two children. He was twenty years older than I was, and I had settled for him. I wanted to experience what most people do — the touch, the moans and groans that come with pleasure. I had heard it with Lillian, and I wanted to experience it myself. Jack was an honorable man, and he made me feel comfortable. We had a house, and he bought me a car, talked to me, and wasn't afraid of me. I liked that about him. When we first met, I felt so complete with him. I thought no woman could feel so complete and not be married. I married him, doubtless and at total peace.

Jean and Lillian kind of bonded with each other. They both loved music, and they moved to Nashville. Olivia didn't agree with the move. When I told her, she used to joke, 'If Jean didn't feel hurt, she wouldn't know how to feel at all.' She didn't understand why Lillian would even fool with Jean at all.

Well, I was a married nineteen-year-old with responsibilities, and I liked this role at times. Olivia became my voice, my soulmate, when I wanted company outside of Jack. Jean had become Lillian's surrogate sister. I called Olivia. Jean partied a lot, and on Saturday nights, Lillian would join her. Lillian had lots of friends. It wasn't like she was looking for love or anything — she had done the marriage thing and understood why I wanted to experience it, but she wasn't at all ready to settle down, so she just had friends. Good friends, mind you. She liked them all the same, and until she decided which one she liked more, she just agreed to have fun, and I agreed with her. She was young, nineteen, pretty, and working as a teacher's aide while she attended school to be a teacher. She had a right to live as she chose.

The difference in Memphis was that my husband owned a store that was the hub of the community, and when I got wind of someone badmouthing my sister, I got their mouths closed fast. A few times, I refused to sell food to a few busybodies, and my husband, being the supportive man that he was, stood by me every step of the way. That might have been another reason why I chose to marry him: He was very protective of my sister and me.

While Olivia joined me at my house, taught me to cook, and shared days with me, Jean and Lillian were becoming much closer. Lillian would only talk to me when she was thinking about settling down, but when the next good thing came along, that conversation ended.

One night, against her better judgment, Lillian went out to see a famous band from Texas called Max and the Blue Notes. The band had a sort of Count Basie or Sam Cooke sound, and they were good. That was how she met Max, the lead saxophonist. There was something about the way he moved and played that instrument that made her see a uniqueness in him, beyond his faults.

Max was tall and well built, with a dark complexion that made women close their eyes in prayer just to meet him. He had a noticeable dimple on his left cheek that appeared when he gave his beautiful white smile. When he walked into a room, all eyes turned toward him, and people either wished to be like him or to be with him. He was well loved all over, especially in Nashville, where she now shared a flat with Jean.

One night after the set, a drink came over to Lillian from Max. Well, she wasn't big on drinking, and she'd had one beer already, so she sent it back. I guess it must have insulted him because he stormed over to the table, demanding an explanation. "What? My drink isn't good enough for you?"

She smiled and explained that she'd already had a drink. Then Max smiled, and she realized he was just pretending to be angry. He sat at the table with Jean and Lillian, and all night he complimented Lillian on her raw Southern beauty. When she got ready to leave, because Jean really wanted to go for some reason, he gave her his phone number and asked for hers. She nervously wrote down her number and ran to catch up with Jean, who was quickly exiting the building.

"Wait, I'm driving! Don't you remember?" Lillian yelled at her.

"It was getting a little stuffy in there. Besides, I got to get up early and make sure Willy gon' be there."

"See if Willy is gon' be there?" Lillian couldn't believe her ears. Jean was actually thinking about going back to Willy, her ex-boyfriend, three times removed, who had kicked her out of the house and burned up all her clothes, when she had a bed at her apartment she could stay at for free.

She opened the car door and drove off, and they each stayed silent, except for Jean asking for a light for her cigarette and complaining about her back every now and then. Lillian knew something else was bothering her friend, and she wasn't totally unfamiliar with the feeling. She didn't connect it right off because she still couldn't believe she was holding Max's personal phone number in her purse.

Then Jean made the statement that took the guessing game out of what was really happening. As Lillian pulled into the driveway, Jean stomped out her cigarette and said, "Lucky you, you just might get the chance to bang Max. I hear he's quite a lover—just what I hear, you know." On that note, she slammed the car door and walked into the house to fuss at a man who was not the man she wanted to be with in the first place.

It was jealousy, plain and simple, but Lillian sort of enjoyed being admired and having others be jealous of her—same thing, except that underlying all jealousy is hurt. Because Lillian didn't like her friend being hurt, she decided that she wouldn't mention how Max's hands felt, how his smile melted her heart, or, to her surprise, how she wanted to marry him although she barely even knew him. For just that night, she decided that she would pretend that Max never happened.

Jean was kicked out that night and came over to stay with Lillian. She got up and fixed herself a cup of coffee, vowing to show no joy over meeting Max at all. That night, she listened as Jean called all men dogs. She watched Jean closely and hoped she nodded at all the right times. Although she was looking at Jean, in her mind, she was listening to Max complimenting her. His words were playing over and over in her head. Occasionally, one would bring about an embarrassing laugh. She always hoped it would be in the right place. Sometimes she was right and Jean would laugh, but sometimes she was wrong, and Jean would say accusingly, "You think that's funny? Try making love to a man knowing he was with someone else seconds before. That can really fuck you up in the head, really it can.'"

Like always—and I came to learn that this was the coping skill she used to face another day—Jean would be really sad one moment, but the next she would begin to laugh and start a brand-new conversation about something. Lillian couldn't ever really remember what they were about.

It took a while to marry Max, but later she married him. Lillian realized her marriage to Henry had deprived her of knowing what lovemaking was all about. Max's reputation was only half told. He was not only pleasing to the eye but was also a warm and giving lover, and she longed for his touch and more. The more she wanted him, the less she thought about the things she needed and wanted for herself. This is the sin in losing yourself to someone else.

She loved the children and her job, but if Max wanted her to travel with him, she did. She went around the world, seeing many places and learning about food, clothes, and manners not often afforded to common people. As a teacher and a lover of books and learning, Max unknowingly tapped into a space in Lillian's soul and filled it. She felt only Max could have done that for her, only he could have given her back to herself. For that, she gave him all she had. He had awakened her as an individual, with separate wants and needs.

She overlooked his obsessive behavior and his lavish lifestyle, which included drugs and drinking, remembering only how he made her feel. He became her world. Everything else in her life came second to him, and she was in love — a love I didn't understand. It was a love that felt unrealistic and unrestrained, one that saw him only in a single, glowing dimension.

I was trying to find the reality of all this my sister was feeling, but it was all rather mind-boggling. We were both in a situation, yet she felt one way and I felt a totally different way. She was so much in love that she stayed up late at night just to get his phone calls when she wasn't able to travel with him, and when he was home, she made sure she got his meals right and his clothes clean to his liking. The house he had bought was built from the ground, and everything in it was to his liking or else Lillian got rid of it. Her world was his world, and she loved it like that.

I married Jack, who was a respectable business owner. We got up early and went to bed early. I cooked, and when I didn't feel like it, Jack cooked. We had children, a family community, and stability. Our home was not the place a guy like Max cared to visit, him with his silk shirts, gold watches, and spit-shined shoes would have been out of place sitting on our lamp porch listening to day-labor men talk about baseball or boxing. I chuckled with Jack when I showed him pictures of Max playing to an international audience, and his chance meeting with Bugeye Blue, who loved Max, and longed to hear him play again, but he was Jack's friend. Actually Bugeye Blue was a smooth-talking, funny little fellow, falling off some bad experience with love that he could only laugh about, although he was married. This joker always seemed to rescue other women and fall hard for them, just not hard enough to leave his wife, which had landed him at times in hot water. And we, with not much else to watch, lived his experiences and exploits, hoping both good and bad would befall him one day.

Even Jack had to chuckle at the thought of this encounter of what Bugeye Blue would say to Max. Max, who had met and played for Muhammad Ali to Miles Davis, and even James Brown. His world was not our reality, and we knew the two should not mix. At first I thought that Jack was a little jealous of Max, but he was just from that other school of thought that basically felt music was a hobby, not a career, and that real men worked with their hands.

Max had hoped that Lillian would marry Charles. He kept trying to make that introduction, but Lillian never showed up. Charles was an older, more stable man who wanted to spend the rest of his life married to the one woman he would find. So, Jack, before he got sick, would bring out all these news reports and shows that revealed a very high Max. He was the first to tell her that Max was on drugs, but Lillian wasn't hearing what she didn't already know, and she knew others knew as well. She was in love, and "everybody did something" was her rationalization.

His main bad habit was being a chain-smoker, and she herself smoked occasionally. What Max did late at night and sometimes early morning, in the bathroom, or in his car, was his personal business. She would not judge him for it, and she also knew she could not stop him. Here's the other thing she knew that clothed her in fear, and branded her sadness: She knew that she could not stop him, but if he had to choose, and she would make sure that this was never the case, but if he did, she knew he would not choose her over drugs.

I, on the other hand, initially liked Max, and this made Jack very uncomfortable, for he thought I might want to leave him for a younger man. I assured him that was not the case. Lillian and I were at different stages in our lives, although we were the same age. I really just wanted peace. She wanted this fast-paced, unpredictable life of Max's, and she got so much more. We were two married women in two very different marriages, living in two different parts of Memphis. We were, in fact, two very different women. She had Max and I had Jack.

Jack was not poetic, and his words did not dance from his lips like a love ballet. He probably never made a woman in his life quiver from his touch. No one in Jack's world waited lovingly to hear what he had to say or looked for opportunities to please him. We had a dutiful passion. Later in our marriage, I took a part-time job a few hours a week outside of Jack's store. I was a legal secretary, and pretty good at it. The law office only had two lawyers and an ex-cop, but now they had me a few days a week, and I liked it. I liked my life and my husband, even though my sister felt my life was boring, and that I had settled for so much less than I deserved. I had been with my husband six solid years, but Lillian and Max's relationship was just really heating up.

They were publicly dating, and the news had picked up on it. Although they didn't always get her name right, everyone knew that was Max's girl. One day, Lillian, out of the blue, came to my house in one of the new dresses Max had bought her from some exclusive store in an unknown city. She was wearing this dress, with an attitude to match. She wanted me to go hear him play. It was this big event. The mayor would be there, and Max was going to be the star of this whole event, but I just couldn't leave the store. Mothers might realize late at night that they needed bread or something. The store closed at 7:30, and my husband expected that I would watch out for things while he was dealing with reorders and paperwork. Surely I couldn't just leave. I could see this irritated Lillian so badly that she gave me a look of pity. Then she asked me a strange question,

"Why did you marry him?"

"What?" I was confused.

"Why did you marry that man that lies in your bed and gives you this, a roadside house, where travelers come and visit and leave. What was it he said to you that was so amazing that you thought this was just a peachy idea, a good thing to do?"

I really wanted to slap that smug, well-powered face of hers and run her in those 6-inch heels off my porch. Then I decided she had a right to know. So I told her with as much enthusiasm as I could muster up. I raised my voice a level in the hope that she could hear the thrill in my voice.

One day, Jack, in his three-piece church suit, black I think it was, well, he walked up as Olivia and I were leaving church and asked,   "Have you ever smelled a lavender flower on a nice bright Sunday morning?"

"What?" I said. I was really thinking this man knew the names of flowers. He appeared to be a labor class man. Was I wrong about him? Then he clarified.

"Well, a lavender flower smells beautiful. I just figured that you are such a beautiful lady, I thought you shouldn't leave this life without smelling a lavender flower." He smiled at me. Then he walked away, and seconds later, a wild-eyed, chocolate-covered, kinky-haired seven-year-old boy ran up and jumped into his arms. Jack tipped his hat to me, got in his car, and drove off. I learned that he grew lavender flowers in his house garden, and you know what, it really is a lovely scent.

Lillian just smiled and said, "Um," like questioning whether that was romantic or not, but I never said I was looking to be romanced. I just wanted her to know that.

That day, I told her, Jack became the man for me, and I wouldn't be running off to an overpriced show in a smoke-filled room, around well-dressed people who all probably smelled like smoke when I could be smelling my beautiful lavender flower. And to add to that point, I said that even if I didn't love him the way she loved Max, she would respect him. I was a committed woman with responsibilities and people who needed me and counted on me. One thing was certain: I knew my husband would never do anything to end the relationship, and I was far too sensitive to end it myself. So I stayed — committed and content.

What I know now, and didn't understand then, is that contentment is the best part of marriage. She loved the version of Max he presented to others—the image he displayed on billboards or around the well-to-do, the man who seemed to belong to everyone. I simply loved Jack and all that came with him.

Jack had lost his first wife of nineteen years from an illness two years earlier. He had been good to his wife and he was good to me. I needed someone to help me deal with the fact that I had everything I thought I wanted, but I didn't have me. I needed someone to show me or help me find that part of me that wanted more out of life. Lillian needed something else.

When Lillian talked about how Max made her feel, and how much she missed him, and how she couldn't wait to see him again, I often found myself justifying my marriage by saying sarcastically, "You know Jack—he'll be home real soon, he's such a good protector and provider." The only tale of glory I had to tell her was "You should have seen how Jack tore into this lady when she dishonored your name, and how we refused to sell her food that day." Lillian enjoyed hearing that. It made her feel good, and she had reverence for Jack. In fact these two men both clothed us in identity and protection, not from others but from ourselves. I think that's why she married him.

Yes, her day in white came, and it was a spectacular event, with the who's who of Memphis all present. In the winter of '66 she married Max. Jack was sick, so he couldn't attend. I needed a big event in my life, so I told my Jack I would go alone.

Lillian had that moment. She got married in a grand fashion, but she soon realized that life after that day was not easy for her. When I got back from that big wedding, things had changed—Jack was not doing well. Although the kids had Jack's sister, their aunt, who really raised them, I became more a part of their lives. They were good kids, and I was always kind to them, but they had a mother and no need for a replacement, and I understood that.

Still, I picked up every report card, cooked for them when their aunt wasn't home, and bought them birthday cakes and Christmas presents. I gave them color, noise, and laughter. But most importantly, I gave them their dad. I made sure he called them every night and visited every other day, until he no longer could.

Remember this one very important fact: People can only give you the love inside them, and it will not always measure up to how much you are capable of loving.

In our thirteen years of marriage, I never told Jack all about my life. I feared what he might think of me after I revealed to him who I really was, which I was still coming to grips with. Brokenness does not heal overnight. I felt at times a little more than Mississippi trash that survived. Your past can sometimes clothe you in protective layers that can be very hard to take off. It's something about dying that reveals what life was trying to teach you.

Jack had cancer. He was bedridden, and sometimes angry, just angry. I left a lot, and only Olivia knew why. I was able to open up to Olivia. She knew I could not witness another death. I remember coming back a few days before he passed, and I got really close to him and held his hands. I was going to experience this moment with him. He was so weak, and he smelled of black cumin seeds, something his daughter told me she gave him to help ease the pain. I thought I could experience that moment with him, but I couldn't do it. I left again. A few weeks later, he died. A few days before Thanksgiving, Olivia called me, and I came home.

He was surrounded by his loved ones. They told me it was peaceful. It wasn't a sad occasion. His younger son, Jack Jr., was twenty-one, and now he was to run the store. I didn't fight for anything. I got the bank account, the insurance policy money, and the privilege of being Jack Hillman's wife. His daughter had been a teenager when I came into her life. She was married now and going to night school. She knew that the house would be their inheritance, and she was pleased with that. While I was in Memphis, we were still very close. I left after Jack's death and moved to Nashville for most of the time. I still came back and stayed with Olivia. I had a room there that I paid for monthly, even if I wasn't living in it. That was going to always be home to me. I dated a little a few times more in Memphis, but they were not like my Jack. They just helped relieve the sting of loneliness. He was my great love.

My mind started to wonder what it must be like to live in bigger cities. My imagination had traveled North long before I landed there, but I was for sure going North. I still practiced the habit of driving to a deeper wooded area, climbing on top of my car, and just listening until the earth became still and God would speak. I was surely going North. I just didn't know when.

Max and Lillian, during this time, were just doing them. I would invite them to things and they wouldn't even show up. I had to go to where they were to get an audience with them. When we did attend parties, those two always found a way to make it about them. Lillian was so in love it was sickening. She enjoyed the fact that everyone wanted a sit-down with them, like church musicians looking for an opportunity to play with him. Some just wanted to be able to drop into common conversations at hair salons, shopping centers, or friends' porches, then mention how they just happened to converse with the great Max, and he gave them a bit of wisdom they felt important enough to repeat, or dropped that he actually invited them to an event they would be privileged enough to attend. People wanted it said of them that they actually spoke with the great, the one and only Max.

It's so strange, because I knew Lillian was not as happy as people thought she was. In a twisted way, I had begun to feel that I was keeping my sister alive, which is why she always wanted me around. She liked what Max represented and what he brought out of others—a power she didn't possess herself—but because she was with Max, she could claim part ownership of this bigger-than-life personality by default.

At one point Lillian started losing weight and just letting herself go. I am sure she visited our little church in the woods and left something there—her soul, I believe—but it's hard to be a twin, you understand. It's like you are living someone else's life, and at some point that person is going to wake up and you are going to vanish. Do you understand?

———

Margarita

I nodded yes.

She looked at me with an intense stare, as if she were trying to read my soul, which gave me a jittery feeling. The truth was, I understood without understanding, if that is at all possible. I knew she had experienced something real, so I nodded yes again.

I wondered to myself if Ms. Leona had forgotten the story she was telling me. She had slipped into a more dangerous place, for she was staring right through me, far beyond this space. I smiled at her, and it slowly brought her back. She seemed to think she had said something funny, but she hadn't. She was back, and I was standing next to her, at the window.

Then she said to me, "I had children in Memphis you know."

"Oh, by Jack?"

"Maybe," she said, almost as if it was a surprise to her." I was young and curious.

"Tell me, I want to know," but she stopped me and said,

"Let's keep the children out of this, okay?" But I will tell you about Phyllis one day.

That was it, she sat down, and so did I. But oddly enough, she had taught me something about love, then she added.

"Love is a choice, and when you choose to love the right person for the right reasons, what a beautiful thing. Coffee?" she asked me.

"I don't drink coffee," I said.

"Oh, right," she remembered.

I smiled, mentally reminding myself that the time I spent with her was always priceless.

PHRASE 12

DISMEMBERED

Margarita

It's funny how seasons change, but your circumstances stay the same. You meet people, and although they go by different names, they are really the same—same motives, same intentions. After talking to the twin about love, I decided I would take it easy on love. Sure, I wanted at times what I felt my sisters had, but I also wanted purpose, and you can't have them both at the same time, or rather, it was wise to pursue purpose first.

Leona was having an odd effect on my life, and my sisters noticed it. Janet and Andrea had waited patiently to see whether or not I would give up relationships. It was a game for my father—guessing who I would sleep with. They were rather disappointed when they learned I had decided I would not sleep with my ex-boyfriend. Then I met another guy. He asked me out, we started dating, and now he was my boyfriend. He wanted the same thing, just in a different way. He was very complimentary but also a little manipulative. He thought if he told me often enough that I would be his first and his last, and how much he cared about me—even loved me—I would give up the gold. I didn't. My sisters booed that decision. They thought he was one heck of a lay. I have to admit, he was close, but I decided not to do it. Eventually, he found some dumb reason to break up with me too. When someone leaves you, it's sad, even if you didn't really like that someone.

My sisters talked with me all the time about boys. Some were in good relationships and some were not. But oddly enough, Leona's stories never really left me. They served as somewhat of a guide to my choices. I was thinking the whole sex experience could wait for college. I didn't know everything, but the more I saw people wanting sex without love, the smaller the light of opportunity grew. If I lost sight of that light, I would be like everyone else, and those were odds I did not want to risk.

I still hoped I would learn more about love, but I remembered that if you have to question if it's love, it's not. I was a teenager—I questioned everything—so love had no place to grow in my life right then.

I was on my way to visit Leona. It was only one bus ride away. Since we'd moved to the West side, my sister Andrea came home more often because now she had a room, which gave her time to spend with her boys. She still did drugs, but just marijuana, and she and Janet both now did the same thing. Sometimes, I called them the two hypes just to hear them say marijuana was not a drug.

It was a hot summer night, when most girls are out at the movies or get humped somewhere, but me—I was on my way to visit Leona. When I got there, she was in good spirits. I didn't have to remind her that we had been talking about love the last time we spoke. She knew, and she was ready. This time she had cooked, not just for me—I could tell she had saved me a small portion from a larger meal. Seeing her in the kitchen, putting things away, she looked like she felt different—more alive, more vibrant.

"It's gumbo soup. Eat up," she announced with pride.

She needed to say no more. I had brought my appetite with me.

She yelled from the kitchen. "We were talking about love the last time."

"Yes, love," I agreed, and I went to stand by the window. That was where we had stood last time, and I liked the small bit of fresh air that carried the smell of gumbo.

"Why are you standing, silly?"

I wanted to tell her that the last time we talked about love, she had asked me to stand, but I didn't. I sat in my chair, and she brought me a bowl of okra, bell pepper, onion, shellfish, and who knows what else. The smell was tantalizing. The taste was indescribable, and good is an understatement.

Then Leona put on some jazz music and started to dance. I had never seen her dance before, but she could move. When she realized I was watching, she let out a laugh so loud and full that I was startled. She bounced into her chair, then moved to the edge of her seat as if she was about to tell me a suspenseful story. There was something different about Leona when she cooked, and I was beginning to notice it. She told me she had been to France and had seen the Eiffel Tower with her own eyes. Then she added with full knowledge,

"What makes Paris so amazing is not just the way it looks. If you want a place that only looks amazing, go to Malaysia. What makes France amazing is the smell of the food and the visitors who give off an energy that something spectacular is about to happen."

———

Leona

In retrospect, without the cloud of other issues, Lillian said she always felt that marriage forced her into a bottomless corner, a small place with very little room to move. She just didn't recognize it because of the sound of the word *love* coming from his lips and landing in her heart. Those words, like his music, trapped her and encircled her in a rhythmic pattern of staccato confusion. It was he who made everything in her life come alive. If he was happy, she found reasons to be happy. If he was sad, she felt it was her responsibility to make him happy again. But she loooved him!

She loved his smell, his talk, his jokes, the way he interacted with people, and the sound of his music, which moved the world and soothed her soul. She felt privileged and honored to admire him as the world did. Or was she just another admirer he happened to sleep with? Regardless, she was at the bottom and didn't know it until she finally turned inward and faced herself.

From the very beginning, things seemed a little one-sided to Lillian. Max wanted her to travel when he felt like it, and when he was tired of her, he sent her home to work or decorate the house the way he liked it. It was all about him from the start, and for the most part, how things start is how things will end.

Max was gone often without her as time progressed, which gave Lillian time to go back to school and get her degree. Lillian was a teacher of a fourth-grade class. She even took the two classes required to be an administrator — not that she ever imagined she would want to be this, but because she had time. Her husband made a whole lot of money, and she spent little of it. He was her master teacher, and he taught her not just sexual pleasure but also intimacy. Lillian told me how she longed to linger in his arms, and I didn't know what that was like.

Jack wasn't romantic at all. On a few occasions, I had woken up to find his heavy arm across my back, which made it hard for me to turn onto my side. I didn't care. He liked rubbing my back, but that was all I got, and that was okay. Max, on the other hand, lit candles and brought wine for them to sip in steaming, bubbling hot water. If only she knew that he built her up so that he and he alone could tear her down, those days would not have been so enjoyable.

It was a dark day in May when Max's throat started to give him problems. He picked up his horn and couldn't make a sound. It was hard for him to breathe. His throat was so shot from booze, cigarettes, and possibly drugs that he could barely talk either. He wasn't healthy. His friend and manager suggested he take time off to get himself together. There was a hot new trumpet player making waves in the music business, and if Max was to compete with the guy, he had to be at 100 percent. So he went home back to Lillian with his bad habits, and even worse, his attitude.

She dealt with Max's declining state the best she knew how: She stayed away from him and did a lot of overtime at the school. This also made it easier for her to hold onto love, or to what she felt for him, for a darker reality was approaching.

As usual, Jean was in an abusive relationship with a man and asked if she could move in with Lillian and Max. Lillian was having a hard time understanding Max, and an even harder time understanding what it was like for him to lose everything and still live. So she said a willing yes to Jean and insisted that she take her time finding a permanent apartment. The reality she had to face was not just approaching, it was staring her in the face, and this was the basis of it: If music was Max's life, his great love, what was she? How did she really fit into Max's world if it was void of music?

Jean was now working with a doctor who used to have a practice in Hollywood, but due to problems never revealed to Jean, he had to leave, and now she was his clean-up lady. Jean told Lillian in secret how she came into his office and told him she needed a doctor, and for him to drop his pants *now*. He did, and she slept with him right there on the patient's table. She really didn't like the old man, who smelled like cheap cologne, but he looked a little like the TV lawyer Matlock, whom she had fantasized about many times. So now she was in a relationship with a man who looked like her dream defender. I thought the old man was losing his mind. He didn't like Jean to be out of his sight at all, calling her at all hours of the night just to talk and calling her in to work at all hours. She obliged, like the whore she was born to be, and was only slightly embarrassed by the whole situation. She wasn't embarrassed that he was married, thirty-five years older than her, and that he cared little about her outside of sex, but she was embarrassed because he was round in the stomach area. All her other boyfriends were thin, but she always added that it was because they were drinking themselves to death.

Lillian stopped her from talking about work in the house. She didn't like knowing this about Jean, but she realized it was Jean's life and she would have to answer to God for herself. Jean continued to work for the man after Lillian refused to let her vent about the relationship to her. Lillian would catch Jean talking to Max about work, but when she got close enough to hear, the talking would stop, so she could only conclude that Jean was talking about the doctor again. Lillian wanted to prevent her from flaunting herself around the house, laughing, and making private jokes with Max, but Max wouldn't have it. He was being reborn in a strange way with Jean being there, for they had a lot in common: They went to the same schools and had both grown up in Memphis, so they were becoming quite good friends. For the most part, Lillian thought that was all they would ever be, for Max used to say Jean was so Black that if you turned off the lights, she couldn't be seen. He wouldn't let her take Jean on certain trips to hear him play, because he said she would ugly up the place. If it wasn't in the South, Jean was not welcome to come.

Jean jokily said that the doctor was going to fix her one day, but I never probed to find out what she meant by that. Then, one day, she came home all bandaged up. A few weeks later, she removed the face covering, and she looked amazing. Her scar was gone, her left eye was raised, her nose was smaller, and her face was pulled back. She looked different. Max and Lillian just sat in her room looking at what this doctor had done, amazed at what money could buy, for who would imagine that she could be made to look so good?

It happened slowly. Jean began losing weight, and soon she was buying beautiful clothes that showed off her new figure. Over time, a different woman seemed to be living under Lillian's roof—one who had never been invited.

When Max wasn't insulting Lillian, he was admiring Jean's face. They smoked and drank together, just as they had when they were younger, while attending the same school at the same time. They laughed and reminisced like old companions.

It was as if Lillian wasn't even there.

Lillian had been the head teacher at the school for years. When the school board announced they needed a principal, she was the only one with any administrative coursework. All she lacked was a financial management class, and she would qualify as the new full-time principal. The school board agreed to not only pay for the class but also for the books needed for the class. It was only one night course, offered in the summer session and beginning in two weeks.

She hurried home to tell Max. He had often complained about money, and now she would be making almost double her salary. Instead of being happy for her, he was upset. He looked at her as if she had cheated on him or was taking this class to hurt him. Max told her bitterly, "You can't go," then lit a cigarette and looked at the sky, not daring to look at her, afraid to see the hurt in her face. But, be assured, he wanted her to be hurt.

"What—what do you mean, honey? This is the opportunity of a lifetime, and it's not as if I would be asking you for anything."

"What about trying to have this baby? You still want that?"

"Yes, of course, honey," Lillian said. "If that happens and it gets to be too much, I will quit, that's all. I get to become a principal, and teaching is my life!"

"Well, we all can't get to do what we want in life. Just tell them no," Max said. "Now, that's it: that's all. I said no."

"All due respect—" Lillian looked at him. The controlling way in which he spoke to her revealed a dislike for her that he had obviously felt for a while. She had never disobeyed Max, and if he asked her to jump off a bridge with no parachute, she would have done it. But not to take this class? She didn't get that one. She wanted to smack that cigarette out of his mouth. How selfish and careless could he be? He was willing to ruin her life.

"Honey, with all due respect, it's my decision, and I made it," she said.

"So, you are going?"

"Yes. It's two nights a week."

"Not caring what I said. Forget it, be gone nights! That's okay. You go, go on to school." He smiled wickedly at her and walked out of the house.

She followed him to the door, but he slammed it in her face.

The seasons had changed in her household. Max was no longer in love with her, if he ever really loved her. Lillian was arm candy for him when he was around that well-to-do crowd. That was no longer his company. No one wanted to hear from an older musician who could not play.

As she walked back to her room, Lillian noticed Jean sitting in the kitchen. She couldn't look or talk to Jean. She went back to her room and cried. She cried until she couldn't cry anymore. Then she decided she needed girl support, so she went back into the kitchen, but Jean was gone. She called out Jean's name, and when there was no answer, Lillian realized she had left—left to support Max. Little did Lillian know that this was how their relationship started.

Lillian felt like her husband was on loan to Jean. She knew all along that they were having some sort of affair, but she couldn't bring herself to fully accept it. For the first two years, she just couldn't look close enough at either one of them. She was in school, working hard, and studying with her new friends in the program. The kids were still the bright spot in her life. Although Max gave her no encouragement, he kept letting her go to school. She was still doing nice little things for Max, like leaving candy on the bed and planning weekend dinner dates, but nothing seemed to make him happy, and he was beginning to invite Jean to everything. If they went to the picture show, he would invite Jean, and Lillian would never say no. She was catering to him, and she knew she was still in love with him. She also noticed that he treated her more like a sister around Jean. He wouldn't even hold her hand in her presence. She asked why one day, and he simply said, "If you want to be a schoolgirl, I'm going to treat you like a child."

Margarita

At this point, a sudden sadness came over Leona. She often switched tenses, and that never bothered me. I simply wanted the story to continue. I didn't want her to say, as she had done in the past, that she didn't want to talk anymore, and the day would end. This story was so interesting. I saw her repositioning herself, and I knew the story would continue. I didn't want to say a word, not even move. I wanted nothing to take her away from this moment. A couple of seconds later, she continued.

Leona

It was Lillian's last day of class. She was the new principal that fall. Little did she know at the time that this also meant her time with Max was ending; she had one year left. Max was drinking and losing money as if he had holes in his pockets. At this point, he had totally given up music. He talked about playing a few local gigs, but it never worked out. He spent his time sitting and laughing with Jean, eating, and watching television. The bank account they shared had been closed out, and Lillian never questioned what happened to the money.

She opened herself a separate account, and lo and behold, she came to realize that she was paying most of the bills around the house.

Jean was developing an attitude with Lillian: She would make smart remarks to her and try to say things to show her up. If she missed a question on a game show, Jean would laugh and throw in remarks like, "And she's the teacher!" When Lillian acted offended, she would accuse Lillian of being too sensitive.

Lillian probably would have lived with it longer had it not been for the townspeople letting her know that something was wrong. Now this was a problem. She had to accept that her husband wanted to live and sleep with two women under the same roof, but the community was beginning to feel that this was some sort of agreed arrangement, and people started giving her disgusted looks. She remembered those looks; in fact, she was used to them, and the strength of her youth revived her.

I came to visit Lillian one day and told her everything. I could see it plain as day. She had heard but not listened to the rumors people were whispering behind her back, or as she walked to and from the store. She had grown up in a small town and was well aware of how to tune out rumors, but hearing them from me, she couldn't hide from not knowing any longer.

Lillian began to watch Max and Jean closely to confirm what her soul already knew was the truth. She banned Jean from any area in the house but the attic, where she had moved her things. She didn't want to see Jean at all, but this didn't last long. The life of a principal was very demanding, and most days she didn't get home until after 8 p.m.

Knowing this spilled over into her relationship with Max, for she no longer admired him. She hated that she still loved him, but she didn't respect him. She slept with him only to flaunt her half-nude body around Jean, who showed signs of being upset, like leaving the house in a hurry or slamming things to the floor. That is what she enjoyed the most about Max and her relationship. She hated his touch, but oddly enough, the more disdain she felt for him, the more he wanted her. When love dies, it just lies on life support, and that is how she felt day in and day out, barely breathing. Max would say to her, after he felt he had done all he did to make her feel sexually pleased and got nothing. "I don't know what got into you, girl, but you better get over it." There were no moans of pleasure when he touched her. She cringed when he tried to kiss her. Unknowingly, what she had gotten over was him. Well, at least in part.

At first, Lillian stopped cooking and cleaning the house, just to find that Jean gladly did all she didn't do. So she went back to caring for her house because it was slowly becoming all she had, and there was something lovely about seeing Jean in a small attic with limited heat in the winter and no air in the summer.

She was being honored as principal of the year in her small school district. Her kids had outscored four other schools, the teacher retention rate was high, her teachers didn't leave, and she had an active parent board. This was a big event, and somehow Max was invited. Max and Jean showed up one hour late. Olivia and I offered to take her out to eat, but she wouldn't hear of it. All she wanted more than anything was to get home and get some sleep. I could see that Max was slowly killing my sister, but this was a battle I couldn't fight for her. She had to go at it alone, but it was taking its toll.

I didn't know until later that Max had moved out of her room to sleep in the guest room, and that Jean had quit her job. She was to work with Max at this new club he was opening, which Lillian knew nothing about. Lillian and I just happened to be downtown one day and saw Jean going into this abandoned jazz club. We followed her and found Max and his business partner, a contractor, talking about the plans. Lillian was so shocked that she sat down and just looked at Max. She couldn't take her eyes off him. I wondered what she might have been feeling, but she wouldn't say. She just stared at him.

Max, feeling the awkwardness, stated in a liar's tone, "This was to be your surprise, honey."

Lillian didn't say thanks or anything. She just got up and walked out of the joint. I did all I could do—there was a box of glasses that I accidentally bumped into—then I remembered it was her battle and followed her out of the place. Olivia was keeping me committed to minding my own business. She would always say, "What if they get back together? Then he would hate you, and you and your sister's relationship would be estranged." I knew that could happen, so even when I wanted to interfere, I wouldn't allow myself to until I was sure it was over, because I could sense it was ending.

The next morning at breakfast, Lillian had found enough courage to confront the truth. She announced that it was time for Jean to leave, if for no other reason than to get their reaction, which was deadly silent. Then she added, "She has been living with us for four years. She's grown, Max. We are not responsible for raising her. You understand, don't you, Jean? Get your own place, settle down, become a respectable citizen."

"I'm already a respected citizen," Jean said in her smart-alec indigent tone.

Lillian shot back, "Okay, then, whatever. Get out, leave by Saturday."

Max, acting as if she hadn't spoken at all, said, "Don't you think we should have discussed this first before you just blurted it out like that?"

"Who are we kidding, Max? When's the last time we sat down to do anything, much less discuss something? You're either drunk or high or both. Pathetic. She's leaving or I'll burn this damn house down!"

Lillian left him to ponder whether or not she would do what she said. He obviously thought she would, because he moved Jean out that night, and two weeks later, he moved out too. He had left her for Jean. She has so much pain, so many questions. Why? What just happened? Everything was so not real to her—air, wind, night, day—there was nothing real, for what she feared had happened, and it had totally taken her out of reality. Then she had to accept the ultimate insult: Jean was pregnant, and if that wasn't bad enough, so was she.

One day Max came home wanting money from Lillian, and of course, she refused. Then he got sentimental. He started helping her remember the first time they met, and he talked about how much he used to like her in certain clothing. She was listening to his words again, and she realized she still loved him. He touched her gently on the back of her neck, and he was no longer disgusting. She gave herself all too willingly to him. She thought and hoped that he would bring back the yesteryears, when everyone who was anyone wanted to be them, when they would walk into a room and give it life and purpose.

Max appeared to be in love with both her and Jean. Lillian thought back on a time she remembered: When Jean was gaining back the weight, she would go for a soda in the refrigerator, and Max would make her put it back and drink milk. All of this she enjoyed. She would smile like a black Siamese cat and drink the milk, then waddle upstairs, for Lillian couldn't stand to be around her and she knew it. She was loving living under the same roof with the husband of another woman.

After Max left her house, all this started to come back to her—everything. She got pleasure out of reliving and revisiting the pain. She loved Max and she hated him. She wanted him one moment, then she wanted him to die. She had her baby, a beautiful little girl whom they both loved, especially Max. This made Lillian use the kid as artillery. He had to stay with her to see baby Phyllis.

It was painful for me to watch Lillian. Here was a principal, earning enough to support herself, still young and beautiful, with a beautiful baby girl, yet she was forcing Max to come over to see the child and would call his and Jean's house, making threats.

She began drinking alone. Sometimes she drank so much that we had to go pick up baby Phyllis. I hired Olivia to take care of the kids because I knew Lillian could not, and someone had to be with her day in and day out.

Lillian was hurting herself, and her work began to suffer. I pretended not to notice the warning letter lying on her bed, its ink blurred by tears. She was slipping. The sound of hope, once loud in her life, had gone silent.

Love teaches you something, though not always gently. It does not fade like age or passing shadows. It remains steady, and sometimes it reveals the truth you least want to see — that the person you loved is not the person meant to love you back.

The very next day, she would assure me that she was done with him and wouldn't ever see him again, but a week or two later, there was Max lying in her house, bringing with him the shame he had lived the night before.

My mind kept on telling me, *We have to have the talk, we have to have the talk*, for she had vowed to stay with him until death did them part, and for all practical purposes, she was dead.

I had waited for this day like a new bride waits for her wedding day. It was something about the way she slipped her coffee, or looked down with eyes that were afraid to look up, that let me know that time had slowed and bowed its permission to me to speak on this situation. Lillian was broken enough to hear. All I needed was a visible crack in her brokenness that would allow a moment of common sense to slip in, and I hoped that the moment was long enough for us to really talk.

I came over that morning with that hope. As I was getting tired, I was almost convinced that I would leave my sister in her misery if that is where she longed to stay. She was using most of her funds to keep together a house that was too much for her to afford. To avoid motherhood so as not to hear the cry of her baby, she had hired a nanny who was mothering her child. The only time she really cared about the child was if Max was near. I was leaving my children with Olivia, just to make sure she was okay, far too often, and I just couldn't do that anymore.

It was on this day, at her kitchen table, that she spoke, voice low and raspy. She was in the midst of telling me how much Max had wanted her back when she lost a little weight, and how he would regret what he'd just done to her: He had called the police on her and had her arrested for destroying his tables and glasses the night before. It was on the news that a head administrator was arrested for fighting at the nightclub. She was too proud to see how bad this looked on her record. She and Jean had been catfighting over Max for the whole community to witness: two grown ladies, both with babies, fighting over Max in public. My sister, the educator, was praising the fact that she won the fight. She had cut Jean's face with a box cutter, and she was so proud of this. I was listening to my sister, mortified by this elaborate tale, and I wanted to slap her pretty face. Memphis papers had it splashed across the Sunday headlines, and none of this registered a rebuke in her small, simple mind. My anger got the best of me.

I dragged my sister by the hair to the mirror in the bathroom. I didn't stop to comment on how her house looked so neglected, how she'd lost time off work, or how her appearance had gone down. I took her to the mirror by her head for her to see for herself.

"Look at you, Lillian!" I shouted at the fragile image in the mirror.

"He's my husband. I have a right to him," she muffled out in a low, prideful voice.

"Look at you, Lillian! You are not the person I know — you're just like them, Lillian. You are just like Max and Jean. Fighting in a club? You have a child's mentality. You are no more than the dirt you migrated from!"

I ran from the bathroom and brought in Phyllis, who at the time was barely more than a toddler. I lifted her up beside Lillian and held her toward the mirror. In the reflection stood fragile images staring back at us — Lillian's bloodshot, drunken eyes, patches of hair missing from the front of her head, and dark circles settled beneath her eyes. Her bruised cheeks were swollen and red, and worry pressed deep lines across her forehead like a neon warning. The only pure thing in that mirror was Phyllis.

Baby Phyllis, as if seeing herself for the first time, reached toward her reflection.

"What do you want for her? Does she even matter to you? If you don't stop this, she will become another misfit statistic—searching for love from people incapable of giving it, letting her heart take her places her feet should never travel. What did he do to you that makes you love him more than this woman in the mirror, more than your own life? Or do you like being treated worse than dirt? I'll say this only once: He is not worth it. Even if you win and get Max, you will still lose, and so will she."

At that moment, as if God Himself spoke through the baby, Phyllis began to cry. It started as a soft whimper—a warning of the storm that was coming.

Lillian turned her face from the mirror and looked down.

The crying continued. Soon, the baby was twisting in my arms, reaching for her mother.

Lillian listened for nearly three minutes while I made no attempt to quiet the child. The cries became screams, and still she stood there, afraid to face her own reflection.

Finally, she took Phyllis from my arms. The baby's face was wet with tears. Lillian held her and began to rock her, and slowly the crying stopped. And though the child would never remember that day, that day, Lillian became her mother.

Her mind was no longer clouded by the fantasy she once called life. Everything was clear now. For the first time, she saw Max for who he was, and she saw herself as well. She recognized how she had neglected her daughter and her job, and how she hid bottles in her desk, under her bed, in her coffee cabinet, and even in her water canister. And how, whenever she felt nervous or sick, she drank again.

Now she understood why her hands trembled, why sometimes she could barely hold a piece of paper. Her liquor had made her sick and weak and had only given her a thirst that could not be quenched, and here was where life had landed her. Somewhere between loving and wanting to be loved, she had lost herself. But that day she learned something: When you let in the light, the viper cannot stay.

She carried the baby to the window, and sunlight poured over them. Things were different now. A quiet calm settled over them, and soon both mother and child drifted to sleep.

Throughout the night, I watched. I slept on the couch while Lillian was cradling Phyllis as if she were a newborn. I heard my sister cry out her pain in whimpering prayers all night. I could not understand the words — they were hidden inside groans and soft, high-pitched sounds — but I knew she was fighting for her life.

There's an inner stench that one smells when rejected, hated, and betrayed by loved ones. Lillian knew she wasn't the Savior, but that night, she died on an invisible cross to something called togetherness, and for the first time in her life, she had to accept she was a single mother.

Months tiptoed past her like thieves waiting for an opportunity to rob. Lillian was fired from her principalship and was now in obscurity. She worked as a fifth-grade teacher at a small private school miles away. Both Olivia and I watched the kids. I watched Lillian stripped of her fancy clothes and high-paid titles. She was just a teacher and mother in a small two-bedroom flat. This do-over was not without its moments of shame, but pieces were coming back together again. She was beginning to feel her new self and embraced her very new life. A few suitors came after her, but she just couldn't bring herself to date anyone from Memphis. At the time, she knew she had nothing to give anyone but her body, and she was too tired to give that. However, men just liking her gave her hope. She was no longer trapped inside Max's life for she was her own person now.

When she had gotten settled in her new life. Max came back, of course. Misery will find you, as it hates rejection. He even promised to leave the club and Jean. She saw right through this. It wasn't that he wanted her back that badly. It was that he hadn't totally destroyed her, and she was doing the unthinkable by getting along without him. It was funny to Lillian how she even flirted with this thought, just for the satisfaction of seeing the failure in Jean's eyes. But she knew that if she accepted the bad things back into her life, good things would take a detour. Max had to deal with Jean and her now two babies, and both of their bad habits, and he was not going to get Lillian to share the burden.

She still had to go to where the two of them lived, which was in an old boarding house above a run-down secondhand store, in which Jean from time to time worked (when she wasn't stealing clothes from the store owner). She had to go visit Max, because I finally completed my secretary program and business degree. My office was relocating to Chicago, and they wanted me to join the firm as a full-time legal research secretary, something I loved doing. I had accepted without even knowing if Lillian would want to go or not. I had given Memphis many years, but it was time to move on to a new chapter.

There was a new boarding school I could get the kids into while I worked tirelessly for the law office, which I really wanted to do. It didn't surprise me that Lillian was all for it.

She wanted me to live a little and explore things I really liked. We would be uprooting and moving to Chicago. It was one last thing we had to do, and with me being in law, I had already had her papers prepared. All we had to do was get Max to sign. He fussed and hollered hell no for about two months, but he needed money, so he asked her to visit him. He was now willing to sign the divorce papers, provided that when the house was sold, they'd share the proceeds. Lillian, I am sure, would have given him the whole house and every dime in the bank had he just asked. She was truly done.

He also asked for the right to see Phyllis, the child he clearly loved. Phyllis loved her dad, and Lillian would not deny Phyllis the pleasure of seeing the good side of Max. She was his only daughter, and she brought out the good in that man. At times it made her a little jealous of how he bowed down to the child. But he loved his daughter, and if that was all he could love in this world, she wouldn't take that away from him.

When night stubbornly bumps back and forth with the light, leaving fragments of itself behind, morning slowly begins to evolve. At this particular juncture in the cosmic struggle, we left Memphis. It had been twenty years, but we never regretted having lived there. But Chicago would be home soon.

I've been told that people come into the world knowing how to love themselves. I do not agree. I think people can come into the world selfishly focused on self, which can masquerade as love, but I will argue that the only way to truly love is to love others. It is the love for a child that teaches how to love yourself. You get these incredible creatures through marriage, or maybe you will birth or adopt them, but when you love children, truly love them, you will learn how to love yourself.

———

Margarita

"For the book," she said, and winked at me before she got up and walked toward the back to go to her room. She told me to let myself out and lock the door, as I thought, *What was Phyllis like?*" She told me the story of Phyllis a little later on. I never thought I would need that story until the season came, and I did.

PHRASE 13

SEASONS

Margarita

I had been visiting Leona for five years. Somewhere along the way, I became more than just a student volunteer in my community. I had become an inspiration — at least, that is what people told me. Kids who had lost their grandparents said hearing about me and Leona helped them imagine what it might have felt like to have an older voice of reason speaking into their lives. I would tell Leona's stories all the time, and my friends enjoyed hearing them. Of course, sometimes I would embellish the story a little, making it more urban, but they enjoyed them all the same.

I encouraged friends, and even a few enemies, to join the foster grandparent program, and many of them did — mostly because they had already heard so much about *my* foster grandmother Leona. Officially, I was part of the organization and she was my assigned grandparent, though she insisted she was not much older than my mother. Still, she was over fifty-five, which qualified her for the program.

Leona hated anything that suggested age. The very idea of being called a foster grandmother made her frown, but I used her name anyway.

I was a senior in high school now. That alone felt good, but what felt even better was that I was up for a citizen's award that would pay a large portion of my college tuition for four years. I had waited for this season for as long as I could remember. Now I had to tell Leona. The thought made me nervous, but it mattered for my future.

Part of the reason I was even being considered for the award was my visits with her, yet she had never attended any of my ceremonies. She was always busy. I had also written several award-winning articles about senior care. Some had been published, and one was being syndicated in a major Chicago newspaper. It focused on crimes against seniors, inspired by the senseless death of an elderly cab driver.

I was still young, but I was on my way to becoming what I had always wanted to be — a journalist. I dreamed of hosting my own show one day. I didn't know exactly what kind yet — not something shallow, but something that mattered. I knew only one thing for certain: It would be investigative. And if I won this award, there was another possibility — the unmentionable one. I could get an agent. A real, live agent. Someone who would open doors I couldn't yet reach. I also hoped to intern at a major newspaper while I was in college.

My heart raced, moving much faster than my feet, as I walked toward Leona's house. Over the years she had become more than my assignment. She was my dear friend. I had listened to countless stories, eaten more good meals than I could remember, watched her favorite old movies, and even learned about fashion trends I never cared about before. But there was one thing I knew for certain about Leona — she was different. Unpredictable.

One afternoon I arrived and she insisted I call her *Mrs. L.* She was dressed up, her face covered in heavy, almost caked makeup. Her lips were a strange bluish color, as if they had been burned. Leona normally wore her soft, natural hair, but that day she had on a long, kinky blonde wig. Everything about her felt unfamiliar. I only stayed an hour. I wasn't even sure I knew the woman sitting in front of me, and for the first time, she had no stories to tell.

A few months later I visited again, and she was completely herself—casually dressed, jazz playing softly through the house. That day we talked about music, all the greats from Sam Cooke to Miles Davis. Music was clearly one of her great loves.

She told me, very seriously, never to fall in love with a music man. "They can take your mind," she said.

We laughed about it, and before I left, she handed me an envelope. Inside was enough money to cover all my senior fees and events.

Leona had a way of knowing things about you before you ever spoke them aloud. I was certain she must have called the school to find out exactly what I needed, because the amount she gave me was precise—down to the last dollar.

It was getting close to the day of the banquet and award ceremony. I had already prepared my speech, and I had procrastinated long enough. I needed education. It was all I knew how to be good at. Yes, I was cute to most people, but not model-beautiful, so I couldn't count on my looks to get me through doors. I was hopeful that I would make it to Northwestern University, majoring in journalism. I keep telling myself that Leona would understand why a girl like me needed this scholarship. I was definitely introverted and strange to some people, and not really endowed with the likability factor like my mother. If I didn't get an education, I wouldn't have a world to live in or a way out at all—and believe me, I needed out. This couldn't be all there was to my life.

My family had come along, for we had only two bad seeds out of nine, but according to Leona's philosophy, they were all working to remain poor. I had an opportunity to become a living organism.

I laughed at myself when I realized that Leona was making sense to me. I was beginning to understand her long poetic parables, and as much as I hated to hear them before a story, I would have much rather she just started with the story. But it was her parables that started strangely making sense. She just had to come to this event. People needed to see that she wasn't just a figment of my imagination.

Before I knew it, I was at her door, and she opened it, facing me in a beautiful pink dress trimmed in white. "Come in, dear, I'm making iced coffee. Have some?"

I shook my head no, figuring that I would just listen until I built up the nerve to tell her about the award ceremony and that she would have to come. I didn't know who had nominated me for the award, but I sure did need it, for it would land me in college without having to work.

"You were to come on Saturday," she said. "I had baked your favorite—caramel brownies."

I sat in my chair quietly, wanting to say, "Look, just come with me so that I can get this money for college and see you in four years." She studied me for a second, then sat down on the couch, crossed her legs, and allowed the room to turn deadly silent—the one thing I was afraid of, for the air was thickening by the minute. If someone didn't say something real soon, the air would be too thick to breathe.

"I got a twenty-one on my ACT test," I said finally.

"Good for you! Now, off to college. I liked college, though I imagine your experience will be much better. I was in night school, you know."

"I didn't know that," I said. "Well, my parents can't afford any money for college."

"I really hope you learn to speak English before you go into the world of books and brains," Leona said.

"You know what I mean," I said sarcastically.

Leona had a way of making me angry before I ever said what I came to say. It usually eliminates small talk. As always, I found myself wondering if this would be the last time I saw her after I told her. Still, it had to be said. I stood there a moment longer than necessary, then finally spoke.

"Leona, I'm being considered for an award."

She didn't respond, just kept doing whatever she was doing, diddling with the pillows on the side of the couch as if I hadn't spoken at all.

"It's for some articles I wrote, and for my involvement in the foster grandparent program. For working with you." I swallowed. "A lot of my college tuition would be covered."

Now she looked at me.

"And I need you there," I said quietly.

"You don't work with me," she replied. "If so, who's paying you?"

"You know what I mean."

"Look, let's establish something," Leona said. "I don't even know what you mean unless you tell me. I can't read minds, and your English is never self-explanatory."

"Will you go?"

"I will not be exploited. If that's what you came for, go back. Truth be told, I rarely see you anyway."

I was not going to let her frighten the words out of me, so I said, "I will have to stay here and go to junior college without scholarship money. I don't come from wealth. I am working with the cards I've been dealt in life."

"I'm not your meal plan or welfare plan, that's not why I'm here," she said matter-of-factly.

"Well, I don't understand," I said.

"Clearly you don't, for if you did, you wouldn't want me to be this puppet, this poor soul that can't do anything by herself and needs a little chocolate child to show her the way. I won't go!"

"You got to, Leona!"

"It's going to be hard for you in this world, granted, and I will help you any way I know how, but not at the expense of my dignity. You got that?"

I couldn't say a word, or rather, I couldn't find the words to say. I was stuck in my anger. I wanted to give her one last look and then never see her again. I hated her and her so-called seeds of wisdom. Who was this woman anyway?

"Don't look at me like that," she finally said fearlessly. Junior college isn't that bad. Who knows? Money can come from many different sources."

"Don't worry about me, old lady!" I said angrily. "I will make it!"

"Of course you will, and if you were a little nicer and didn't carry this poor girl privilege mentality, you would make it sooner and it would be easier for you, but you'll do okay, I'm sure of that.

"How dare you say that to me? Like you had it made so easy. Being white as a ghost never made you privileged? I thought you knew."

"It was an advantage, but that's not the point. I just need you to know money is not your only handicap. That's the point."

"That is not the point! I don't have any handicap, and that includes money. Everything you have ever told me was pointless. You lived a very pointless life, so now deal with it. I'm not ever coming back. Tell your fairy tales to someone else. There's another chocolate child out there somewhere who may listen."

"Just walk out, just like that," Leona said.

"Just like this." I took a deep breath and made a move toward the door. My legs carried me where my heart did not want to go, out the door, and for practical purposes out of her life.

The look of surprise, which quickly dissolved into disappointment, crossed her face. She said, "Wow, what a girl you turned out to be. A seven-year relationship gone because you want me to sit on the stage and pretend to be hopeless and helpless so that you can get money for college. Valuing nothing more than time! What would I have done without you, dear, in my life? Kill my damn self, I imagine."

I walked out the door, not wanting to give her the satisfaction of seeing that I was conflicted, and started to cry. I walked out, content but not happy that I wouldn't see her again, but I knew somehow that I would. She had taught me not to give up so easily. I wouldn't give up. I just needed her to give in.

UNPAVED

Margarita

When there is an unpaved trail from your past, go back and trace your tracks and pave that road. Otherwise, the journey of your life will always be filled with bumps and buried places. I often found myself retelling the stories Leona told me, sometimes to just think about the characters and other times to decipher the possibilities of her stories. I was never really sure if she told me stories for pure entertainment or if there was truth hidden in the parables, fables, and allegories. For some reason the story of Phyllis stayed with me. She died around my age, and as the timeline reveals, probably a year or less before I met Leona. Leona slowly dripped into the fabrics of her stories that she was dealing with two deaths when I first met her. I wondered about that often. It was still kinda strange how the two boys fit in, but apparently, they were here before Phyllis, and my guess was that they were around ten to twelve years older. She never really liked talking about her children. She would always say to leave the children out of it, but she told me about Phyllis.

The thoughts about Phyllis had me doing somersaults in my mind. I didn't yet understand why it weighed so heavily on me, but as I contemplated what I would do in just two days if Leona did not attend, the memory started returning on a winter day, just after my birthday. She hadn't wanted to celebrate. She only wanted to talk about Phyllis.

She stood the entire time she told the story, and I could tell the pain was something she could not sit down on. I remember wanting my birthday present, childish and impatient, while she kept trying to give me something else —

the truth. I sat on the edge of my chair as she talked, and now, years later, I could still hear it as clearly as if it were happening again.

———

"You don't drink coffee, right?"

I looked at her, thinking, this is a no-brainer. My mother told me coffee makes you hard-headed, but what I said was no.

"She would have been your age now. Freshly in high school, she liked writing too. She was an old soul, and everything she touched in life changed other people's lives. You might have heard of her. She was on her way to stardom. She loved the sound of music, the moves it created for the world to bodily mimic. It is a sad story, but some gifts are not meant to stay with you long.

"I can make you hot tea if you like," she said.

I didn't want anything but movie money, but I felt that would have been inappropriate to say, so I just nodded my head no. Then she continued with her story.

"You see, we migrated from Memphis, bringing with us three kids, two boys, and one girl. The boys are still writing their stories, and it will be their story to tell one day."

As I listened intently to this story, I felt an immediate sense of guilt. Most days I came here, I needed her, her space or ear, or even just her stories, to take me away from my own thoughts, and now it appeared that she needed me, and all I wanted was to hang around a few silly kids. I sat back in my chair to relax but hopefully to tell her I had time, and I wanted to know, not just to listen but to hear. In a few seconds she continued.

———

Leona

Max had fallen from the town's hero to something closer to its cautionary tale, and people seemed to take a strange pleasure in reminding him of who he once was. There had been silk ties, confident speeches, and respect that followed him into every room. He had been one of the few men the police addressed as *sir* instead of *boy*. Now he was just another man — perhaps even less — because everyone remembered his height before the fall. Max was a supernova, a star that had burned too brightly and then collapsed, forced to walk the earth as a wandering shadow of himself.

Lillian and I took him the papers, and he never looked up. He was lying on a mattress on the floor with a lamp with no shade to give him light. He looked tired, just plain tired. He lit a cigarette and pointed to the door, so we closed it. He didn't want to hear anything, just wanted what was happening, which was full permission to destroy his life, to be done, over. The house would sell soon and he would get half, and of course, when he got back on his feet, he could see Phyllis. That was all he wanted, and she agreed.

Jean was in the bathroom. She didn't even come out. That was good because Lillian still felt a little sore toward her and probably would have caused bodily harm to her in some way. Lillian walked out, and that chapter closed with the door.

We stopped by Olivia's house and said our goodbyes. She had prepared a basket of chicken and grits for us to eat on the road. She never stopped being my friend. I was going to Chicago to be a legal research secretary to a well-established law firm, and this amazed her. She just couldn't stop hugging me, but we said our farewells and we were on our way.

On our way North, just before we crossed out of Indiana to Chicago's border, we met two cops, and they got us a small taste of what the North would be like. Let me digress. I think this little encounter will be important in the future. So, we stopped off at a small-town pit joint, just to feed the kids and get all the restrooms out of the way. We noticed that people were looking at us. We were used to people staring at us, but not so much like this. I mean, what's wrong with two preteen boys obsessed with their video game and a little girl traveling together? We thought maybe it was the fact that we were two women. I nagged Lillian, letting her know this was not the place to stay long. We needed to get back on the road. We still had around three hours before we would see the location that would house us. My law firm had arranged for me to stay near downtown Chicago, close to the job. Lillian and I had decided to share an apartment until she started teaching, for she was told that her certificate would be honored, and in due time, she would be back on her feet.

We were feeling good about life in general before this encounter. We were forty-something, employable, single, and strikingly attractive. What more could life offer? Lillian was also waiting for her house to sell, which would give us a big check to chill out with. We had paid the bill and were heading back to the car when we were stopped by two police officers from the great state of Indiana. It was so embarrassing: They made us put our hands on the car and searched our car thoroughly. Then one of them looked at Lillian and said in the meanest of tones, "Bet you running away from that nigger boyfriend, now you got those nigger babies to raise. Serves you right. What does he do, beat you? Did he beat you good? I remember a day both of y'all would have hung from the nearest tree. Serve you right," he repeated as he took our clothes out of cases and sort of had things all over the place to further embarrass us.

We lived such a sheltered life. We rarely knew what people thought of us. Only once in our lives did someone think we were White. It was the one time Clare took us into town to buy a special kind of sewing material, and the sales clerk gave us candy because she thought Clare was our nanny. The truth of the matter is, we never really knew what to call Clare. We were fed well enough and we had a place to sleep, but what do you call that person? Clare nodded yes, and we ate the chocolate, and the sales clerk thought we were mute. We just weren't used to being spoken to so kindly. The sales clerk smiled and walked away.

It took a while before we realized she must have thought we were little White girls. Our hair was combed to the back in one plait. We didn't really recall having a mirror or even looking in one, which would come much later. Clare had one in her room, but that was it. Yes, that was the only time in our remembrance that we were considered something other than Black, but it was certainly happening now. Lillian and I just looked at each other. I didn't know what would happen next. The South was known for racism, but we had never experienced such a thing. In fact, as I come to learn both lands, I would say that the South is more into separatism and the North is straight-up racism.

Lillian had always been the type who quickly assessed and adjusted to her circumstances. I had always been the one to react in most cases, which had served us good and bad, depending on the situation. Lillian held Phyllis close to her in a very nurturing way and spoke with a Southern accent much thicker than I was used to hearing her speak. "You are right, sir, when you say this is my child, for it is, but I didn't have it.

One of the Black ladies gave her to me to raise." I thought to just leave her, but she would have no one if I did that."

I know why Lillian said this; she wanted to protect the child, and if she made the child a victim, that could bring protection. It was a good idea at the moment, but it would later have its consequences.

Embarrassed and hurt for Phyllis, I wondered if she had marked the child that day. For as the little girl grew, she always felt like she wasn't Lillian's real child, though we both knew Lillian loved her. The police officer looked at the boys, and I didn't say a word. I just smiled. They were mine, and not even to appease these racist cops would I take that away from them. I let him assume they weren't mine, but I never said it verbally.

The policeman eyed us suspiciously. Then he muttered out, "What the hell do you want to raise a coon for?"

"Well, I just didn't want to see them given to the state, sir," Lillian said.

I figured she had started this line of rationalization, and she would have to end it.

For just a fleeting moment, these cops became interested in me. Besides, I was bothered slightly that Lillian had disowned her child. I knew my sister liked to pretend and mess with people's minds, but I didn't think that was a good way to accomplish her *dough* of make-believe. So, as the "good cop" was running my license and plates, I jumped into this game of make-believe.

"We actually may have a little negro in us, you see," I said. "That's why we're headed to Chicago—looking for our papa."

"Sister, why do you want to tell those men all our business?" Lillian asked me.

"Excuse me, please, sir," I told the cop, "but I just convinced my sister not to kill herself. She had decided that if she had one ounce of Black blood in her body, she would jump off a bridge."

"She would kill herself?" he said, smiling, yet half heartily believing it.

"She would," I said.

"Well, it was just a thought!" Lillian shouted nervously, looking around. In all her play, she hadn't thought of that line of defense, but she was loving it.

The cop signaled for his partner to come over, and the two stood facing us. "What did you get?" the partner asked.

"These two ladies might have coon nigger blood in them and was thinking about killing themselves."

"I sure in the hell would," the other cop said confidently.

"Why don't y'all take down your hair?" he asked. "We could tell you right now, so you won't have to visit or see that papa of yours."

"Why your ma didn't tell you?" asked the other cop. "Why she make you wait until this late in life?"

"She wasn't going to tell us at all," I said, "but she was dying, bless her soul, so she figured we needed to know. What an unfortunate situation we find ourselves in."

The two cops watched closely as we took down our hair, which we knew wouldn't have a wave in it at all, for we had freshly permed it before we left. Because our hair was sandy brown, it looked blonde in the sunlight.

"It's hard to say. What do you think, Jack?"

"Get to cutting your throat, young lady, cause you don't look pure White." You can stop hoping for anything else but one of them.

"Oh, don't say that, sir," I said. "You gone cause her to cry, and we won't be able to stop her."

They laughed at each other, amused by our conversation. "She was really going to kill herself, huh?"

"Kill herself dead, had it not been for Mama dying so soon, and she having to raise little Phyllis. It's all complicated. My mother, being a good church woman, just wanted us to know the truth."

"What you gone say to this nigger when you find him?" the cop asked.

"Just may have to kill him," I said.

The two cops laughed a knee-slapping laugh. I was no longer amused but insulted. I wished I had never started this game in the first place.

"Well, I go to church every Sunday, and sometimes killing is justified. What do you say, John?" referring to the other cop. So one of them was named John.

"Happened in Bible days all the time," John replied.

I knew the answer to this question, but I just needed to hear it, for it was becoming clear to us that in this great North, it was better to be dead than a negro.

So I said to these law-abiding lawmen, "So, you think, sir, that we ought to kill our papa when we do see him?"

"Well, when you come to think of it, he wasn't in you girls' lives."

The other cop nodded in agreement and gave me back my license, but I could tell he wasn't ready for us to leave. I figured we could entertain them just a bit longer and try to understand how they thought so we could better understand the mindset of those folk we called Midwestern.

"That's true, he wasn't," I said. "Then again, if he was in fact colored, my ma wouldn't let him around us girls anyway."

"I still don't understand why you would want colored babies in your house. Where is she going to eat or sleep at?"

"Eat at tables and sleep in beds like everyone else, I guess."

We all gave a half-hearted laugh. I had just gotten smart with the cop, and I needed to cover it up somehow.

"Well, she is still a child, you know," I said. "Let's get back to our dilemma. You cops are helping us out a great deal. Back home, our preacher sort of told us to love."

"Love who?" he asked.

"Everybody, I suppose, but you say something else."

"I say, you should love those who love you. Jacob I loved, Esau I hated. Even God hated — it's in your Bible."

"Well, what do you know? Now we must learn to hate," said Lillian.

"You already hate," said the cop. "Wasn't you gone kill yourself if you had nigger blood in you? That's hate, little lady. Now, as I look at you, you got it in you."

"Well, if she killed herself, who would I have?" I asked. "I guess she better start learning is how to love herself, even that nigger part. If in fact we are, for we are just as White as the folk back home."

His eyebrow raised and his face turned red, letting us know he was mad. He was mad for real — so angry that if he'd had a tree, all five of us would have hung from it. The boys had started to shift in their sleep, eyes still closed and bodies quiet. I prayed they would not wake. It was clear the thing he hated most was boys who would one day grow into men.

Deep inside I knew I was dealing with something dangerous, a kind of beast I had never encountered before, and he could easily have killed us. Only later did I realize how close we may have come to our end. If our identification had not been safely in our purses, if we had not been standing in a well-lit place with people coming and going, I believe that day might have ended very differently.

He stepped toward Lillian, speaking in a tone that sounded less like conversation and more like a warning. He even suggested she might be White — as if crossing some invisible line they never wanted us to cross again.

I would not have believed what happened next if I had not seen it with my own eyes. Lillian grabbed the officer's hand and squeezed with such force that he fell to the ground and released his gun. The second officer, silent and visibly shaken, immediately dropped his weapon as well. For a moment no one moved.

We hurried to the car and drove away. I asked her where she had learned to do something like that. She only said there had been times she had to put Max back in his place. In that moment I realized she had protected us from something only she understood.

As we pulled off, one of the officers managed a weak wave goodbye while gathering himself. The other still stood frozen, staring. That day, Lillian and I knew we were coming into a much different place, and it was, as always, the boys we had to protect. As soon as possible, they would be on their way back to boarding school.

A few years later I was sent in to do a deposition of a new client who had married rich, and his mouth had gotten him into a lot of trouble; in fact, he was on his way out of the political circus if he was found guilty of openly referring to a

Black man as a nigger and spitting in his face. My firm took the case and won, and that man and I became good friends, but he knew never to mess with me, and although I didn't want to keep in touch, he often did. Some of my biggest connections came from that man. I like to believe I taught him a thing or two about race, as he would one day release himself from the assigned hate sold to certain Americans by the pound. It's just funny how things worked out in life. It can sometimes be those small encounters, those moments of brief passing, a warm smile, or a firm handshake, that come back and save the day.

That was our introduction to the North in so many ways. As time would reveal, us girls needed someone. The boys were getting bigger, and of course Phyllis was growing up, and even she picked up the saxophone and played. Music was her gift.

I met Sam at one of my boss's events. Now, if a Black person was invited to my boss's event, they had money and lots of it. Sam was loaded and single, with no kids. I liked Sam, although I didn't like his name, but I got over it. My Sam was an undertaker who was good with accounting. He worked with the city. He also worked with the mob and buried many unknown. Sam made money all over the place. But he wasn't one of these flashy negros. He was rather plain and easy-going. He hired a little help around the house, but that was for me. For the most part, Sam did his own cooking and washing. He moved me to this condo, and we adjusted to each other's ways.

Lillian, my dear sister, went through three boyfriends before she met Buddie, a short, colorless man white as paper, but a Black brother. He was a nice guy, I suppose, although a little dishonest. They say he was good with those numbers, and during income tax time, he had lines of people for income tax. He was known for hiding and creating stuff. I knew she would choose safe this time, for she'd already had the good supporter and then the wild thing. Now she had settled for safety and would grow to love safety, for she and Buddie lived together and got married right in their South Holland home.

Back to Phyllis. She was around ten when they moved out that way. But she was an enlightened ten-year-old. She understood the world at a fast pace, always thinking about how to defend the things she wanted. She had a way of just knowing what was important to you, as to make you feel good and bad. Buddie told Phyllis, "I'm going to be your new daddy." That was a mistake because that was not what she wanted or needed. She decided at that moment that she hated him. Besides, they didn't look like a family to her; in fact, people never saw them as a family. They always asked if she was adopted.

I think she wanted people to notice she had some of her mother's beauty, but they never did. She was a really pretty girl, but she looked like her father—smooth, dark-skinned with large, round eyes, and long, coarse hair. I just imagined a child who looked like that stuck out in a family with albino paper white Buddie and her mother, who was a tanned-looking White woman. Phyllis talked about Max all the time, and I got tired of hearing about him. She wanted to play like him. She watched his old video recording, which she somehow got a hold of. She looked up to him, the man who simply made her laugh over the phone but kept not one single promise to her.

I convinced Lillian to send her to Olivia, and he would come see her a few times, just to show her stuff on the saxophone, and he would be off again. Lillian often explained to her that she looked up to the wrong man. Buddie was paying for her to go to private school and take music lessons, and Max was getting all the credit. All she knew was that Max was getting high and being a poor father to his two growing boys, one boy the same age as Phyllis and one two years younger. Yet that dude was what she talked about, to the point that Buddie stopped wanting to be in her life. He even started to bring around his one child, to sort of let Phyllis know that he didn't have to be her father to her because he was already a father. This didn't bother Phyllis; in fact, Phyllis became a friend to the girl a year younger than she was. In her writings, we learned that the girl was a part of the mission she was on.

Now she didn't want Buddie to be her father for two reasons. She helped that little girl feel good about herself. She was so good at that. She knew how to pinpoint your needs and meet the exact one you needed to help you be a better person. Too bad she couldn't do that for herself. Kids can be typical. In many ways, she was typical, a kid in need of space and time to grow, but she understood what it meant to be a living organism. I think she always knew. The words *Living Organism* was one of her stellar poems. If she wasn't composing, she was writing poetry.

Max would make very little effort to see the child, but he called all the time. I used to think he called to upset Lillian or maybe even mess up her relationship, but I later learned that he probably called because if you stayed around this child for minutes, you wanted to do better.

With Lillian's permission, I had Olivia's contact number for Max so that Phyllis could call him when she wanted to anytime she wanted, and often she would wait until Buddie was home to call. I used to think maybe this child just didn't want to see her mother happy. That was not the case. She had to call later in the afternoon because that is when she knew someone could call for her Dad.

When Phyllis was ten, Lillian let the visits start. She was supposed to live with Olivia, but of course, she wouldn't stick to that agreement. If her father lived in filth, so did she.

At the age of eleven, Phyllis was more like a middle-grade student. She had made three doubles. Learning was easy for her. It was as if her mind could not contain enough learning in a day, so she was moved to the eighth grade, and here is where she started listening intensively to Max's music. She watched her father play and started to mimic his movement and facial expression, not to mention the sounds that came out of that saxophone.

Lillian thought the child was cracking up. Night and day, sometimes for hours, she was listening and learning, and although Lillian had put her in music, she wanted more. Phyllis was like a man dying of thirst. She just wanted more lessons, better teachers, special seminars. Because she was so young in the eighth grade, she had very few friends and was growing further and further apart from Lillian. Lillian, who was working as a schoolteacher and surrounded by children, didn't quite know how to pull herself back from the kids she loved at school to the child she was struggling to love at home. To make her home a little more peaceful with Buddie, she settled for a distant love relationship with Phyllis because she figured she would have more time with her. She was going to grow and one day need a relationship only a mother could advise on. *There will be more time*, she reminded herself. How wrong she was.

I can only imagine how hard it must have been for her. She had overcome abuse and alcoholism. She really couldn't handle the stress of Phyllis's demands. What was really odd, even to her, was that she actually liked her husband's daughter more than the child who lived under her roof. They had more in common: fashion, clothes, and cooking. It was Phyllis she loved but really didn't like, and Phyllis understood this and didn't blame her for it; she just wasn't going to do anything to correct it. While Phyllis stayed in her room and talked to her few friends while listening to and playing jazz music, her mother was bonding with everything and everyone but her.

Phyllis began to play and actually do shows. She was going to be so much better than her dad, and I think he neglected his whole life at that point, plus his other kids and all, to make sure he coached her three days a week. I hear he gave up his drug money and lay sick on his house floor, throwing up and trembling, to make sure he was there to coach Phyllis.

————

At this point I put my head down. I was mentally exhausted. Margarita said to me, "I don't have to hear this story. We can talk about something else." I could tell she was searching to think what else we could talk about, so I started telling the story again.

————

I just know how hard my sister fought to love her child. I mean, she loved her child. She fought hard to find a way to express how much she loved that child. She thought that if she just let Phyllis have her way, sort of giving her permission to raise herself, it would express the deep love she felt for her. Lillian hoped that later in life, Phyllis would view this act as something akin to love, and when she got older, they would have a loving relationship. However, deep inside, Phyllis thought Lillian never saw her. In one of her poems, she wrote,

To my mother,

I am not there,

you can love an invisible seed.

But she did love her, she really did.

Lillian's husband didn't make the situation any better. He preferred to compete with her instead of just loving her. This competition between child and parent brought hardship to Lillian's marriage — one reason that the marriage ended.

At twelve, the superstars were calling for her, the girl with the saxophone. Max let someone hear his daughter play, one of his old connections, and the gig was booked. She would be playing on a television night show. She played Stevie Wonder's "Isn't She Lovely." It was spectacular. Steve Wonder called and congratulated her. Can you imagine getting a call from Stevie Wonder? It was at this point that Lillian figured she had done the right thing. Her daughter wanted music and so she gave her music.

Phyllis had been invited to play at a big award show. Max paraded her around for a week, just letting people meet his daughter. Lillian talked to her on the phone every night, and for the first three nights, she was speechless. All she could say was "Are you eating and sleeping well?" Phyllis had a problem with sleep. Her brain some nights just wouldn't turn off. Oddly enough, she was working out her problems with Phyllis in this distinct time together at night. She told her one night, and she did not know why, but something inside of her had to say, "You know I love you." Phyllis was quiet. These words had shut down her thoughts, but she was able to say to her mother, probably for the first time ever, "Mom, I love you too." They talked about the show — about the free food on the set of the show, her name on the door, the way it felt when people clapped so loudly for her. They talked. That night would have to carry her through the midnights to come.

At twelve, Phyllis was writing eloquent letters about how she longed to be with her heavenly father. She was writing about finding an eternal home, death, and time travel. When most pre-teens are thinking about their first encounter with love and friendship, Phyllis was writing about death.

After her short stay with Max, she came home, and Lillian felt like she could trust him a little more. She hoped that Phyllis would stay with Olivia, but she didn't. She stayed with her father and she survived. She came home to a new reality. Max had secured her an agent, so she was doing talk shows and morning news shows, even in Chicago. Lillian didn't like the fact that Max had let her get a tattoo, but she had her child back in one piece, and *that* she was grateful for.

Phyllis was the kind of kid who always understood true purpose in life, and it was because of her that Max stopped using drugs. She told him if he used again, she wouldn't ever see him again, so he stopped for good. No more visits back to the drug stop. That didn't stop Jean. We were told she started using more. Even though Max was now able to afford her a small home in Memphis and she didn't have to work, she still got high. Phyllis was all the revenge Lillian needed when it came to Jean. This was the one person Max wouldn't go against. Phyllis didn't hate Jean. She said in her poetry that Jean was not her mission field. It was her dad and her mother mostly. She talked to her father and had a really good relationship with her siblings. Jean was a non-factor in her life.

A year later, with Phyllis's newfound fame and Max off drugs, the school district picked him up to teach music classes after Mississippi State gave Max an honorary doctorate. That's the kind of person Phyllis was: If she could change your life, she would. She was so proud of her father. She had accomplished the only thing she wanted to accomplish in life and that was seeing her father whole.

Phyllis was accepted into this summer camp, upstate New York, A camp for gifted artists. Lillian really didn't want Phyllis to go to that camp, but she was a teenager, turning thirteen soon. Max couldn't go to Juilliard School of Music camps, but he wanted his child to go. Rumor had it that he was going to move to New York when she got into the school, and this camp was a feeder school for Juilliard. So, right before Lillian let her go, she wanted to visit Olivia and see her dad.

She had written the nicest letter to her mother and gave her a book of poems. She also wanted her brother to have all her newly composed music. Before she left, she gave Lillian the biggest hug. It was almost as if she was suffocating her, but it felt so good. Lillian renewed hope in the fact that she and her daughter would have that loving relationship one day. But that ended when her dad was at work.

Phyllis and one of her other siblings (the boy her same age) were sleeping in the house. A fire broke out and took them away with the smoke.

———

I stood up and opened the window. Maybe I didn't want her to see me cry, and maybe she didn't want to see me cry.

———

A part of my sister died that night with her child. It was comforting to know that Phyllis knew she was special. She was smart, articulate, and musically inclined, she had much to live for, and yet she didn't care if she lived or died, for she had inherited the part of Max that we all feared—the unexplained pain that only revealed itself through her poetry and music. Happiness is fleeting for the tortured soul, and she was indeed a tortured soul, but if only she was with Lillian. Maybe she could have grown out of that state. These are things you tell yourself when you are looking for a reason in insanity. Lillian knew the truth. Phyllis felt that at twelve, she had lived long enough. She wrote poetry that included her very own funeral song, and she fantasized about death. This, of course, made Lillian very uncomfortable, but oddly enough, reading her notes and poetry helped her understand exactly who her daughter was.

We should have gone back and paved the road, trying to find ways to fill her emotional gap, for we knew it was deep. We just didn't know how deep. Phyllis wrote about being a living organism. It may seem simple, but living things only stay alive to help other living things live. Phyllis knew even at her young age that part of living is helping others live, and she inspired people all around the world when her book was finally published.

I remember, no matter how hard I try to forget, the day she left here to visit Max. I could tell something was off. She had a plane ticket from Memphis to New York, but we changed it because Phyllis didn't want to take her writings to Memphis. She would go there for a few days, make a pit stop back home, get her journals and music notebook, and the next day head out to New York. Had we known more about her suicidal thoughts, we could have intervened. They all said Max wouldn't ever leave Jean. The day after we put Phyllis in the ground, he left Jean, moved in with Olivia, and taught school to all the little Phyllises in Memphis.

The hardest thing I had to do in life was put that girl's ashes in the ground. There were times I wished I could have forgotten, but I couldn't: When you lose someone you are close to, everything around you reminds you of them. Her clothes still had her scent on them, and her favorite color glared at me, even if it was on a cereal box. If I saw no other colors, I saw gray, blue, and orange. Everything about her absorbed me, and I was slowly losing myself to regret, I mean, my sister. My sister was as good as dead. The book, the book written by Phyllis, saved her and Max's lives.

———

Margarita

Leona gave me an envelope that day and said, "Go to the movies. You have around thirty minutes to get there. A car will be waiting downstairs to take you there, birthday girl. I just wanted you to know about her. I felt like talking about her."

"Thank you, living organism," I repeated.

She smiled and went to her room, and that day went on for me, but not without my wondering several times about Phyllis.

That day happened years ago, but it was fresh in my memory, as if she had just told me yesterday. Why did she share that story at that particular time? Why did that story come back to me? I jumped up and asked my father to take me back to Leona's house. I knew I would see her again, but just not this soon. When I got to her complex, I didn't ring the bell in fear that she might not let me in. I simply slid in behind another guest and knocked on her door. I know what I would say, and I prayed it would work.

Leona opened the door, dressed in all black as if she was going to a funeral. She smiled when she saw me and said, "Not a good time. Next time call, but I'm glad to see you."

I said two words: "Living organisms."

She smiled at me and didn't say a word.

Then I gave her the address. "3345 W. Hampton, first floor. Seven o'clock." I walked away.

A couple of days later, I would see her again, sitting in her assigned seat, dressed like a princess. No one there was dressed better. She had on a soft green two-piece. Her long, light brown hair was pinned up, and you could see her high cheekbones and narrow chin.

I read my acceptance speech, as I was one of twelve people who received the scholarship. Leona was there, and she had to accept my praise of her even if she didn't like it, and she probably didn't, but she was gracious. Leona gave me a soft kiss on the cheek, greeted my parents, and left. I was elated. I was actually going to college, hopefully my college of choice, all because I thought of Phyllis.

PHRASE 14

UNHINGED

Margarita

It was everywhere—on the news, in the newspapers, across Chicago. A high school student, Marion Johnson, had been killed at seventeen—a senior headed for greatness, his life cut short. Another case of gun violence. Another senseless death that was slowly becoming the norm, leaving a community shaken and unhinged.

Hands were thrown in the air. Heads shook in disbelief. Voices among us spoke of the blame we all had to share and the heavy cloak of poverty we wore—our faces painted with fear and despair. The entire community was questioned, yet there were no real answers. That upset me deeply because as surely as it had happened once, it would happen again and again.

I didn't know when it would end, but I did know Marion. He didn't like being pitied. He stood firmly on what he believed in—even if he was wrong—and if there were consequences, he accepted them. Death would have been a consequence he would have accepted.

So where did this leave me? Lost emotionally, looking for a compass to guide me back to common sense. He was the second boy I'd dated in high school. A romantic at heart, always whispering sweet nothings in my ear. My sisters had wanted him to be my first and I'd said no. Now I questioned that decision. Maybe, had I said yes, there would be a part of me, a memory I would always have, and he wouldn't be forgotten.

Now what I seem to remember in his death is his mother's red-stained eyes as she tried to force an everyday smile—one that revealed her strength more than her sorrow. I can only imagine that for her, even more than for me, nothing would ever fully make sense again.

I told her I was sorry for the loss of her son. But I was more than sorry—I was mortified. I was angry. She answered not with words but with a half-smile and a soft, gentle hug that told me she had nothing left to give.

I was to go to the funeral. I told myself I would go, knowing I wouldn't. On the day of the funeral, I called Leona to make sure she was free, and I found myself headed to her condo. I didn't want her to help me make sense of this situation, as I had resolved that this was not possible. I guess all I wanted was for her to understand.

For some reason my mind drifted to my sister, Andea. She was supposed to do my hair again—I had already paid her— but now she was back in rehab. I wasn't surprised. She did good for just so long, then it went back to bad. Janet, my older sister, was still her best friend, but to Janet's credit, she did not do the hard stuff. Andea had a choice of rehab or jail, and she chose rehab. I kept hoping she would not die when I was angry. What I really hoped was that that man would die.

Everyone called him "that man" because we could never quite decide what kind of man he was. It was clear he was a committed drug addict who somehow managed to stay out of jail and stay just as successfully out of his children's lives. Yet he had one quality that made the wondering deeper—he was likable, a really funny guy.

He would help you if he could, even while knowing you had just been talking about him. We needed that man when a car wouldn't start or when rodents had to be cleared from a basement. He always had a running car, a willing pair of hands, and a strangely forgiving heart. He wasn't a bad person—just a strange one. Obviously gifted in many different ways, yet he chose to do nothing with his life except hang around in dirty blue jeans and old black Michael Jackson T-shirts with holes around the collar. He would smile at you with those rotten teeth. He had even spent time in the Army. You'd wonder why he never got those teeth fixed.

That man.

The state had asked my mother to adopt my sister's children, and being the true addicts they were, my sister and that man had a problem with this. They didn't want to raise their children, but they didn't want anyone else to raise them either—mainly because, I'm thinking, they wouldn't have custody of them and could no longer use them as "bargains" when income tax time came around.

I wondered why I cared to think about all this, but then it hit me: It was my life, it was part of the package deal I inherited. That's the life I lived, and oh, Marion was still dead!

When I got to Leona's house, she fixed me a tuna sandwich, and I sat in my chair, wondering which story she would tell me now. Maybe she would retell a story. I didn't care, I just wanted out of the hood, even if it was just for an hour. I told her about Marion, and she didn't say a word but rather started playing "Amazing Grace" on the piano. After she played, she said,

"People will die, right? Just appreciate the memories he gave you."

I smiled, not knowing how to respond.

"Was he your first love?" she asked. And I knew what she was really asking: Did we sleep together?

"You told me that if love is questioned, it's not love. But he was a friend I loved.

"Why are you so sad?" she asked.

"My friend died," I said.

"That's not it, but okay."

I didn't argue with Leona today, as I sometimes can. I didn't know where this anxious energy was coming from, clouding my mind and twisting my emotions. I didn't know until she said it.

"Have you heard back from that college yet?"

Then it hit me. Many of the kids got their acceptance letter but not me. Well, I did get accepted to a few colleges, but not from the one I wanted to get accepted to.

Then Leona said, in a very assuring way. "You will get in."

"How do you know?" I questioned.

"I do. Let me let you in on something. By now, I thought you would have picked it up, but you, my dear, have a superpower—a way of helping others overcome things. You can help people begin to heal simply by being bold enough to point out their weakness, which is why you must never succumb to depression. So, start using it."

"That's my superpower?" I said sarcastically.

"It really is," she replied reassuringly. "You want pie? My son brought it over. It's one of my favorite apple pies."

Leona had mentioned her sons only a few times. I wished she would tell me more about them, but she didn't.

I did want pie. So I let her cut me a slice, and we ate in silence. Words would have taken away from the moment, creating superficiality. The quiet created room for us to breathe and think. We had what we needed — the soft clicking sound of forks digging deep into the pie and the warm apple-cinnamon filling that nearly melted the moment it touched our palates.

"Hey," she said, "I need to take your picture and show it to my sons." She took pictures of us sitting side by side, eating pie.

I enjoyed these moments with her just as I had enjoyed her elaborate stories.

Three days later, I received an acceptance letter from Northwestern University. I was going to be a Wildcat. After telling my parents, the next person I called was Leona. She congratulated me, but I think she already knew. If the light had once been small, now it had widened.

I was going to college. And I had an agent.

I decided to write about my friend, Marion, and my agent placed the story. When it was published, I brought a copy to his mother. She smiled — a smile that reached my heart.

That will always be my lasting memory of my friend. Rest up, Marion, rest up.

PHRASE 15

KALEIDOSCOPE

Margarita

My first year of college was going well. Still, I hadn't written a publishable piece in weeks. All that came to me were glassy images — colored fragments of a life I had slowly blended into. I kept telling myself that I was in college. Very few people were being published yet, but I wanted to be the exception.

The wind cut through my jacket, and I turned backward to walk. Yes, I was back in Chicago — back in the city close to the lake, where the wind hits your face so hard it makes your mascara run.

College, if attended conscientiously, gives you no choice but to move toward success. I had a window seat to how the other half lived, and I wasn't about to give that seat up. In fact, I hoped to join the cast before the final curtain. I rehearsed my lines daily and learned the proper etiquette. I had lived on both sides of the fence, and this side was by far much better. I hadn't slipped into this world easily, and I certainly didn't have the right calling card to present to the doorman. I had to work for it.

It was the early 2000s, and the world had gone technical. I just needed the right story — and more connections. I had a knack for writing tantalizing, gossip-like stories, and one day I knew I would find the one that would break me out of being just a hometown celebrity and turn me into something much bigger.

However, my mind could not stay fixed only on my hopes, dreams, and small successes. I'd come back to Chicago for two reasons: One was that I needed to face Leona and try to apologize for my sister Andrea's desperate will to survive. She and her now husband were two miserable, commiserating souls who thrived on self-pity. I was so angry at both of them that I could have slapped them silly, but for the sake of my friend Leona, I held on to the hope that one day they would correct their ways. What they had done was not only insulting—it was an embarrassment to my family.

We were a respected family in the neighborhood, almost like a religious fixture in the hood, with a reputation to maintain. My sister stealing checks from Leona's purse and cashing them through my mother's account made us look like lowlife crooks. I had to remind myself to stay calm, to remain on the path my parents would want me to follow.

Although I didn't see Leona every day, we still talked often, sometimes for hours. She wanted to hear everything about college, and in many ways, she helped me navigate the nuances of a bicultural world. It was different, though not necessarily better.

Among Black people, we often said a lot and meant very little. Among these people, you said very little and sometimes meant nothing at all. Everything seemed to be about hiding who you really were, and at times that kind of living was exhausting.

I felt a lot more responsible because it was I who reintroduced this couple to Leona. She had met Andrea when we were children, and she had hoped Andrea would have changed by now. I felt responsible because when Leona needed someone to fix something at her home in South Holland, I was the one who thought of that man. Because of that, her purse was left out for no more than ten minutes, Leona told me, and in that short time she was clipped for four checks.

They cashed a few of them and used the money to buy things they could sell quickly. Leona didn't want to press charges, but the state picked up the case anyway. Now both of them have to serve a year in jail. That man is going to jail. At least something good came out of a bad situation.

I planned to give her the money back. I was making enough now to begin paying her in installments, and I would insist she accept it—for the sake of my family's name.

Secondly, I was back in town for the untimely funeral of my father. I can't think of him without laughing or crying. He was a good man of faith, and family. He worked hard to support his family.

As I walked to Leona's house, tears welled up in my eyes, but I smiled because I knew that laughter pushes back tears. I still had my mother. That little lady had all her senses and she was still the rock of our family. My dad's favorite color was purple, so she demanded we all get together and go shopping for purple. Seeing my family and Leona were the only things good about Chicago. Tomorrow, I would go shopping with my family and find purple, but for now, after I asked for forgiveness on behalf of my family, all I wanted, more than anything, was to sit in my chair, drink a cup of peach tea, and immerse myself in her tall tales. I didn't want to hear myself talk or think. If I was really lucky, I just might escape into her world.

I heard music when I got to the door, and before I could knock, she had opened it, exposing her dress to kill. She was dressed in red, with a gold scarf, long gold hoop earrings, and her hair pinned up, as if she had just come back or was going to a dinner party.

"Come in, girl. Look at you."

She started to pin up my hair, and she went to her jewelry box and brought me out a pair of gold dangling earrings.

"Child, you gained a little weight." Are you going to eat, walk, or simply trick? What is Bruce feeding up?

"Bruce," I said. I was surprised. "How did you know about Bruce?" I had been dating Bruce for six months. My family didn't really know about him, though I had been dating him for about six months. Bruce and I had actually met during my first year of college. We didn't date then. At the time, he was dating someone I called Ms. Hollywood, and I was just the girl on the sidelines, watching how messed up their relationship really was.

I liked that butter-brown-skinned kid from the moment he opened his mouth, and his intelligence rolled out so effortlessly, it almost seemed unimpressive.

I didn't realize how much Leona's stories had shaped the way I saw my own life until I nearly made a mistake. I never went after Bruce. I just secretly crushed on him. He was the one who eventually broke up with the girl I called Ms. Hollywood.

Miss Hollywood wasn't a typical girl, and I could even see why he was attracted to her. She was biracial and understood cultural differences in a way that made people feel comfortable around her. She never treated me like I was less than. She was friendly, and unlike me — who sometimes struggled to make friends outside my culture — she naturally gravitated toward people who were different from her. If you were around her long enough, she would find something you had in common, and suddenly there you were, having a conversation.

Bruce dated her and did all the things she liked. I watched from the sidelines, thinking that he and I would probably be happier watching a historical film together instead of going to the kinds of events she loved. But that was their world, not mine, and when things ended, I didn't force a relationship with me on him; I was just his friend—the friend he one day kissed and loved.

Leona went in the back and brought out a red loose-fitting dress. She looked at me sternly and said, "Well, put it on."

I was almost afraid to say no, but I was a junior in college, and at some point, our relationship had to move to the adult realm. So I said, almost breathless, "I have a funeral to go to in a few days. I didn't really come here to play dress-up.

"Oh, I'm sorry," Leona said, "Have I ever played dress-up with you before? I mean, we did have fashion week, and I showed you how to dress, but I am just not into playing dress-up."

"Why are you giving me clothes to put on?" I asked.

"Oh, I promise I will explain it all, but I just figured you might like this, so when your mother told me you were on your way over, I thought this event might be just what you need to sort of get your mind off things. Oh, by the way, my sympathy because of your loss. I am sure you have lots of fond memories.

"Of course, but really, I wanted to apologize to you because, you know, the checks."

"Don't say another word," she said firmly. "You never have to answer to me about something you had nothing to do with. I don't mean to be rude, but a limo is picking us up in ten minutes. Can you put on the dress?" She smiled in a way

I have never seen her smile before. It was a half-smirk, half-smile.

"Leona," I mustered up the courage to say. "I am just not sure I need this in my life now." I looked down, hoping to convince her I was sad, because I was a little sad, and I had my mind set on a whole different encounter.

"Get dressed. You need this, trust me."

I don't need this, I thought to myself, but I obeyed. I wasn't sure what this would be, but I was going.

In the limo, I noticed how dolled up Leona had gotten. She had her nails painted red, which matched her dress perfectly. She was very stylish. We got out of the limo and were ushered to the front seat of the church, and it was at this point that I realized we were at a wedding. A wedding. I sat next to Leona, watching her, but she didn't want to catch the attention of my stare. When the vows were shared, I realized that the man's name was David and the lady's name was Samatha; he called her Sam for short. Could this be her son David? Did this woman just invite me to her son's wedding?

After the vows, it became really clear that she had, in fact, invited me to her son's wedding. After the wedding, I was to meet David and his new wife, Sam. I also met Darnell. He was very humble and very articulate. He kept saying, "So you are real to me," and that made me a little uncomfortable. If they assumed their mother had made me up, they were wrong. I know they had at least heard my voice. They'd called a few times and spoken to Leona, and I was there. On meeting me, they were both treating me like a ghost. Talk about tables turning! I sort of understood how the twins must have felt growing up. But it could have been nice—the stares and sometimes blank looks from total strangers.

Darnell was David's best man, and honestly, the twins didn't do too badly. Their boys, who I imagined were older than me, were lookers—handsome in different ways. David stood about six feet two with broad shoulders, like he might have played football in a former life. He had a light complexion and very dark eyes. His hair wasn't black, though—it was more of an auburn brown. Thick eyebrows framed his eyes, and when he smiled, two deep dimples appeared.

Darnell, on the other hand, was tall too, though not quite as tall as David. He was slimmer, almost like a model you'd see behind a computer screen in some advertisement. His brown eyes were larger, his eyebrows just as thick, and his teeth a little whiter. His hair was straight Indian-black hair. He had only one dimple in his chin, and his complexion was just a shade darker than David's.

Leona was in full social bloom that night—gracious, classy, and perfectly put together. She nursed a single glass of wine throughout the evening, and she seemed to float through the room, introducing me to politicians and businessmen alike.

At one point I met a man who worked for NBC, and he asked if he could look at my portfolio. Like a kid unwrapping a present, I could hardly wait to see who I would meet next. Either this Sam was somebody important, or Leona was far more connected than I had ever imagined.

I even took a little walk down fairy-tale lane as I met some of the very people she had told me stories about, and they were exactly as she'd described them.

One of the people I met was a police officer who was now an assistant mayor of Chicago. He asked if Leona had ever told me about their encounter. She had indeed, which made me a little wary about shaking his hand. Then he burst out laughing and said, "Leona actually thought we were members of the KKK." He pulled her into a hug as he laughed. "We were just pulling their chain. It was funny. You should have seen them when I pointed to a tree—they went into full defense mode."

Leona shook her fist at the gentleman, which made me wonder just how many of her stories might have been slightly embellished. Still, I was thrilled when he told me to call his office on Monday because he planned to give me a press pass.

The night was nothing short of incredible, and I couldn't help but feel grateful that Leona was in my life.

Around 7 o'clock, the family planned to visit my sister in jail since she couldn't come home for my father's funeral. At that moment, I decided I would go with them. At first, I hadn't planned to, but something inside me had shifted. For the first time in a while, I felt infused with hope.

We laughed and ate. The food was delicious, and the event ended. While David and Leona had their mother-son dance, Darnell came and sat next to me. Then he finally said, "Sorry if I made you feel a little weird."

"Oh, no, I guess I could look like Phyllis, a little."

"A lot," but no one deserves to be stared at up and down. You are good for her, you know. She calls you her treasure box."

"That so?" I said.

"Hey, let's dance." He changed the subject as the crowd emerged onto the dance floor. As odd as it appeared, I felt like I'd known him in my life, like we were somehow connected.

We took pictures, and Leona insisted that I be in the family pictures, and so I stood in a few. I felt guilty after a while. I was having so much fun two days before my father's funeral. The boys knew about the death of my beloved father, and they gave me their condolences. I felt relieved to be happy a little while longer. This day was somewhat therapeutic for me, empowering me to face the days ahead.

After three hours of blissful fun, I found myself back in the car with Leona, and she was taking off her jewelry.

"You can have that dress. It's too big for me."

"Liar," I said.

"Ok, I brought it for you, and watch your mouth, young lady."

As she took off her earrings, words from her past started to flood my head. I put my head down to stop myself from having a panic attack, and hoped she didn't notice my heart speeding up. Should I say what I'd just realized, or should I not? As we approached my house, I decided I wouldn't.

"Thanks for taking me to meet all those people. It felt good not to think, you know."

"I do; I do. You are very welcome."

"Will you come to my father's funeral?" I asked.

"No, but I will stop by the visitation and sign the book. Tell your lovely mom she does not have to send me a card. I simply wanted to help out.

I was tired but so excited, just happy to have had that experience. "I will tell her," I said, "and thanks again."

"You like him, don't you?"

"Who? David and Darnell? They were both so nice."

"Of course they are, but I'm not talking about them. I'm talking about the little lawyer-to-be at your school."

"Hey, how do you know that?" I asked curiously.

"You are not the only one who likes gossip. By the way, your sister and her boyfriend will be at the wake tomorrow." Get there a little early so you can see them."

"It cost too much to get them out for it. My mother couldn't pay."

"They will be there for around twenty minutes, so tell your family they don't have to go visit. She will be there."

I didn't ask. I knew she had paid. To get an inmate to a funeral, you have to pay for security and transportation, and we just couldn't afford it. I was so happy to know they would be there. All I could say was "Thank you, Leona, from the bottom of my heart."

"One less road your sister will have to pave." She winked at me and motioned for the car to drive off. I got to my porch and watched the limo driver take her back to her world in downtown Chicago. I would have to stay in my world alone for the next three days. I would try to tell my mind to stay away from my love life or the lack thereof, but I guess she was right. I did like the lawyer-to-be, but I had also liked a few other guys on campus, and it didn't turn out so well.

I would also try hard not to think about the weird thing I noticed that day. It would cause my mind to overthink, and for some reason, I didn't want to think. In a few short days I would see my father in a casket, and I would see what it felt like to lose the only man who had ever unconditionally loved me. But that was not this night, and the life of what to do after the funeral was entering and exiting the door of my mind, until I finally locked it out. I just wanted things to happen, days to be experienced, and days to end.

PHRASE 16

MEMORIES

Margarita

There are certain things in life you never forget. Sometimes you wish you could, but you don't.

By then, I was engaged to Bruce. I was a fully grown woman carrying her own scars, some healed and some still tender, with questions both answered and unanswered. I had the number-one podcast in the United States, a column called *The Mysterious*, and a popular book about unsolved mysteries. My column and podcast focused on dramatizations of the mysterious, and I loved it.

Leona — with all that she was, all that she loved, and all the life she had lived — came back to me picture-perfect. So when David called me to see his mother, even if I wasn't going to see my mother, I was going to find a way soon to see her. He didn't say why. He just wanted me to see her. What's also a sidebar reward is that I'd kept in touch with David and Darnell. They were like close older brothers I'd never had. I have brothers I love, but we were never close. I made them promise to attend my wedding, and both of them agreed. So, when they told me their mother had asked for me, I packed my bag and was on my way.

Another bonus was that I would be seeing my own mother for an extra weekend. My mother had aged, but she was still active. I had bought a three-flat building in Oak Park, where she lived with Cindy, who was married and stable. She took

Mama to church and made sure she ate and was taken care of. My mother was independent, and she could cook if she wanted to, but on those days, when her legs couldn't move and her hands were too tight to open and close, she had Cindy. She was not a quiet storm as she had been in the past. It had been ten years since my father had died, but my mother kept him alive the best she could with pictures and his sayings floating around, knowing that if he were still alive, he would have intervened. Nia and her husband lived on the first floor, and they paid rent to Cindy at my request, and that rent was used to pay taxes on the house. Janet and Andrea paid a little something every month, and that money also went to Cindy to make sure the property was kept up, which was good because that money didn't necessarily come in monthly.

Andrea worked at a secondhand shop in Oak Park. She had visited jail a few times before she called it a day. Now she was off drugs and working a stable job. I guess what finally did it for her was when that man—who had helped her land three drug possession convictions—ended up going to jail himself for a second time. While he was there, he met one of his cellmate's sisters and married her right in jail.

Janet was that sister anyone could live with as long as you kept your space clean. She was already raising the boys, who were both in high school, along with her own daughter. So when Andrea asked if she could move in, Janet was fine with it. I suppose they were both trying to get over loves that had gone bad.

The house in the big OP (Oak Park) became our safe haven. All the Thanksgiving meals were at this house, and when common hurt touched us all, this house was our sanctuary.

My family lived vicariously through me when it came to Leona and my relationship. I told my family that I would be visiting Leona, and of course, Janet and Andrea wanted to know about her sons, which in my opinion were out of their league, but they had every right to dream. I honestly think they were more excited about meeting David and Darnell in person than actually attending my wedding. I dropped my stuff off at Cindy's house, and I was off to see Leona.

In the car, my mind skipped back and forth on the times we had shared, the lessons I had learned, and the words that made no sense at the time but now walked in my mind like a silhouette of truths leading me mostly to places of comfort. I had talked to her over the phone, though not as often as I would have liked, and in her elderly state, she had become even more unpredictable. She was losing things more often. There were times I would call her cell phone and a stranger would answer. I knew that meant she had misplaced her phone again.

When I made it to her house, Leona buzzed me in at the outside entrance. When I made it to her door, it was open for me to let myself in. I was hoping to see David and Darnell, but they weren't there. I walked into a house that looked as if it was getting packed or painted. Leona, in a very common gray knit dress, pointed for me to sit, letting me know that she was busy but that my company would tolerate it. I came slowly in and put my stuff in my chair. She was busy, moving about, collecting books in a particular order only she understood. I thought my sitting would last longer, but she asked me to come quickly with her to the back room as I watched her sort clothes into two bins—one for clothes she would keep and one for clothes she would give away. She had a much different energy that day. Everything felt rushed. She was telling me about boys, particularly her boys, thinking she required them to think for her. Then she was reminding me that she had her own mind and that she would do what she wanted. She had a loft in a West suburban town that she had to live in. Then she told me off topic, "Sometimes life calls you back to sort of pave the road so that a trip back to that place and time is not so bumpy, you know. It sort of slides through your memory portal.

She looked at me for an intense three minutes, as if she was figuring out something about me. I felt she was judging my fashion sense, but I was dressed quite simply with a white T-shirt and blue jeans. I was going to hang out with my mother on Sunday and attend church, so I had freshly permed my hair and pinned it up.

"You have a nice grade of hair."

She said it to me deliberately, slowly, as if she had never spoken those words to me before. In fact, she had. Leona's hair was long and a sort of dirty blond color. It had a light curl pattern, mostly at the ends. I smiled, trying to hide the fact that I knew she had said those words to me before.

After looking at me for a few seconds, she said, rather breathlessly, "Let's have tea," as if this was an event we had never had before.

I nodded yes, and we walked arm in arm to the kitchen so that she could put on the water. I could see that her kitchen had been opened up a little more, which provided a little nook area. She was modernizing her place, but she didn't mention it to me, so I didn't comment on how different the apartment was. I actually liked the way it was. She put the teapot on and took out a small container with assorted tea bags.

"You still like berry?" she asked.

"I never liked berry tea," I said.

"Oh, no, don't tell me, you like chamomile. You like to feel relaxed after you have your tea, right?"

She was wrong. I actually just liked plain old lemon or peppermint tea, but I said yes because, truthfully, all brands of tea relaxed me. Something I saw in her eyes did not let me correct her. She was fighting to still know, and I wouldn't take that away from her, so my favorite tea would be chamomile for her. I looked around the now-opened room and saw freshly made tea on the table. This was not like Leona at all. If she took it out, she would immediately put it back. She was a clean woman, and her house was orderly and well put together. It was apparent she had not remembered about the tea and had made more tea.

We walked to the living room and I sat on the couch next to her. She looked at me with reservation.

"You don't want to sit in your chair?" she asked very quietly.

"No," I said, pointing out that I had placed my purse and light jacket in the chair.

"It's okay. You can sit next to me. It's nice to just remember." She paused. "Can I ask you something?"

"Of course," I said.

"I just wondered, have you ever experienced, you know, black spells? Where you simply black out and then wake up again? You're still living, still doing things during these little black spells. You sort of can't stop yourself from living. In fact, you have no control over the set of events. Life just happens, and you just watch it — much like watching a good movie."

"I'm not sure," I responded, but in essence, I did have moments in my life when everything sort of faded to black, but I wasn't sure she was talking about those moments.

"Well, you are still young. It's just sometimes I feel like I am living life in reverse, so I guess it really wouldn't be a blackout. It's more like —. I don't know. I must sound silly to you.

Well, you don't sound silly, Leona. I just may not be able to fully connect.

"Well, that's okay. I wanna tell you about Clare.

"I think you told me about Clare," I said, somewhat confused.

"I didn't tell you the whole story. Life happens in phases. This part is important, so listen. You are going to need this part for your research. This part is told in five parts.

I looked, still unwilling to correct her, as I had learned her reasoning was much different from mine, and that was okay.

Then she continued. "Sometimes the ghost from my past invites you back so you know the full story.

I sat next to her and listened as she unpacked another one of her fascinating stories.

She smiled at her thoughts, then the smile quickly resolved. "I don't think I ever told you we did, in fact, go back to Mississippi. We had to go back, and we knew we would. You see, you live better when you pave those roads; it is a smoother drive."

She got up from me and walked to the piano, as if she had just noticed it was there. She played some bluesy jazz songs, and she actually sang. I had never known her to really sing, though I knew she could play. After she played, she held her warm tea as if it were infusing her with power and words. She spoke calmly, carefully leading me back to an obvious place of pain. I could see she was fighting not to relive the pain, but she wanted me to know.

———

Leona

They stay with you like a Kodak picture, frozen in place, never to be forgotten or changed. The image becomes reality.

Lillian and I were sitting at my kitchen table, flouring down a pan—no, we were cooking chicken, coating the wings in flour, a meal for our husbands—when the mail came. It was a letter from Belzoni, Mississippi.

I remember walking into the kitchen, my hands covered in flour, holding the letter, speechless.

Lillian took the letter out of my hand and read what I'd read. In what looked to be the writing of a child, it read, "Clare is sick, expected to die soon, come home."

Lillian turned on the water so as to drown out the thoughts, feelings, and questions that revisited our minds every five seconds or so. Silence dominated the room for about ten minutes. Then I announced to Lillian, "I just got a new car. My husband bought it for me, and they say it gets good mileage."

She agreed that that meant we were going. After twenty-one years, we were headed back to our birthplace to see Miss Clare one last time.

We didn't want to talk about it, but we both knew we would go back. Besides, it was time. We hadn't seen that place in years. We were older now and married. I was living the second journey of our lives, which included raising children.

I had told my husband all about my past and how we grew up, for we shared everything. I was sure he would support our decision to go back, and he did. We were at a good place, as happiness was presenting itself in a fresh new way. We had children, and they had laughter. Even when you can't laugh at yourself, just listening to the laughter of children sings to you. It makes you want to hum along. It lingers, like the smell of flowers or unkind words — lingering, breathing the story of what was once unheard.

The ride to the South moved like death on rocky roads: slow, long, and boring. And like death, when you know it is coming, at some point you wish it would hurry up and be over with already.

Lillian and I talked mostly about the new Cadillac convertible my husband had bought me. Sam liked doing nice things for me, and he liked seeing me happy. He wanted me to give up one thing, and my mind was approaching that thought with the hope that one day I would.

We each wondered, though we never mentioned it, about our friend Tara, who had left the South for fame and fortune when she was in the twelfth grade. We wondered if we would see Lillian's first husband, Henry, and the high school kids who had made our lives a living hell. We wondered if the rumors would still tiptoe behind us, blocking others from seeing who we were.

We arrived at the place described as home at around 3:30 p.m. on Sunday afternoon. We stopped off at a new corner diner for a bite to eat, and we agreed to stay in the motel if our house wasn't in livable condition, which we hoped it was. We wondered how someone had found our address to send the letter. Then I remembered someone had been looking into buying that house and contacted us, for we were still paying the taxes on the property. We thought about selling the house, but we knew it would be hard to sell, for the rumors the town had created around the house would beat any Hollywood movie any day of the week. Therefore, we had decided to just hold on to the house and maybe give it to a really special person one day.

As we sat and ate, we noticed that people were staring at us, almost in amusement, and eyeing our car like a lion would eye its prey. We walked gracefully out after paying for our meal and leaving an eye-opening tip from "two hometown girls making it big in the city." We would have toned down our appearance if we'd known how, but we figured that we'd never cared what they thought about us before, so why start now?

We arrived at our house in the woods around 4:30 p.m. that day. Belzoni had grown a lot, but it still didn't have a livable motel or hotel for its visitors. We expected to find the house dark, dim, and full of cobwebs, but that wasn't the case at all. In fact, it was livable. Surprise does not describe our response. It was as if someone had prepared the place for us. The furniture was just as we left it: a cup left unwashed in the sink, our room exactly as we'd left it.

We sat down on the bed, which had absolutely no dust from not being made in twenty-odd years. How could that be? We sat in silence, both taken by what we were seeing. Lillian finally stood up and announced that the next morning, we would have the furnace updated so that it would no longer be necessary to cut wood, and we'd repair the front of the house. A new paint job was all that was really needed, although we both agreed to fence in the place for protection. We didn't know exactly who we were fixing this house up for, but we both had a feeling that it should be fixed up.

Although we had not been back for quite a while, it felt like we had never left the place. It was an unexplainable familiarity that bonded us with our past. The memories were painful, but they also helped us appreciate how far we had come. It was good to look back, but thank goodness we could move forward.

SEEING HER

PART 1

Leona

In the coming days, we were to see Miss Clare. No longer able to talk or walk or pierce our souls with her haunting looks, she lay helplessly in bed.

The house looked much smaller than we remembered, a house that had outlived its glory. There were bigger and better houses nearby, yet it seemed to be trying desperately to hold on to its former pride. The walls were now a dull white, with thin cracks in the paint, and the lights no longer hung with self-importance. They were simply fixtures now— remnants of what once represented a comfortable middle-class status. The piano she'd loved so much was covered with a white sheet. We dared to lift it and discovered that the once sparkling white keys were now yellow.

We walked into her room, a place she'd never wanted us to visit but where we were now welcomed. And we saw her. The stroke had slightly twisted her face, but yes, it was her. Her hands were no longer long and graceful. We could only imagine how her fingers had once played across the keyboard because now they lay across her stomach, shriveled and unmanicured.

Her lips were drawn tightly together, with no teeth to give them the nice curve they used to have, and her face was covered with untraceable, thin, vine-like lines that were exposing time. Her hair was wiry gray and matted to her head, like mothballs. Lillian wiped the sweat from her face as we sat on her bed and watched in silence as she confronted death.

The nurse who was looking after Clare for the last ten years said that Clare spoke very little and that she had mentioned us maybe once or twice. As we thought, she'd gotten our information from a broker who was looking into selling the house and had searched the tax records. Clare had requested that the house be willed to us. The fact that she left the house to us, we couldn't understand, but there we were and there she lay.

The nurse was a chatty woman of around thirty. She told us what the townspeople had been saying. To them, we were almost like ghosts — not real at all — and they told the story of our parents quite differently from what we believed we knew.

You see, the nurse had heard that we, Lillian and Leona, were the children of Clare's husband — that we were his outside family. Apparently, rumor had it that Clare and my father had plotted our mother's death. It was supposed to look like a suicide, but in his rage and anger, my father made far too many mistakes.

He shot both victims multiple times, and he knew the police would never believe that a dead person had somehow come back to shoot himself again. So my father fled and vowed never to return. He never did.

According to the nurse, Clare asked about Daddy often. Whenever she heard a knock at the door, she would say, "John, is that you? I knew you would come back." She did this quite often until recently. Then one day, the nurse said Clare suddenly looked up and gasped, as if she had seen a ghost. From that moment on, all she could do was stare at the walls

Lillian and I laughed, totally unimpressed with this small-town gossip. Clare was married to our father. Funny, we chuckled. Our father was the town's representative. I know this because we saw one picture of him behind a red, white, and blue flag. Now the town had married him off to Clare. I always thought my mother was too adventurous to be a married woman; she was more in love with thoughts and words than anything else, so a part of me did wonder if this could be true, but the town had always made up ghost stories about us, so why should this be any different? Hearing the new version of the story made us hate this place all the more. We had understood Clare and Daddy's relationship in a totally different way. We knew we had to find the truth, or a way to rebuke the town's lying lips, if for no other reason than to ease our minds.

We sat on Clare's bed and reminded her of the few good times we had shared. Later that day, we went back into the secret room and began searching through everything, hoping to find something—anything—about our father. She was still calling out for him, which meant he must have kept in touch with her somehow.

We were fortunate enough to find an envelope postmarked fifteen years earlier. It was addressed to *1541 W. Bell, Springfield, Illinois*, but it had never been mailed. Could our father be in Springfield? We continued looking, and then we found it—inside a sealed envelope, a marriage certificate. Lillian and I both began to cry, not just for our mother, but for what our mother had been.

Lillian hugged me and reminded me that nobody is perfect. The truth still stood: Even if they had been married, it didn't give him the right to kill her.

We didn't want to see it, but we were beginning to understand another side of the story. I remembered the nights my mother sat on the porch waiting for Daddy, who never came home. We had always thought he was working late. I could still see the cigarette smoke drifting from my mother's hand as she listened to jazz music. We always felt that my mother had lived with us, but somehow her life existed somewhere else.

I made up my mind that we would go to that address. We had to pass that way on our way back, but Lillian really didn't want to go, so I immediately objected. I said to her, "Look, Lillian, we don't know what happened that night. Everyone has a right to know the truth, Lillian, even us. We deserve to know."

Lillian started to protest, but was greeted with my strong counterprotest.

"They took our mother and turned us into a couple of freaks—ghosts! We are not even real to the majority of this community. I don't give a damn about these folk around here, but our father and Clare changed our destiny, and we deserve to know the truth."

When one of us was bent on doing something, we could go through hell or high water and still not change our minds. It was settled, we were going to see John. We walked back into Clare's room and resumed our quiet positions by her bedside. The nurse wanted desperately to ask us many questions, but she didn't, and we didn't volunteer.

For one solid week, we watched Clare and fed her in silence. The silence she gave us submerged our souls and took away the love for sound. She had suffocated us with silence for years, and now, when she needed sound to ease her into the afterlife, all we could give her was silence. Then, one afternoon, she opened her eyes wide and closed them in fear. We could feel her heart beating faster, as if she was being chased. It finally slowed down, and she squeezed my hand tight and gave up the ghost. We kissed her on the forehead to say goodbye and walked out of her room.

Maybe for the first time we realized she might have been another victim. Maybe she wasn't aware of the killings. Maybe we were just as much of a surprise to her as she was to us. When Mama was around, nothing good came out of her mouth about Clare. Our mother held all the characteristics of a loose, privileged woman.

We made the arrangement for Clare's funeral, and the townspeople said we put her away nicely. We gave her house to her beloved church. That is what she would have wanted, I am sure. We didn't want the house, not even for money. Yes, Clare would have wanted this. What we didn't expect after giving the church the house were all the kind words said about us. Now, we were well-raised young women. and when word of the house being gifted to the church floated and landed on perched ears, we were greeted with smiles from folks who had previously frowned at us—folks who had handed down ghost stories about us, gift-wrapped for the next generation to open and embellish and pass down to their children. Now these community novelists were pronouncing our names with Southern proper interpretation. These same people now gleamed with pride and respect because we had made it, and we were a part of them. We, for the first time, were treated as people with lives they cared to know about. We were forgiven, my sister and I. We had earned that gift along the way and kept it. This community of forgiving mortals would get our thanks for the many compliments, but little else.

After Clare was buried, we decided to do a little work on our house, the one that sat in the woods. This place was not our home, but it did house our memories of the past.

The motel was right off the road in Belzoni, and we had just freshly painted the house, so we decided we would spend our last day there. Lillian and I decided we would throw ourselves a little party. We went to town and bought popcorn, soda water, sandwiches, and candles. It was going to be like old times.

Just as we were walking out the door, we saw Tara. We didn't recognize her at first. She was wearing a long blood wig, loud red lipstick, and red blush that looked as if she had just spread it on her face. She looked as if she was going to a costume party. Lillian started to ask her just that, but when I looked her in the eye, I knew this was Tara's poor attempt to hide her physical and mental scars. She was still thin, but it was an unhealthy-looking thin. An older man holding a bottle, bending to the side, waited for her. It looked as if the both of them could have used a bath. He held a cigarette in his hand, which was smoking itself, because he was standing sideways in one spot. Tara took the cigarette out of his hands and he swiped at her and missed. She smoked the burning cigarette anyway, walking slowly, waiting for him to pick up his pace. We noticed that every few steps, he had to stop and stand still.

We both shouted "Tara!" and she slowly turned around. She instantly recognized us, and we ran to her and gave her a hug. We laughed, the joy of seeing the only person in this small town who had treated us like humans made us emotionally charged, and tears just flowed.

"Twin!" she exclaimed. "Man, it's been so long. Shit, how y'all doing?"

Tara swearing? We quickly got over the shock of her appearance and speech and hoped there was no surprise in our voices. "We are just fine," I said, "and yourself?" I frowned a little after releasing those words, because you had to be divorced from any form of truth not to know she wasn't okay.

"I'm still living. It ain't taken me out of here yet," she said.

"Look, Tara, why don't you come over and celebrate with us? We're leaving soon and just decided to throw a little party, like we used to do."

"We're a little too old for pajama parties, don't you think?"

"Never too old to have fun. Girls' night out sort of thing."

"Someone was saying y'all fixed up the ghost house," Tara said.

We both hesitated to answer her after she referred to our house as a ghost house.

"No, we fixed up our house."

Tara, of all people, knew that we were real. We had confided in her. She had confided in us. We had laughed and cried together. Then we realized that maybe she was drunk and this was just a slipup, so we forgave her on the spot.

"You're invited. Come on, who is it going to hurt?"

"Tara, let's go," the drunken old man who was with her interrupted as he walked ahead of her.

She looked at us, not acknowledging his presence or words. "Where you staying?"

"Roadside hotel," I said.

"Okay, I'll see y'all tonight, okay? Y'all know y'all look good. I mean, shit, I should have went with you girls. Is that y'all's car out front?"

"Yes," I said, embarrassed. For a moment, I wished we didn't have it so good.

"Shit, you must be turning flips in bed to have something like that. Well, I'll see you tonight." She walked away.

———

Tara came over at 11:30 that night, way after the party was over. She wanted coffee, so we let her in. We shared with her our plans to visit summers. Words were hard to come by, for we kept looking at her and noticing how she had changed for the worse.

Then she said in a very low, hoarse voice, "I'm sick, twin." We knew just what she meant by "sick" — it meant she was dying.

"I got AIDS," she continued. "It's okay if you don't want to hug me. Figured I'd just let you know right off. Started not to come, but all my life, when I thought about who was there for me in the world, it was you two. Always been so good to me. At times I really didn't think you guys were real. I think the only time I was treated like a person was around the twins."

She smiled, and although they had given her a death sentence, through her smile, we saw life. Before she told us her story, we embraced her warmly and without prejudices, for we all would one day have to take that temporal nap in death. We listened as she told her story, and I will tell it to you as if she were telling it herself, for you never know a person's story until they decide to reveal it. Although she had been through much, Lillian was right: She was still Tara, our friend.

TARA

PART 2

Leona

Tara, where do you start? She was and is a trailblazer. She always wanted to be somebody, a star, a person with admirers all around. Maybe she was a little like her dad. Maybe in my heart she understood him more than I would have liked to, for I, too, longed to be a hero remembered.

———

Tara

So I left with Mike, my mother's friend, who actually was my mother's lover and later became my lover. Once you start falling in life, if you have nothing to hold on to, you will quickly hit the bottom. I can't ever say I'm proud of my life. The only thing I can say is that I've lived it.

New York was the place of the arbitrary hustlers, everyone trying to make money. It's like it must have been written somewhere: Move to New York, make money or die. Mike was one of those people who wanted to make money and die, so being with him, I was doomed from the start. His first objective was to be rich enough to die, and I was a moneymaker.

Mike got a gig at a place called the Blue Light the first week I arrived, and I was singing seven nights a week, sometimes three times a day. Things were actually going great. I had a little cup on the side, and every night it was filled to the brim with money. This money Mike let me keep, but I heard through the grapevine that the manager was giving him more money a week. By that time I had caught the New York bug, in that I wanted money and lots of it. I had seen the lights and I wanted my name in them. I was cursed with self-absorption. In other words, I had successfully assimilated. When I asked Mike nicely for more money, he frowned and explained that the rent in New York was expensive, and the conversation about more money was dropped.

If I was to earn more money, I didn't just need a voice—I also needed an image. I had the body, but the face was lacking, so Mike paid for me to have a few alterations done to my face. I hated that he did this, and after the operation, he reminded me countless times that he paid for me to look good. He was controlling my mind, and when I attempted to think, he would punish me by leaving me in the nightclub without cab money to get home. I didn't learn his address until three months after I moved to New York.

I figured I would have a better chance of leveling the ground if I got into Mike's exaggerated self-image, like most of the women who hung around him. He was like a boy toy, pleasant to the eye, but I never really liked the guy. He always had this sort of dark cloud above him, and he could never stay happy long. I remember when I was asked to open for a hot new group. He was so happy, he kissed me because one of his acts had finally gotten a headlining opening, but ten minutes later, he was sad and angry that they weren't paying me as much as I should have been. It always had to be something with Mike. He never allowed happiness to get hold of him and settle in him.

I admired the way Mike got jobs and talked me up to managers. He made me feel like there was nothing I couldn't do. I was the next Billie Holiday, or newly on the scene, Mrs.

Queen of Soul herself. I was blessed in that I could sing like the best of them, and my voice didn't tire easily.

One day, Mike brought me this nice gold-sequined dress. He asked me to try it on, and I did. Then he asked me to take it off, and I was about to walk to my room, but he grabbed me by the hands and said, "Right here." So I undressed right before his eyes, and then he started touching me, and suddenly all the love songs I had sung came to life inside me. I hungered for his touch, felt an itching in my heart, wasn't no mountain high enough, and it was a wonderful world, as I gave him the only remaining thing he didn't have of me, and that was control of my body.

Strangely enough, each time we slept together, it seemed as if Mike hated me more. He knew I enjoyed his touch, but it was almost as if he didn't want to touch me and it was a struggle for him. I once jokingly told him that each time he touched me, it was as if he was making a bet with himself, like "Man, I bet you can't do it again," or fighting to convince himself, "You can do it, man, you can do it." When it was over, he was glad he was able to make love to me but hated that he had to. He smiled at me when I said things like that, and then he would drink until he couldn't feel anything, for deep down inside he knew I was right. As nice looking as he was and as many women as he slept with, I was beginning to think that either he didn't like himself or he didn't like women.

Mike was the kind of guy who would put one bullet in a gun, put it to his head, and pull the trigger right before your eyes. He was totally unashamed of his disregard for his life, and at times I thought he was begging for death. Nevertheless, after I got into a relationship with him, things changed. The band members treated me with more respect.

Mike started to give me play money. I was happy, I guess, doing my thing, and I felt important because I was admired. At nineteen, I was singing in most of the major nightclubs in New York. I shared a stage with the Four Tops. I was moving up in the world.

One day, a man came by and wanted to sign me with this major record company. I was scheduled to go into the studio, and when I did, that was when I saw it: Mike was kissing another woman, and he looked at her in a way no one had ever looked at me. Her face was pretty to him, you could tell, and maybe she could one day mean something to him. That was not at all how he looked at me. He just treated me like an object. There were men all around me who gave me warmer looks, and I wanted to go out with them, but when Mike knew I was into someone else, he would play the nice game and I would be content with him again. He had a way of making me feel like he cared for me and only had my best interests at heart. I believed the lie every time. I guess I needed to feel like someone really cared for me, even if it was a lie.

I watched as he kissed this little cutie and hit her on the butt. My heart dropped to my stomach and I had to sit down, but I couldn't take my eyes off them. They went out the back door, and my hopes of being loved by Mike left with them.

Revenge set in. My heart was harder than stone and getting harder by the day. Like a revolving door, my mind twirled around, picturing all the things I'd lost by dealing with this man. Because of him, I was estranged from my mother. For years, my mother couldn't look at me, and when she spoke to me, it was generally not good. She'd even slept with Mike after she had learned of our so-called relationship, and she didn't do it for the money. I was sending her money, lots of it, to take care of Rose, but she didn't care. All she wanted to do in life was hurt me. Well, later on in her sad, pitiful life, she met the Lord, and then she had a place to condemn me to — hell. As sad as it may sound, I didn't mind being condemned by my mother because it meant there was finally a place for me in my mother's heartless heart.

Okay. So, I was to sign this contract. I figured I would just be cool, let Mike be Mike until I signed this deal, and then I would fire his ass. I had told this to a few of the band members, thinking they were my friends and all, but they told him, and he set my ass up. He very innocently introduced me to Albert, who was a controlled junkie — not at all typical — and a smooth talker. I loved the feel of his hands. They were so soft and warm, and he dressed so flashy. He came quietly into my life and promised to take all my fears and doubts away. I hit my first hit and was hooked. We started getting high together, and I loved the way it made me feel. It felt like I was floating into a new body, floating closer and closer into perfection each time I did it, but no time was like the first time. In fact, I guess that is why I kept doing drugs: I was hoping for the feel of that first hit.

Now Mike had control over me once again. He supplied my day-to-day high. The day I was to meet the executive of the music label, he made sure I got high the night before, and he made it my responsibility to get the taxi and make the appointment. I was so high the next day that I missed the appointment. After that major disappointment, I started getting high for days in a row. I would wake up and not know what day it was.

The monster he had created, he now had to destroy, so he started abusing me. I had low self-esteem and no self-worth. I was like the gum under his shoe, padding for his shoes to walk on. I was nothing to this man. I would see him just laughing at me for no reason, just looking and laughing that pitiful laugh. I once told him words I didn't have sense enough to believe myself: I told him I was going to get myself together and stop getting high, and he just shook his head and walked out of the house. He hated me, but not half as much as I hated myself. Twins, when you hate yourself, there is no low too low.

The gigs were few and far between. I was losing weight, and Mike was watching me kill myself and enjoying the show. All I had was my voice, which, surprisingly, was still strong. He was holding all the cards, and I had nothing until his secret was revealed.

It was after a show, and I had just gotten high. I thought I was dreaming at first, or that Mike and Albert were wrestling or something. I was still living with Mike, but I had no room. He'd kicked me out of his room and made me sleep on the couch. He complained about how I was becoming a burden to him, how he'd never really liked me, and how making love to me made him throw up. If it was mean and he knew it would hurt me, he would say it. I heard all the mean things he said, but I didn't care. I was like, "So what, what's new, whatever."

That night, I was so high that my mouth was bone dry. The hit was good. I stumbled into the kitchen to get some water or something and saw Mike and Albert in bed together. I was like, "Hell naw!" But it was beginning to make sense: He'd kicked me out of his room, he'd asked questions about where Albert and I were, and as the last straw, he'd moved Albert into our apartment to share his room.

Albert had a girlfriend, but he never spent any time with her. He was always over at our house, getting money and clothes from Mike. The puzzle was complete, the enigma solved. I knew. Now, Mike was raised by his grandmother, and if he had respect for anyone, it was her, so I figured he was waiting for her to die to tell his secret. Knowing this about him, I felt like I had a little power. I was just waiting for the right time to reveal it.

For the next month or so, I watched both of them carefully, just to be sure the drugs hadn't made me paranoid. Mike got a little jealous, wondering why I was all of a sudden staring at Albert. I smiled, Albert smiled, and what I suspected was confirmed. I was sort of embarrassed by just how little any of this mattered to me personally. As long as I was able to get high, he could have married the man right under my nose. I wouldn't have cared.

It started to bother me when I was becoming the only burden to Mike. He was getting tired of me. He had started moving in with other women, not to sleep with them, but just to show me up. They were shapely and pretty, and he was their manager. I still had the voice, but I didn't have the looks.

I had gotten a show, but it was a small crowd, and I was afraid I wouldn't make enough money. Mike had threatened me, saying that if I didn't bring home two hundred dollars, I was on the bus back to Mississippi. He called me the country clown everyone laughed at, and I was like, "Please don't send me back South. I will sleep with anyone and everyone just to not be on a bus back South."

I'll never forget that night, for I was dope sick like never before, but I had to sing, and I was singing my little sick heart out. There stood Mike, dressed in clothes he had not earned the money to buy. I had. His hair was freshly done and his nails were shiny and pretty. I watched him fold his arms tightly across his muscled chest, looking angrily at me. On my break, I was barely able to hold my head up, but I watched his hands count my money. He frowned at the money he was counting and told me in a very threatening tone that my bags were being packed at the door.

I had no family and no hope. All I had was my high and that couch, so I shouted, "You always talking about kicking me out! Hell, I ain't the only person living in that house — what about Albert? Why don't you kick him out? Naw, you wouldn't do that, 'cause then who would you fuck?"

It was like the whole little dressing room stopped and looked at him. He stopped counting my money and nervously looked around, wondering if all eyes were on him, and they were. I could see the disbelief in Mike's eyes. He was angry that I had called him out in front of all his peers, but the look he gave me — it was like he didn't know himself that he was gay. He didn't say a word, just walked out of the dressing room, taking himself far away from the stares and blank expressions.

I went back out on stage and sang. I think I had over two hundred dollars in tips when I went home. I was ready to give the money to Mike. I prepared myself to throw the money in his face, taking out just enough to get high. I walked into the house and found all the lights on and the television playing loudly. I didn't feel like talking to Mike, so I lay down on the couch and went to sleep.

I woke up in the middle of the night and found it strange that the lights were still on. *Something must be up with Mike*, I thought, for he never liked to sleep with noise of any kind or any lights on. He had to have total darkness. I walked into his room and found him sitting directly in front of the mirror with his head bowed, his body slumped in a chair. Blood had soaked his clothes and half of the carpet. He was dead.

All I could do was scream. I yelled so loud, I couldn't speak. I called the police, and they came along with cameras, lights, and newspeople. They asked me, "What do you think would make him do such a thing?" and I told them I didn't know, but inside I knew.

I took the last two hundred dollars and came home, back to the same deplorable conditions I'd left. I was broke and physically messed up, and I had the added benefit of being on drugs. I got high down here as much as I could. Not that it made me feel good — it really didn't make me feel any way at all — but I got high with the hope that maybe it would help me sleep or think. Twin, it was like a dark, heavy presence following me, nudging me to get high. I heard voices in a low, seductive tone, encouraging me to go get high, go get my happy, that I was really nothing without it. Then the voice would tell me that I couldn't sleep without it. Ever since I saw Mike like that with a hole in his head, I haven't been able to sleep, and it's been years. There is a part of me that feels like I killed him, which was why I didn't stick around for his funeral: I couldn't face the people he loved or the people who loved him, because if I had just kept his secret, he possibly would still be living.

Three years later, I discovered that Mike had left me another secret: He had infected me with AIDS, and now I was dying. I started to wonder if that was why he'd killed himself. Albert wrote and told me to get tested, for he had revealed his condition to Mike the night Mike died. Albert never knew what happened at the club and blamed himself for Mike's death. It took him four years to face up to the fact that he, too, was dying, and so was I. When you have a death ticket and many reasons to die, why try to live? I wake up every morning just to ask myself what the hell is the point. Maybe if I had just waited and left with you twins, I would be rich.

———

Leona

"We're not rich, Tara, just working-class folk," I said humbly.

"Life just ain't right, fucked up, and I keep asking myself why I deserved this. I'm not proud of the way I lived, but I did some good—didn't I do something good? When I sang, people listened, and all their problems went away, even if just for that night. That was good, wasn't it, twins? It had to have been good."

She began to cry, and all we could do was embrace her and help her understand that we understood. She had been given a bad hand to deal with in life and made some really bad choices, but we understood, for it hadn't been easy for us either. If anyone ever wished for a different hand to play, it had to be us. Hugging our friend, we reconfirmed her as the person she had lost in the heartache of life. We were able to say that it didn't matter what she went through in life. If she was alive to tell about it, it was worth the living, if for no other reason than for others to learn from her mistakes and know that there was a way out.

Tara was surprised to learn that she had graduated and was now able to go to college. Before we left, Tara started talking about going back to school and giving up the bottle, and we helped her find treatment in Jackson and a support group for people living with AIDS. We helped her find a nice small house, even helped her fix it up in Jackson, Mississippi, near her support group. We hadn't planned on staying that long, close to six months, but we did. Our husbands sent us money, and they even visited the place, but we had work to do, and we weren't going to leave until it was done.

You can put that in the book, my dear.

LADY JANE

PART 3

Leona

The day before we left for Belzoni, we had received a note from someone stating that Lady Jane wanted to see us. We had spotted an older lady in a long black coat following us and checking us out as we made our way through the city, but we thought she was part of the curious crowd, and we had long since stopped wishing to fulfill others' curiosity. At the funeral, this Jane lady watched to see if we would cry. Of course, we didn't, for we had no reason to cry. Clare had served us loveless, and we had buried her loveless, and now the score was even.

This woman had requested to see us. As we packed to leave, we decided that we would stop by to see what the woman with the long, knitted gray hair wanted to say to us. Ten minutes, we said we would give her, and that would be it.

We got to this woman's house, a small house painted black on the outside, with unkept grass and black curtains. *What is this lady, a witch?* we thought, but we went and knocked on the door anyway. She opened the door and let us in — inside lived a very dark, cold soul. She was an unusually tall woman with long hair and nails and strong Indian features. With her light-colored eyes, she almost looked like a man in drag, but she was female. She was dressed in a long, black silk dress, and she smiled, showing a perfect set of white teeth. She liked to be called Lady Jane. As she explained, she was a lady of wisdom concerning the living and the dead, but she cautioned us not to confuse her with a witch, for she assured us that her spirit was from God. The only thing I remember about her house is that it had a ghostly feel to it, with lots of curtains and cluttered with books and candles. I mean, there were curtains for doors, curtains to the bathroom entrance, and curtains in a circular pattern that made private a small table with three chairs. I know she said she came from God, but there was nothing godly about that room, and the way that house made us feel. It just didn't sit right with my spirit.

She insisted that we sit at that small table, but I chose to stand. I wasn't afraid; I was curious. We must have stared at the woman for a good fifteen minutes, for surely we had seen her before, but we couldn't place where. She was old but age defying. Then it hit me! I remembered where I had seen her before. She was at Clare's house a few weeks before our eighth-grade graduation. Lady Jane was Clare's friend.

After that, we were willing to stay with her for hours if she could help us in our quest for truth. She offered us coffee or tea, and we refused. She smiled, and then we realized this was a friendly visit.

"Why are we here?" I asked pointedly.

"Well, I just figured maybe we could help each other," said Lady Jane.

"Help each other?" I questioned this notion, but was willing to give her an ear.

"That's right, help each other," she said.

——

Lady Jane

When I was a little girl, I could see and hear things no one else could see and hear—spiritual things. In a small town, you struggle with such a gift, for somehow everyone knows you have it. Some folk can sense it.

I met Clare one day at the market and told her that I saw a very beautiful lady following her. She cursed at me and called me a liar and made me take it back. Three years later, she sought me out and asked that I describe the lady. I described a lady much like you, Lillian, and she began to cry, saying she knew the lady. She wanted me to get the lady from around her. I told her it was possible, but I needed to know the whole story, for spirits don't just hang around you for nothing. There had to be a reason, and if I was to help her, I needed to know the whole truth.

Clare was weary and tired and needed a soul to bare all to, and I was that person. She made me promise not to tell anyone and said she would deny it if I did. Then she told me her story. I figured that if you heard it, you just might understand the lady who raised you after all this time.

You see, Clare and John were childhood sweethearts. She made him promise not to tell a soul. She was a little embarrassed by him, for he didn't dress that nicely in school, but mainly it was because she was the church's junior musician, and church folk always frowned on girls getting too grown for their skirts. Old people's jargon. She loved the country in him and all. He was her first, and they were inseparable. The townspeople knew they would be together; it was expected. They did, I think, get married. I wasn't exactly invited to the town's affairs, but Clare said he was her heart. Then he met your mother, somehow, and they were together. Clare never did explain this part of the story to me, but you see, Clare had plans for her life. She was being asked to speak in Washington and travel with politicians. She was so smart that some even thought she would go far, and your father supported her.

I only met your mother one time, and when I did, she referred to your dad as her husband. This infuriated Clare when I later shared this with her. Then the rumors started. It just didn't look right for a councilman to be having a relationship with other women, and Ruth May was not the only person rumored to have slept with your dad. Small towns move more than just feet. Clare told John to just leave Ruth May, but when they paid her to leave, she came right back when the money run out. She was never going to go away.

Clare told me she went out to this club in Jackson one night, dressed like she never knew the inside of a church. There was this tall, nice-looking musician named Randy there, and she just knew that if Randy met Ruth May, he would go for it. Now she paid Randy to just take Ruth May away. But the two of them didn't do that; in fact, he decided to tell Ruth May what Clare did, and now they both were blackmailing them. Ruth May was getting money out of Clare, and Randy was getting money out of Clare. They were two peas in a pot that needed to be cooked and tossed out. Turns out Randy had been knowing Ruth May a very long time.

The whole car breaking down chance meeting was just a joke. The worst part of this whole situation is that Randy was now admitting to Clare that he was in love with Ruth May. Clare had to laugh at this whole situation, and I actually had to laugh with her, because as it looked, they had two very cocky people, Ruth May and Randy, committed to hanging around and taking their money. Both were professional crooks. They wanted Clare to have a home built for them in Jackson and send money down monthly to take care of the kids, whom they claimed were John's kids, but at this point, Clare didn't believe a word that came out of their combined lying mouths.

She knew for sure that she was not only in the history book as the first African American school leader, but she was also asked to join the secretary staff of a national political party. She would be in Washington, D.C., and she could bring her husband along, who was running for the town council. They were meant for history books, and those two in the back of the woods were meant for the trash. She simply wanted them erased from this world.

She whispered this plan to John, who must have agreed because before the summer ended, both Ruth May and Randy were dead. I'm sure there is more to this story, but this is all she shared with me.

After John killed those two, he left. He was to return. But he never really did. He left her to raise his responsibility. She ended up just waiting on his return; she felt as if her life could not move without John in it. She didn't get the job in Washington, D.C. She remained the head teacher but kept thinking about John. Having to explain over and over again that John was on the reservation, taking care of a sick mother, got tiresome. She was becoming distracted. The stories just kept getting stranger and stranger. Everyone she felt was looking at her and questioning her about John. I assured her that most people probably didn't care, but she had long convinced herself that people had hope for John and her, and they would carry that hope to their graves. Then she told them they divorced, and that switched to him now deciding to live on the reservation with his mother. The story kept changing. She even started sending herself gifts from John just to appease a community that probably cared less than she realized. Not to mention, everywhere she went, this lady would be following her. She couldn't see the lady, but at night she swore she heard voices, laughter, and footsteps. She had unexplained things happening in her house. At night all of a sudden, the water faucet would just turn itself on, or the porch light would be on. She would smell cigarettes or beer just out of the blue, and no one in her house smoked. If it wasn't for the hope of John one day coming home, she probably would have killed herself.

Clare told me the story because there was no one else she could tell. She hired me to go places with her and clean out her house. I worked for a week to get that spirit out of her house, but to no avail. All this was very real to Clare. Clare still couldn't sleep nights, for the light would just come on. She heard laughter in the middle of the night and felt cold hands around her neck, so tight that she could barely move. She had to fight some mornings to get out of bed, for her legs would feel as if lead were on top of them, so heavy she couldn't walk or stand. She was convinced this woman was holding down her legs. I did all I could do, with prayers and all.

Then I told her that maybe the spirit wanted its children, which was why I think you had to get out. I didn't exactly tell her to kick you guys out, but that's how she interpreted it, and the next thing I knew, bags were put on the porch. When you guys left, for a while things did get better. She didn't hear the laughter and see lights, and water stopped coming on, but now she was obsessed with finding John. All she talked about was finding John. Clare's body was being broken down. She could barely function at work and she had to retire early. She had turned into a mess. She couldn't date, couldn't sleep, and most painful of all, she couldn't have John, the man she loved.

She was soon to learn that he had started over. At this point, I think my friend's life ended. All she would say to me is "Bring him back, can you bring him back to me?" Then she accused me of not being able to do much. I drove out the ghosts, but they would just come back. She got so angry with me, I couldn't be around her. Her energy was so strong that when I walked past her, I almost tripped. She was losing. Her eyes were getting dimmer, and her arms were weaker. Her bones were beginning to push forward, almost coming through her skin, and her back was now a little arched. She wasn't this tall, elegant woman we had known and admired. Your mother was beautiful, but Clare was gorgeous, skin flawless, tall, model thin, her coarse hair hung in a curl pattern to her shoulders, and her speech gave words distinctive sounds. It was like listening to music. Yet people thought it was my friendship with her that cursed her, which wasn't the truth at all. If Clare was cursed at all, it was due to her own conscience.

"Clare paid for what she did to your mother. I just wanted you to know she was punished." She got up and came close to us, holding a handmade mirror. "I told you what I felt you ought to know. Now you tell me which one of y'all is real."

She held up the mirror, and we watched her in confusion, for if she had any spirituality at all, she would have known the truth. We had been a freak show all of our lives, and we wouldn't be one that day.

We walked out, knowing more than what we'd bargained for. We had a greater understanding of Clare's life, which helped us understand our childhood better. If what the lady had just said to us was the truth, that could be why Clare's soul was so closed. Maybe she was struggling with some form of mental illness as a way of coping with what she did. We couldn't witness all of what Clare claimed was happening in the house, but knowing that she might have thought it was real, we understood her more.

As we went back to Illinois, we even cried for her, for surely she had reaped twice as much as she sowed. The person at the center of this was our father, and we wondered what he would have to say about all this.

MEETING HIM

PART 4

Leona

Lady Jane had left us in a frantic search for our father. As we drove back to Illinois, we knew we had much unsettled business that had to be finished. The address, 1421 W. Bell, continued to float in and out of our minds.

I told Lillian not to be disappointed if things didn't work out. Maybe the man was dead. Maybe we wouldn't ever find out if the gossip was right or if we could trust the things we remembered—the bloodstained sheets, the cake-like dirt on my mother's lover's face from being dragged outside, our father walking around the room nervously, picking up the phone, then hanging up. We remembered the dreadful goodbye our father made us say to our mother, the blood sprouting up to soak the sheets, her face still beautiful and polished. I had run out and Lillian had said goodbye.

Now the vision was trapping us: Was it a crime of passion, or was it premeditated? Lillian was the more verbal one, but on this issue, we still had to know.

We arrived at Bell Street at 5:30 a.m. and decided to wait until the rooster crowed to see if our father actually lived there. How would he look? We were asking ourselves so many questions. I really had to see him—not because I wanted to know the truth, although that was part of it. I really had to see him because I had to. Secretly, I'd been holding on to a love-hate relationship with our father. I wanted to know if deep down inside, he loved us too much to hurt us or scar us for life. I didn't remember much about him, but I did remember, or hoped I remembered, that he loved us. I guess I had to see him to know this. It hurt to believe that Clare had actually plotted with our father to kill our mother. She was coldhearted, but surely not that coldhearted. I couldn't believe my father had ever liked her, much less loved her enough to plan our mother's murder. It was hard being in the middle now and being in the middle then, and I guess we just wanted out.

At around 6:30, dawn began to break and the sunlight took a sneak peek at the wonders of this world. Eventually, the sun illuminated the sky, and it took our breath away. The thought of God and his realness intruded on my thoughts, giving me the grace to accept whatever I needed to accept. The sun and all of its beauty assured me that no matter what happened, there would be a tomorrow, and a sun to illuminate that day as well. Even if we weren't loved by our father, our mother, Clare, or our ex-husbands, we knew we were loved by God, who created beauty that could not be contained, and created it inside us. I felt free and ready to get it over with. I knew I would survive.

It was now 7:00 a.m., time to see if the man was alive or dead. And if he was alive, would he remember us? I guess we took pleasure in recalling what might happen. Actually, we were afraid as we walked to the door. We heard a dog barking in the yard. I really wanted to do it, but the sound of the dog barking made me want to turn back. Lillian squeezed my hand, and I realized that the only reason I could be so headstrong about this meeting was because she was feeding me the energy. She wanted to do this too, except she just didn't know it.

A young man came to the door, and he looked just like our father.

"Is there a John McDonald living here?" I asked.

"No" he said knowingly, and then we heard a woman's voice from the back. "Who in the hell is ringing my door this early in the damn morning?"

"Sorry," he said as he began to close the door.

"Wait a minute," we both objected. "Please, if you don't mind, what is your father's name?"

"What?" he asked curiously.

"Your father. What is his name?"

"Douglass James," he said, rather confused.

So, he was living under a different name. "We would like to see him—Mr. James, that is."

"He's sleeping!"

"Will you tell him he has visitors, please?"

"Visitors." On that note, he closed the door, and I hoped he would come back. Ten minutes later, he did. "My father said he doesn't have visitors, so who are you?"

"Well, we are. Can we come in?"

"Who the hell is this lady?" the woman shouted.

"I would give you our names, but I want it to be a surprise," I said.

Out of desperation, he led us into a junkie shotgun one-flat house. It was apparent that someone liked to read newspapers, because they were piled in every corner of the house, some so old they had faded from black and white to mustard-yellow and gray.

From a distance, we saw him sitting there, gray-haired, his face still dark and attractive but bearing deep wrinkles. He sat straight up without a bend in his body. She stood there tall, dark, and beautiful, right by his side, and we knew she had carried him a long way. She wore a scarf on her thick, long black hair. They shared a son, sluggish and unconcerned, who walked us back to a round table, where he sat and she stood beside him, handling a frying pan with hot scrambled eggs.

Then our eyes met his. He looked at us, surprised. I'd never seen a dark man turn colors, but he did that day. He turned dark blue. His gray, aged eyes teared up. He never looked at Lillian, his eyes stayed glued to my face.

"Well," the kid said, "here's your guests."

Our father didn't take his eyes off Lillian.

"Who are you? I'm single, you know." The kid had chosen one of us. To this day, I'm still not sure which one. All I know was that as a boy of maybe twenty-five, he was revealing his growing hormones.

"Where do you come from?" the woman asked, but we stayed focused on our father, and he stayed focused on us, and the truth had not to be spoken. It was revealed on his face. He cleared his throat but didn't say a word.

"Well." That wasn't what I really wanted to say, but it was the only thing that came out.

"Are you related?" the boy asked, and we had the pleasure of not answering.

After our father looked at us long enough to make sure it was us, he put his head down, and that was enough. We had seen his guilt. We knew all we wanted or didn't want to know.

"Well, who are you?" she repeated.

"Ask your husband," I said. "Let's go, Lillian." When I said "Lillian," he looked up, because I guess he couldn't tell us apart. We were still identical twins as adults: same long brown hair, green eyes, and olive skin, and like our father, we had not aged that much at all. He looked at Lillian and me as a father would look at his little girls. He loved us.

"Well, let's go, Lillian," I said again.

"Why did you make us say goodbye?" Lillian cried out. "Why did you make us see her like that?" She was becoming hysterical. I hugged her and helped her head to the door. He never said why.

She broke loose from me and ran back. "Why?" He pushed the plate of eggs away and walked shakily to what we guessed was his bedroom.

Lillian said angrily, "Goodbye, John McDonald!" She ran past me and out the door, and I watched him go to his room and close the door. I think his wife knew, but the son stood there speechless.

We left with as many answers as we could handle.

The young lad ran out and met us in the car. "My mother said who are you?"

"It doesn't matter anymore."

"But who?" he asked, almost begging.

I looked at this kid who needed to know, rather, who wanted to know. If he didn't find out, he wouldn't ever live a complete life. He would wonder who we were until he had to seek us out, and we really didn't want to be found.

"We are your father's long-lost daughters. I'm Leona and she's Lillian."

He cleared his throat and said softly, "Sisters." Wait a minute, there're two of y'all. This had not only taken him by surprise but also out of his world of logic, for we could see that despite his laziness and sheltered life, he was a thinker, and something had seriously confused him; confusion was coiling around his imagination, and he was entangled in thought, which totally tripped up his words and ability to speak, so I spoke.

"We live in Chicago," I said.

"Oh, nice, er, nice meeting you."

"Maybe one day you and Dad here can tell everyone the truth, so that we can live with just a little more knowing. I tossed my business card on the table and walked out.

We got in the car and drove off. "Why did you do that, Leona?" Lillian asked me.

"Because he deserved to know. They plotted her death. I believe they planned it together. You know his ass should be in jail or hanged to death." The canopy that had covered his lies was beginning to crumble. He didn't think he had us to deal with ever in the world, but guess what, we survived.

"But it wasn't his idea," Lillian rationalized, too afraid to admit that even with the killing of her mother, she still loved her father, and I, in my anger, did as well.

What happened, how it happened—I wanted to know the whole truth, and the person who had that knowledge had put it in a vault and wasn't going to release it. I hope he will tell one day, and if you hope for something long enough, you will get it. Before John died, he did, in fact, tell us all we needed or wanted to know.

DUST FROM THE CHOCTAW BOOTHS

PART 5

Leona

After three years and no word from John, we had all but given up hope that we would ever know the truth about who those people were. We had moved on. Hurt has a way of teaching you to hold everything loosely. Eventually, you stop wondering. You stop searching for answers. You simply move on. Then one day, it came in the mail.

It was an early October day. There was no return address, just a three-page letter. Lillian and I held onto that letter for about a year. We didn't open it—we just looked at it. It was strange, but twins really do move in unity.

One day Lillian asked if I wanted to take a ride, and right before she uttered those words, I had suddenly felt ready to take one. So I did. We did. We drove to a small wooded area somewhere in Iowa. I had driven all the way there, turned off onto a back road, and stopped the car. The stillness of nature stopped my thinking and froze my expectations in place. I knew that on that day, I would finally know.

Lillian opened the letter. I lay on the hood of the car while she rolled down the window and sat inside with the doors open. She handed me the letter. I guess it was something she needed me to do. Lying still on top of the car, feeling the cold steel against my half-cut T-shirt and listening to the quiet drip of a nearby water brook, I began to read the letter.

Hello,

The opening of his letter took me back a little. He greeted us as if we were casual acquaintances. I tried not to choke or cry. I was fully grown by that time and aware that he simply didn't have a connection with us. Still, I continued to read.

———

Dad/John

This isn't an easy story to tell. I will try. I will also try to tell it as I have lived it, as truthfully as I possibly can.

I was raised by my grandmother on my father's side. My father was killed in the Civil War. After his death, my mother—who was a full-blooded Indian—left. Apparently my father and mother both drank a lot. When my father checked out, my mother went back to the reservation, a place she didn't think I would be welcomed. So Granny took me in.

My granny was a good woman—tall, dark, with broad shoulders. She was bent on making a better man out of me than her son had been. My father, I heard, was not just a drunk but a man who went from loose woman to loose woman. As beautiful as my mother was, it didn't keep him home.

A few months after my dad died, I was around seven or eight. My mother left me without saying a word. She didn't even look back at me. It could have had something to do with me stepping on her baby kitten until it died. It stopped moving underneath my slipper until it was dead.

My ma gave me a familiar look. It was strange—almost as if she saw the monster tucked away inside me. She looked at me as though she could see right through me.

Granny thought I just played too rough and chalked it up to that. With her bare hands, she removed the kitten from under my feet and threw it outside. I sat quietly at the table, ready to eat Granny's delicious meal and wash it down with her watermelon punch. My mother was still watching me. I didn't know what she was waiting for. All I knew at the time, being a kid and all, was that killing that kitten meant nothing to me and that I was hungry.

My mother came slowly behind me and whispered a phrase in my ear. Then she gave me a small feather in a glass case, about the size of a silver dollar. I guess it was to let me know where she would be. Then she walked out of my granny's house and never looked back.

After dinner, my granny took me into the washroom and fixed me a warm bath in a large gray tub. Then she put me to bed.

I always hoped my mother would return the way she left, but she never did.

My grandmother became my master teacher. She taught me how to build a house from the ground up. She taught me how to lay a roof, paint, and put up walls. Everything I needed to know, she taught me. She even taught me how to read.

We were poor, but I had more than some because my grandmother could do almost anything that involved using her hands — sewing, making clothes, or cooking a nice Sunday meal. She was truly an amazing woman, but hard — very hard and stern. She never talked to me much or asked my opinion. She just wanted to make sure she was putting the necessary things inside of me.

She didn't believe in me spending long hours listening to the funnies on the radio. She believed in work and nice Sunday meals. Granny wasn't really much of a religious woman. She attended church when her customers invited her, and she always cooked. I didn't grow up hearing many prayers or gospel music. When Granny listened to music, it was jazz. She would drink a little moonshine if she felt inclined. She smoked too, and the smell of cigarettes was always around.

In the South, preachers traveled from church to church. When it was their Sunday near Granny's house, we attended church once a month. Every other Sunday we were out fishing or learning how to lay planks.

Life as a youth was a series of small lessons. My granny taught me how to run electricity through the walls of a house. She had watched it done one time, then came home and taught me how.

I didn't have many friends, but I had Clare. I think I liked her because she reminded me of my grandmother. She was tall, broad-shouldered, and smart. All the guys liked her, but they felt inferior and too afraid to talk to her. I wasn't afraid. She was really the only person I knew how to talk to.

Granny always wanted Clare to be impressed with the things I learned. I didn't just learn how to repair houses; I memorized speeches and poems too. When Clare's family visited, Granny would set a place for me to perform. Sometimes Clare would play music while I recited poetry or gave a speech. We even put on small shows for the town. If folks didn't know anything else, they knew those two kids were going to be something someday.

Clare's parents owned the biggest colored store in town, so they had money. We started high school together, but I only stayed two years. Granny could no longer manage the house and chores alone, so I left school to work. Two years of schooling was more than many colored boys had anyway.

Granny filed the papers and started a small business. I became the town's "fix-it man." She also pushed me into speaking for the community. Before long, I was traveling around the South, repairing houses, and giving speeches when leaders came through our town. One year I spoke in Jackson, and the next year we got a post office. The whole town celebrated. Apparently, I was responsible for the government giving a post office to our small town. I also got in the paper that year. I always liked seeing my grandmother smile with pride. She had done what she set out to do — raise a better man than her son had been.

But the thing that truly made me feel alive was killing chickens. One evening I killed ten of them, each in a different way. I chopped off heads, wrung necks, and shot a few too. It happened after a big speaking engagement when everyone else felt proud of me. I went behind the barn and found myself laughing while I did it.

Granny came out and saw the mess — blood, feathers everywhere. I stood there breathing hard, hoping she would look at me instead of the ground. Maybe then I would have to tell someone the thoughts inside my head. But she didn't look at me. She simply said,

"You were only supposed to kill three chickens for Easter. Now we'll have to invite more people. Pluck them and clean them."

She made me promise not to do it again. I didn't — at least not that many at one time.

During Clare's final year of high school, she announced she was leaving for college. Granny looked surprised and later asked what I thought about a girl like Clare going away. I told Granny I was afraid she would come back married, and Granny gave me that look that simply meant do something about it. So Granny invited her to dinner.

After the meal I gave Clare a suitcase I had made out of wood. I told her if she accepted the case, she had to accept the hands that made it in marriage. She said yes. The whole town celebrated, and it even made the newspaper.

Clare and I talked often about the future. While she was away studying, she wanted me to build our home. I had already bought a small place in the woods to practice on while I purchased more land. That summer, she left and I went to work designing what I hoped would be the finest house in the country.

Granny loved hearing me talk about it. I even bought and repaired a grand piano and kept it stored out back, waiting for the day it would be moved into that house.

Still, after Clare left, I found myself searching for something that would make life feel complete. I thought perhaps Clare and I could build a happy life together, at least for a while. Instead of my own happiness, my mind often drifted to how happy Granny would be when Clare and I married. The feeling that I could live normally returned, but it still didn't last. I was a sad person and didn't know why. Part of me thought the thoughts in my head were normal, though deep down I knew they were not.

Clare and I often took turns appearing in the papers. When I repaired the church, it made the paper. When I attended meetings with White leaders from nearby towns, it made the paper. I would cut out the articles and give them to Granny, and she always framed them. Sometimes she would mail a few copies to my mother, but we never got a return reply, so she just stopped telling me when she mailed a clipping.

About a few years later, Granny began to decline. She stopped eating much and no longer had the strength to keep up the house. I would spend part of the day working on the house in the woods, then come home to take care of her place.

I could smell death on her. It smelled like sour milk lingering in the room. It stayed with her, through the thinning of her hair, the darkening circles under her eyes, the weakening of her bones, and lips drawn together like a dried plum. Standing hurt her. Sitting hurt too. It was hard to watch a woman who had worked with her hands all her life become so fragile, her hands now unable to brush the sweat from her face.

I knew I had to act quickly if Granny was going to see one last piece of happiness. Clare still had a year of college left, but when my name was mentioned for a colored council seat, I drove to Memphis and asked her to marry me right away. She stood there surrounded by her giggling friends and said yes. When I walked back to my car, I heard one of the girls say I was a good-looking man. I think I smiled, though the thought crossed my mind that she shouldn't admire another woman's future husband. That night, I rushed home and told Granny. She nodded and smiled. That was enough for me.

That same year, Mr. Walter stepped down as head teacher and recommended Clare for the position. They traveled to her college in Memphis to interview her about becoming the town's first colored female head teacher. Everyone was proud. I kept waiting to feel something shift inside me when I read the article about her success, but it never did. After a while, I stopped wondering why I had to pretend to care. Later, I read that people like me sometimes struggle to feel the things others do. I suppose the experts may be right. Still, I often wonder why people like me exist at all.

When Clare came home for Thanksgiving, I showed her the house in the woods. Her first thought was that it felt isolated. I told her we could even raise chickens there, but she wasn't impressed. My hard work meant nothing. The house was fully renovated, everything was new, the best line of products, and it didn't matter to her. Two days later she showed me a different house—one her parents had bought for us as a wedding gift. It sat on a large lot near downtown Belzoni. She described everything she wanted: A wraparound porch, lamps along the drive, and a shed beside a concrete slab for the cars. It was different from what I imagined, but I liked the challenge.

Once she returned to school, I began restoring the place. When I wasn't doing paid work, I was fixing that house—varnishing the wooden floors, repairing the fence, painting it black with white trim. The work kept my mind busy and distracted me from watching Granny grow weaker each day.

One afternoon I brought Granny out to see the house. She smiled and said there was room in the back for a small farm. That excited me. I noticed a small shed behind the property that I hadn't paid attention to before. I imagined enlarging it, turning it into a proper workspace. I ran to inspect it and was so excited I didn't hear someone calling for me.

When I returned, Granny had fallen to her knees. I lifted her into the car and rushed her to the hospital, but about an hour later, she died. People used to say she got her wings. I hoped she believed I had become the man she wanted me to be. Losing her was the greatest loss in my life. Yet when the doctor told me she was gone, something inside me shifted in a way I had long waited for.

I felt relieved and free. Now my thoughts could be my own, with no one holding a measuring rod over my head, judging every good and bad thing I did. All that nonsense was done with because I knew I was more bad than good. Now, I could uncage the images in my head.

His name was Mr. Bell. He would be my first death. I saw him hit his wife. He was drunk, probably like my father and mother, and he never smiled. He sobered up and begged for his life. He didn't deserve to live. I burned him in a fire, cooked him like a bird. I learned that fire was not my preferred way of killing; it takes too long. His wife asked me about him, and if I wasn't busy planning my own wedding, I would have buried her in fire. She later told me she believed he ran away, left her, and that saved her life.

Clare and I married. I continued running my construction business and speaking for the community. I thought perhaps I could control the thoughts in my head if I kept busy. I even considered becoming a deputy, since most people trusted me. Clare laughed it off and said I was only grieving Granny.

Clare quickly became an icon in town. She had bigger ambitions than she let on. She arranged for us to attend a dinner with a congressman. We sat in the back with the kitchen staff, but we still managed to get our photograph taken with him. She believed my future in politics might reach beyond the local level. I didn't know how I was supposed to feel about that.

Around that time I began visiting a small club in Greenville where live music played. My granny loved jazz, and hearing it performed live stirred something in me. That is where I met Ruth May Bullock.

She was bold and full of life. People believed she was the daughter of a mulatto couple who once lived in our town, but she had never even heard of Belzoni before I brought her there. She told me she was a cousin of Lena Horne, and I believed her. They say people like me cannot love. That may not be entirely true. I felt something for Ruth—stronger than anything I had felt before.

Most people believed Clare and me were happily married. I wasn't happy at all. Every few months I would go out hunting, shooting animals and people and burying them. It was the only way I knew to quiet my mind. But when I saw Ruth, those urges paused.

I visited that little club often just to watch her. She was beautiful and sassy. She had adopted much from her Black side of the family, although clearly she was something else. She sometimes sang, though she mostly managed the place.

One night she argued with the owner and suddenly jumped into my car, telling me to drive unless I wanted both of us shot. I drove toward Belzoni, wondering where to take her. Then I thought of the house in the woods.

I told Clare a White woman was hiding there from an abusive husband. At first Clare felt sorry for her. But when she finally met Ruth, her sympathy vanished. She wanted her gone. She noticed that Ruth had something about her that was beautifully Black. The more Clare pushed against her, the more I felt drawn to Ruth.

At first nothing happened between us. But Ruth had a teasing way about her, and it soon became clear that Clare had my name but Ruth had my heart. Ruth would ask me to do something for the house and I would do it immediately. When Clare asked, things often waited for weeks. I could never say no to Ruth.

One day Ruth told me I wasn't going home, and I didn't. It was the best and worst day of my life. She made love to me with a kind of cruel confidence — like I had to want it and hate it at the same time. In a strange way it kept me from feeling anything else. While I was with her, I didn't feel the urge to kill.

As months turned to a year, I began to believe she had come into my life to destroy me, and part of me wanted that. She was exactly the kind of woman my grandmother would have disapproved of. Still, I kept going back. When I tried to stay away, she would come into town and provoke Clare. Then she became pregnant. I was running for councilman at the time, but she didn't care who knew. Clare stood by me, and I still won the election.

That night I thought about my grandmother. Ruth might damage my life, but she wouldn't erase Granny's memory in this town. I decided then that my life would be with Clare. Ruth was part of my past.

I stayed away from Ruth until she had the babies. Twin girls.

I didn't know how to relate to babies. I only wanted to see them once. They were beautiful. I wished my grandmother could have met them. It didn't take long before I was back in Ruth's bed.

Since Clare had no children yet, Ruth started behaving as if she should take Clare's place in town. She would come to my office, kiss my cheek, and bring me food. Sometimes the food wasn't even cooked—just wrapped to look that way. It embarrassed me, but I didn't care. A part of me wanted her to do more bad things. I wondered if Ruth had my thoughts, and if we both were meant to work together, but she didn't. She was tricky, but she respected the lives of others. I told people she was a sick sister who had come to town. No one questioned it. When she dropped the babies off in baskets, people believed they were my nieces.

Ruth loved money, so I warned her that if she ruined my position, she would lose the life my income provided. That quieted her for a while, but not for long. This went on for six years.

She burned my clothes in the yard, scratched Clare's car, and even showed up at council meetings demanding money. By then Clare had had enough. She said she would raise the girls as her own if Ruth disappeared. For once Clare and I agreed completely. It was at this point that I realized Clare and I was one and the same. She was capable of the same things I was capable of.

I went to Ruth's house, intending to tell her to leave Belzoni for good. When I arrived, I saw a man sitting on the porch drinking a soda meant for my children. Ruth came outside laughing and kissing him while my girls climbed into his arms like he was their father. I watched as if I was watching cinema. Something broke inside me.

I went home and told Clare. Outwardly, I pretended to be relieved that Ruth might finally be out of our lives. Inside, I felt nothing but anger. For a week, I shut myself away in a room Clare had decorated beautifully—a canopy bed, soft carpets, polished furniture. It felt like a king's room, but I was a king without a heart. I couldn't stop thinking about Ruth and the man. I remembered watching them together—how gently he touched her, how she laughed with him in ways she never had with me. Watching them through the bedroom window gave me a strange sensation, like witnessing a final showdown in a movie. I knew it had to end, and it had to end badly. I thought about burning the house down, but that would have been too kind a death for them both.

Finally, I decided to go get the girls and end the situation once and for all. I wanted them only because Ruth loved them as much as she could love anyone. And maybe, I thought, if I had them, I would still have a piece of her worth keeping.

Clare understood what I meant without me saying it. She told me to go.

With Clare's encouragement, I brought the gun in case Ruth started throwing things or attacking me like she had before.

When I arrived, the house was quiet. The girls were asleep. I walked into the bedroom and found Ruth lying peacefully against that man's chest. I shot him first.

She woke up screaming. The girls came into the room. One of them grabbed my leg. Ruth rushed toward me and I shot her.

Then I kept shooting.

I remember watching myself do it as if I were outside my own body. When the gun was empty, I placed her back in the bed beside the man.

You girls had run and hidden beside the stove. One of you stared with your eyes wide open, too afraid to blink. The other had your eyes squeezed shut, too afraid to look. If there had been more bullets, I might have killed you too.

Instead, I told you to say goodbye to your mother. You asked me about this, so here's the answer, and it is not as noble as you might think. It was only a way to give myself time to leave, though in truth it spared your lives.

When I got home, Clare had prepared a full meal. She hugged me and said, "It's over now. That wretched woman is gone." I didn't understand how she knew. Then she asked if the children were safe. I nodded yes.

She said she would arrange the scene to look like a robbery and told me to leave town, just as we had once discussed. When I dropped the gun from my pocket, she calmly wiped the fingerprints from it.

Only then did I realize something.

I had never loaded the gun.

Someone else had.

I left that night.

They say people like me can kill without feeling anything. That's not entirely true. When my granny died, I felt something—I felt free. I didn't understand then that the feeling meant I wanted to kill. I also felt something when Ruth died. Out of all the books I read about people like me, I always wondered why they never mentioned one simple fact: Though you can't feel, you can certainly remember.

I didn't stop killing. I killed a man and took his name, stole his wallet, and kept moving. I killed a couple for smoking in a store. When I suggested they put the cigarette out before it caught fire, he gave me the finger. I cut off his hand. I buried them in a muddy grave. I took their car and kept the newspaper clipping about their unsolved murder.

I killed—never for a good reason, but for reasons.

They also never mention the torture. The memory stays sharp and clear. You want to sleep and forget, but the mind won't allow it. At first, remembering is almost like the day you hit your first home run and everyone cheers. But as you get older, you reach the point where you want only to forget, and reliving your killings becomes torture. I see their faces before I black out, only to wake and see them again. It's like living inside one long nightmare.

Sometimes when someone turns around in a store, their face becomes the face of someone I killed. Age has weakened me now. My health has declined. I wonder who might hurt me, so I avoid people, especially strangers. I am afraid all the time. It's like something dark is creeping up behind me and I can't run; I just have to feel that way. Nothing ends the pain.

I see things. I hear things. Laughter. Voices. The sound of the man I shot. If you wonder whether I paid for what I did, I will tell you this—I would have rather lived in prison for the rest of my life than inside this mind.

People say men like me have no regrets. That isn't true. What we have is worse. Memories.

The second time I ran away, I married another woman. She had a son, and I helped raise him. I gave them a roof over their heads but nothing more. I had no feelings left to give.

Now I am weak and frail. I can barely walk across a room. But the memories remain strong. Small pieces return every day—the limp arm falling from the bed, the look on a face just before the bullet hits.

I try to forget, but I can't. At night it feels like cold hands are pulling at my soul. I hear cries. I think someone is behind me, but it's only my own mind. I become both prisoner and torturer. The fear becomes constant, like a dark cloud pressing down on me. I live quietly, barely speaking above a whisper, waiting for death to come. I would take back every life I took if I could.

My grandmother knew something was different about me as a child, but she didn't know how to help. My mother saw it too. When she caught me killing that kitten, she whispered something to me. I didn't understand it then, but I do now.

"Dust from the boots of the Choctaw Indian will summon the wind to curse your memory if you kill again."

They say what I have is a disease with no cure. If you ever feel something like what I feel—even now—something that never quite goes away, there is something you can do. It is possible to push back the memories before it's too late. One day the thrill will leave you dry and impotent, and fear will become the only emotion you truly know, until you do to yourself what you once did to others. I don't deserve to give you advice, but I will anyway, just in case I am speaking to someone like me. So here it is:

Choose differently. Choose better.

Not one of my kills was worth it. It will not end well for me. I know that now.

———

Leona

We closed the letter and sat quietly. Lillian climbed up beside me on the hood of the car. What we had read was more than we had ever imagined.

After a while I said, "It's like a hyena eating its prey alive. He was eating himself alive."

She wiped tears from her eyes. Then she said boldly, "He was a monster."

I shook my head slowly. "A tortured soul."

Lillian repeated it again, almost angrily. "He was a monster."

"He was what he was," I said. "But we are who we are. We are not monsters, and we never will be. Good can come from bad. That's the lesson."

She looked at me, still unsure.

"Maybe that's why you became a teacher," I told her. "You can tell those children that it doesn't matter who their parents were. They can still be better."

She nodded slowly. "We are better," she said.

"Got that right," I answered.

Then we got into my car and drove back to the city.

Now we finally know.

PHRASE 17

LINGERING EFFECT

Margarita

I had been married for a few years and lost my dear mother a year or so earlier, so my time in the city and visiting Leona had been limited. One day I got a call from Darnell asking me to come see her.

"She's dying," he said. Darnell did not sugarcoat it.

I had too much life in me then to think about death. The future felt new and unimaginable. We were trying to build a life. I was doing well. Yet this was the moment she chose to die.

I'd told Bruce, my now husband, about Leona through her many stories. Looking back now, it seems strange how almost everything good that ever happened to me in life came through some connection to her. That thought lingered as I dressed to see Leona, probably for the last time on this side of heaven. Her sons told me not to worry about their mother, but they appreciated that I was coming to see her.

A winding road lined with tall oak trees led me to a quiet place beside a brook that sounded like soft, steady rain. When I arrived and signed in, I was told she already had visitors. David and Darnell were there. They looked tired, especially Darnell, but were gracious to see me. We talked for a few minutes at the door of her room while Leona stared out the window. When she heard my voice, she asked the nurse to place an extra pillow behind her head.

David and Darnell said they would step out for a while to give us time to talk. They kissed their mother on the forehead and quietly left the room. I stood waiting for an invitation to come closer. She motioned for me to approach.

When I entered the room, I noticed she had decorated the space with a photograph of her and Lillian playing the piano.

She had flowers surrounding her from friends. I smiled and held her hand. I did not want her to die, but with all that I had, I could not stop or delay it. The hurt lingered like a cloud of smoke in the air. My mind was searching for something good to say, just to not have to talk anymore. I would no longer be able to feel her long, gentle touch or feel her stern glance, which let me know that this was not the time to play, or hear her wisdom and uncanny sense of discernment. All of this would be absent from the world when she died, and absent from my life. I turned my head so as not to cry. I took a deep breath. "No trace of fear," I told myself.

I looked at her with what I hoped showed no trace of fear. She was different but yet calm. She looked refreshed, but she could no longer hide the traces of life. Sandy-colored hair was mostly gray now, and thin, but I could still see the wavy patterns hanging past her shoulders. Her eyes were a little dimmer and more gray than green now. She looked tired and ready.

"How are you doing?" I asked with as much genuine curiosity as I could muster up.

"This ride you got to take solo," she said very clearly and cohesively. She was very aware of the fact she was leaving, and she didn't seem bothered or afraid but more at peace.

I knew what she meant about this ride. No need for her to explain, as I knew she wouldn't. She smiled at something I knew was not in the room. Then she said, slowly and clearly, to make sure I understood every single word, "I have lived between worlds a long time. "It's good to finally feel this way, you understand?"

I didn't, but I nodded yes. What I did understand is that she had lived a life that many wouldn't have endured, yet she was still standing on her own. She started to pull down those imaginary strings, but she quickly stopped and turned her attention to me.

I said, with nothing better to say, "You look fresh."

She smiled, letting me know the word *fresh* may not have been a part of her vocabulary, but she understood that nowadays people used it and that it was a compliment. Then she finally said, "Marriage, huh? Four years."

I smiled and said, "Not bad."

She asked me if I saw those falling stars.

I smiled and said nothing. I covered her up just a little. It was a little cold to me in that room. I noticed it took a little more effort to breathe. I saw her inhale and fall asleep. As I was headed to the door, David and Darnell were coming back into the room, so I told them she was sleeping.

Darnell looked at me, smiled, and said, "She does that a lot. Hey, thanks for coming."

We gave our hugs and I was headed for the door. I knew it wouldn't be long before she would leave me, but what she left me with would certainly not die with her. I was more hopeful now than ever before about becoming a mother, as everyone needs to speak to souls that will hold their truths as mines hold gold.

PHRASE 18

FOLLOWING INVISIBLE STEPS

Margarita

I wish people could be renovated like houses—floors rebuffed to perfection, walls torn out, toxins removed, and light fixtures modernized to shine.

Leona died. She died in September. She always called September a month to remember. It didn't happen right away. I was able to see her a couple more times before she took her eternal nap. My sisters and Bruce attended the service. It was just as I imagined Leona would have liked it—loud. A school band played "Oh When the Saints Go Marching In." A lady prayed far too long, and I read a poem. I think it may have been written by Phyllis. The poem had no name and no author. I didn't understand it even then, but I read it all the same. David and Darnell gave a joint electrifying eulogy. It was a wonderful service.

After the funeral, family and friends came to the Green House ballroom and ate. We did the pleasant thing; we laughed and told stories about the woman I had grown to love and respect. We greeted, we smiled, we listened, not knowing really how to feel but trying to be strong in the moment. I was ready to go home. Thoughts were popping in and out of my head, all centered around Leona, who was indeed dead.

I hope she knew that she was my rock. On ice or in a tried fire, she was my hideout to dry out, a hangout place to talk. She was my water for my spiritual drought, my fearless teacher, who laughed out loud. She taught me so many lessons, but one that came to mind in that moment was to not look down on no ONE, not even myself, and to love everyone, including myself. I would have lived a much worse reality had she not shared her stories and brought them to life for me.

She was dedicated to the end. Rest up, my friend, Leona.

JUST CALM

Margarita

It was a gray day, so dark it almost looked dark brown, and the leaves lay still on sunbaked yellow grass—slightly frostbitten and slightly melted, somewhere between seasons and somewhere between emotions. Just calm.

I found myself sitting in a room now cold and empty, with the lingering memories of twins still in the air. It had been a while, a few weeks, and for the most part, I had come back to this world. On a day like this, a cup of tea would have been nice. I wondered who would listen on days like this, and I realized she was still very much needed.

I decided to write a small tribute to Leona. It wouldn't be a book, just something like a thank-you. Besides, Leona was a mystery—one I felt like sharing with the world. My column and podcast were usually about mysteries and the sort of things that grow out of gossip or hearsay. But this time my column would read a little differently.

On that day, though, I would just tell a little of the twins' story and leave it at that. I didn't care if the ratings were high or if many people read it. I felt it needed to be said.

I wrote my story, and it was published. A strange thing happened, though it had happened before. After the death of my mother, I was restless until I took my name off the three-flat building in Oak Park. It was a family building, and I knew my mother especially would have wanted it that way. When I took my name off the deeds, I was finally able to sleep.

Now that I had written that tribute to Leona, I felt released. I was back on the road to simply living again, and trying to have the baby Bruce and I both wanted so badly. The story was written and published in the morning paper.

Around noon, my editor called, and he was thrilled! The whole twin element intrigued him, and a whole lot of people. This surprised me because I knew why people read my stuff. It was full of gossip, fake news, and what-ifs. But this was mysterious. It was clear. And it was liked. In six hours, it had been shared over 3.4 million times.

I got a text from David. He wanted me to come over for dinner. Then it hit me, I probably should have run the story by them first. I mean, it was their mother. I accepted the invitation, and I had to face them eventually. Bruce, my husband, loved the article. He shared it with all of his friends, and they shared it with theirs. He thought this piece showed diversity in my writing, proving I was more than just a high-paid gossip columnist.

Bruce and I were trying to have a baby. I texted him and told him one hour, because I had to meet David and Darnell at around 4:30 for dinner. I looked at the viewership, and downloads of the article were at 20.9 million. People all over the world were reading and liking this story.

On my way to grab a quick bite with David and Darnell, I got a call from Rubin, my agent. Rubin was a character who only wanted what the numbers wanted. His quote to live by was, "You are never bigger than your numbers." When he negotiated my salary, he always told me it was a numbers game. With all the views I got on that short tribute to a friend, I wondered what he would have to say about my numbers now. I had been trying to get him to get me a syndicated mystery talk show.

I picked up the phone to hear him speak in his high-pitched voice, which sometimes irritated me. "You know, love, we have pitched several different ideas, none of which stuck, but people are into this story, love. I think it will work, you know, if you really go and investigate this mystery. People are into visuals now. Look at all the videos coming out. Big superstars can't sell records without a video."

"So what are you saying, Rubin?" I was now in the car, hoping I could quickly eat a bite so that I could get home to my husband.

"I think you may have done it with this story. I am thinking of a six-series pitch. I will put the rest together. What do you think? I will be the first to tell you ABC is already on my speed dial. It's the numbers, girl, and you got numbers, love. The truth about the twins is that it's sellable."

"Okay," I said, "I think it will be okay. I am meeting with her sons in just a few. "

"Tell them the good news, love. I got work to do." He hung up before he got an official yes from me. Of course I wanted to do it—to have a series with a major network. It wouldn't even be for the money or fame. I simply wanted the experience, but before I got too excited, I had to meet with David and Darnell. I arrived at the meeting spot and sat in the car, then got out of the car and walked into the restaurant.

PHRASE 19

SERENDIPITY

Margarita

I just knew that Leona had somehow orchestrated this. She liked a good mystery, and she loved telling stories. If she were there, she would be glued to her seat watching this show. I smiled, knowing this was what she wanted.

We came face-to-face in a popular eatery known for greasy burgers and good coffee. It was serendipity, a wonderful accident that had bonded us together, and I was glad to see them. I knew I would be okay the moment I walked into the restaurant and both David and Darnelle hugged me.

Darnell was explaining, as we walked to my seat, that this place had the best burgers ever. He greeted the owners and chatted with them for a bit while David walked me to our booth. One could only assume that married life with kids could be draining. Now David had two children, and I could see he had that settled look about him.

When the three of us were finally seated together, the first thing they did was tell me how much they loved the tribute to their mother. I smiled but couldn't really take credit for it, so I told them the truth.

"I slept good after I had written the story, and I guess that means it was a good thing."

"A good thing?" said Darnell. "It was spot on, and now I've got a fan club."

We laughed. Then I said jokingly, "Maybe it's time for you to settle down, playboy."

He shook his head no and smiled, and I could tell he liked the trading off of women every now and again.

I said to them," I take it you liked the article," trying to stay modest.

"That article's going crazy!" Darnell said, "What was it, 60 million?"

"Come on," I giggled, but I knew he was right.

"I was so surprised that so many people liked it. I mean, 60 million?"

"Yeah, well, it feels good to know people are reading my work. But first, know that it was supposed to be a tribute, and I had no idea that so many people would be interested."

"Well, how could you?" David interjected.

"I am sorry I didn't run it by you guys first."

"Can we get paid?" Darnell said.

This broke the ice. We all laughed. "Okay, Darnell, the paper did do well. I figured out a cut and give it to you both."

David smiled and took on a more serious tone. "You know he is joking, right?"

I smiled. It was, after all, Darnell, and he may not be joking.

Then David said very calmly, much like his mother would speak when she didn't want me to miss the point, "Darnell and I did our own research. One of the reasons we stayed in boarding school was because my mother had a dual personality disorder. Doctors call it a dissociative identity disorder. We found the house still standing in the woods. And we learned that my mother's twin died when she was around nine. She lived a very complicated life. She always had two homes because she had two very different personalities. I gasped. "But I saw Lillain in the coffin? I touched her dead body!"

The boys looked at each other. Darnell grinned. "Mom used to be married to a funeral director. She got tired of Lillian and asked her husband to put a notice in the paper for her. Then she got dressed up and lay in an open coffin to see who would come by."

"And she said, 'I prayed for just one child, any child, to visit that funeral home. And that child was you. He's still answering prayers,'" I whispered. "It's like she was trying to tell me the truth from the day I met her."

My mother called you her treasure box. You know that, right?"

I nodded yes.

He gave me several sheets of paper, some signed by Leona and some signed by Lillian. The last one signed by Lillian was in '95.

"What is this? I mean, what are you saying?"

I am saying that my mother, when she was Lillian, had two girls, Phyllis and Felicia, and you look like the other twin. I am not saying you are, but she believed you were, and we simply don't know.

I was feeling very uncomfortable in this meeting. So, I said, "Are you trying to say my mother lied to me? I was totally in disbelief at these two guys.

"I'm not saying anything," David interjected. "Maybe she didn't want you to know. If your mom met Lillian, it was probably good to never tell you." He leaned back, thoughtful. "Lillian, she was wild. The kind of woman who didn't scare easy. A fighter. She also did drugs back then and drank a lot, according to reports. Just not the kind of person you want the child you are raising to ever know. We interviewed a couple of cops during our research. One of them became a close friend of my mother's. He swore up and down that 'Lillian' beat him and his partner on some dark back road heading into Chicago. Said she moved so fast he couldn't even tell if it was one person or two coming at them."

David shook his head slightly. "From everything I've heard, the Lilian side of her wasn't a nice person."

"You got us as family now, and that will never change. You can say no."

"Okay. No," I said boldly. "Glad you liked the article."

They both gave me hugs. I reached to throw my plate away, but David said they'd got it. They gave me a gray folder, and I walked out.

There are words that don't leave you easily, and memories that never really find a resting place in your mind, and there are times your spirit will tell you *not now*.

PHRASE 20

THE LIGHT

Margarita

It took five years from the moment we began this journey for the stick to finally turn pink. I was pregnant. In that instant, images of David and Darnell flooded my mind.

We had spoken often over the phone, but the last time it was just the three of us in the same room, and it felt too surreal to revisit. On the phone, I avoided the past. I clung instead to the safety of the present — birthdays, graduations, new jobs. Darnell had gone into real estate. Simple things. The kinds of things that made it easier to stay connected.

But the truth is, I had followed some of their steps. And in doing so, I found pieces of Lillian — the girl who died at eight. I opened the gray envelope David had given me and retraced a moment in the memories I had shared with Leona. That day, I chose to walk the path of someone I had known for years — not with a camera, not in search of attention or fame, but with a quiet, genuine curiosity to understand.

After convincing Bruce to come with me, we headed back South — the birthplace of Lillian and Leona — to see what still lived and breathed beneath the stories I had been told.

My first visit was with Harmony, the daughter of Tara — Lillian and Leona's best friend. She had never met the twins, but her mother spoke of them often. Harmony was a young woman carrying the weight of losing a mother she believed never truly loved her. With care, I shared what I knew — the good and the painful — and helped her see that the distance she felt wasn't born in her mother, and the move away from her was planted through years of rejection and hurt.

Harmony introduced me to Rose, now living in a memory care facility. Though her memory slipped in and out of time, she remembered the twins in a way that stayed with me: "One you could hear and one you could see."

I couldn't meet Oliver, but I spoke with his son, who told story after story of how Leona had helped his mother out of debt — quiet acts of loyalty that never asked for recognition.

Then there was Willie. Age had settled on his face, but not enough to hide the handsomeness he once carried. He spoke with a heavy honesty. He admitted he had stepped outside his marriage, first drawn to a cheap distraction because he struggled to accept just how good a wife Leona truly was. When she found out, she didn't yell. She didn't fight. Something in her simply shifted. She began taking more trips to Memphis, saying she needed to care for her sister. Years later, it came to light that she had two sons he never claimed — until David and Darnell asked him to take a DNA test seven years ago.

He loved her. He said she was nothing like her sister. He had encountered Lillian — the other side. A woman lost to drugs, drinking, and harsh words. Later, he was told she also had a good heart, though it was harder for him to see. That, he believed, was the only thing the sisters truly shared.

Now what haunts Willie is the realization that he once held a love that made him better and let it slip away. He wonders what might have changed if he had said two simple words: *I'm sorry.*

But he was too stubborn. Too proud.

In Memphis, Leona began caring for an older man. She stayed with him until he died, perhaps because it was easier to watch that ending than to witness her own marriage fall apart in the same way.

I went to Memphis and read about a famous jazz and blues trumpeter named Max, whose family died in a fire—possibly caused by a girlfriend lost to drugs. Another story shaped by love, loss, and destruction.

I followed the path to Clare and John's—a big brick home in downtown Belzoni—and I followed the trail one lonely girl must have followed back to a small house tucked deep off the road, nearly hidden behind a tall, protective willow tree. I stood on that quiet stretch of road and imagined how Randy might have become stranded there, how he walked up to that porch only to be met by a woman searching for love and acceptance.

I often wondered about Ms. Bell—how she connected to the twins. The only nearby home belonged to an M. Bell, and it seemed likely she had been the only friend their mother had in that isolated place.

Then I found Lillian Smith's gravesite. It was there, standing in that stillness, where I touched something real—something heavier than stories. For the first time, I didn't just hear about her pain. I felt it.

I couldn't stop seeing them as children: two frightened girls with only each other to hold onto, to love, while a madman claimed their mother's life. I imagined them huddled together in that small kitchen—one of them shot, blood pooling, life slipping away—and still, somehow, trying to protect the other. Shielding a sister whose eyes were too afraid to open.

And now, standing on the edge of motherhood myself, I understood something I hadn't before, and in that understanding, I wondered if maybe another conversation could finally be had.

Now I was at home with my own thoughts. All the good things in my life were in part due to my knowing Leona. I had just completed another show, and until the next year, I was off and most days bored. Bruce was transitioning from an office space to home. When the baby would be born and I had to leave on weekends, he would have to watch them. I pushed him, trying to turn him over. The log that my husband moved slowly. He was asleep and I couldn't sleep, so I turned on the light, hoping that Bruce would get up and give me an ear, and he did, so I whispered, "Why do you think she would have kept it from me? If it is true. "

"Honey, your mother took total strangers and claimed them as her own. Maybe it didn't matter. Andrea was adopted, but she knew her mother. Maybe you came to her in a different way. Maybe she saw the Lillian we learned about and felt it was better to keep you safe.

I tried to rationalize. "And I just show up, and not even the older sister knew?"

My husband looked at me as if I should have known. "She was at times heavier. She could have, and maybe they knew, but they just didn't really understand. They weren't that much older, honey. Your mama was popping them out every other year! Dad was busy."

In memories of my mother, I pushed Bruce, reminding him that my mother would not have liked that kind of language.

"Okay, just saying. What if you were left at the small church in the woods in the car? Look, honey, your sisters are going to always be your sisters, and Darnell and David, not leaving either. If they did what you think they did, they already know the results. They haven't said a word. They know. The question is, do you want to know?"

"Ice cream," I said.

He laughed before he got up and went downstairs to get his six-months-pregnant wife ice cream. Then he came back up and said, "Honey, knowing will not change much. Got your sisters, that's not going to change, got me and the new baby that's coming. You got David and Darnell, that's going to change. The question is, do you want to know? And only you can answer that, honey. Now I got the big baby ice cream, so that I can get some sleep."

KNOWING THAT'S THAT

Margarita

About a month later, I invited David and Samantha over for lunch. I was always in contact with them for birthdays, holidays, and just early morning chats, mostly with Darnell. I was pregnant, and I needed to have this conversation. Of course, David showed up, he and his wife Samatha, and now that I was going to be a mother, she insisted on helping to decorate the nursery, which I welcomed. I warmed up pizza bites and made tea, and we took it on the patio. I put on light music, and the vibe was right. One thing they knew about me is that I normally just say what it is I want to do, so today would be no different. So I said rather casually, "I got to ask you a few questions, sir."

"Oh, my, I am in trouble, Sam," he said to his wife.

Sam gave him a slight hug, so as to let him know she'd got his back.

Then I continued, "I'm going to always keep it real with you every step of the way, but there is something I need to know now. To be truthful, I have done a little research myself. I'm going to be a mother myself, so I do understand choices a mother can make, even if I don't agree with the choices. I also read some of the files you shared with me, and I understand more about personality disorders.

David smiled and said, "Oh, so it's this conversation we are having. It's cool, I always keep an envelope with me, just in case we are having this conversation, and apparently, we are having this conversation."

Then I admitted that I thought there were two babies.

David nodded yes and didn't say a word.

"David, the million-dollar question, did you take my DNA at our last meeting? Is that why you didn't let me take the plate?"

"You caught that?" David said, shocked.

"I peeked. So, did you run the DNA?"

"You know I did."

"You should have asked me, David."

"I told him that!" Sam interjected.

"Well," David said, his honesty landing heavier than he intended, "I didn't want it to be your choice. Darnell and I, we've lived with gaps our whole lives — empty spaces no one ever explained. We were just trying to close a few of them. We needed to know. And if you didn't, well, that's your truth. Knowing might not have set you free," he continued, his voice softening, "but it could've completed something for me and Darnell. Now that I hear myself say it, it sounds selfish." He paused, almost ashamed. "Truth is, I didn't want to risk you saying no."

He looked at me then, really looked. "Meeting you felt like seeing a ghost, and yet there you were — alive, standing in front of us, looking just like our sister who's gone." He exhaled slowly, as if the weight of years sat in his chest. "Our whole lives, we watched our mother change like the seasons — never the same woman for long. And somehow, she always found a way to clean up Lillian's messes, to smooth things over like they never happened."

His voice dropped to something quieter, more vulnerable. "Maybe knowing you was her way of fixing one she couldn't outrun. And we—" he shook his head slightly, "—we just needed to understand."

"Still, David, it was my choice to make."

"I'm sorry," he said sincerely. "I'm a lot like my mother."

I smiled because he was right. Leona was going to get her answer at all costs.

"I said to myself," David said, "that whenever you were ready for this conversation, I would have this to give to you." He took an envelope out of his pocket. "Okay, here's the results. I won't ever mention it, nor will I bring it up. If you want to know, you open and read. The only thing I want you to promise me is that, whether you read it or not, we will always be family. Just like we are now."

I took the envelope from David and nodded yes, but he was waiting to hear me say it, so I said, "I promise."

David and Sam kissed me and left. I looked at the envelope. I thought to myself, *People can look alike. I could just be a lookalike.* I look closely at the closed envelope, seeing if I could possibly see through it. Then I thought *How silly. This is over.* I walked around the patio and settled onto the stool pulled up to the small wooden nook. I began the senseless motion of tapping the envelope against the wood until the sound started to irritate me.

I started to tear the corner of the envelope when it suddenly hit me. I knew who my mother was. My mother was that bad watch-your-mouth, hat-and-heels-wearing, hips-swaying, Bible-toting, salt-of-the-earth woman better known as Ms. Annie.

That was it.

I took the envelope and laid it flat on top of one of the burning candles. The flame burned through the center. I stomped out the fire, opened it, and was able to read just enough to know.

I smiled to myself, then placed the remaining envelope back into the fire and watched as the white paper burned to ashes. Some of the ashes fell to the floor, and some drifted away, but with them went my worries and concerns, and that's that.

ABOUT THE AUTHOR

Creola Thomas was born and raised in Chicago. Creola's writing gives a front-row seat to the other side of the hood — the side where parents, even in poverty, raise their children with love and firmness. Her characters are deeply real, ripped from the pages of her childhood. Creola, in her own magical way, finds the joy and humor of growing up *hood*. She is a mother, a minister, and a teacher, as well as an advocate for adopted children and foster families. These books were written to not just entertain, but also to enthusiastically explain, explore, and inspire the wonderful imaginations of kids who grow up poor yet powerfully creative.

Contact Creola at creolaxoxo@gmail.com.

Other Works

Fiction
Adventures with the Shortiez: Portal to the Unknown World

Nonfiction
Stop Being Weird: 5 Simple Steps Toward Wholeness for Christian Singles
How to Resurrect a Dying Church
Lying Lips Sink Ships
Why Must I Wait So Long?

www.ingramcontent.com/pod-product-compliance
Lightning Source LLC
Chambersburg PA
CBHW021242060726
47590CB00005B/1859